Praise for

Elizabeth Berg and *The Last Time I Saw You*

A #1 *Chicago Tribune* bestseller
A *Boston Globe* bestseller

"This novel is hard to resist."   —*The Boston Globe*

"A delight . . . Readers will care about every character."
                                                   —*The Oklahoman*

"High school reunions call for humor, and Elizabeth Berg infuses that spirit into [*The Last Time I Saw You*]. . . . These characters are so familiar that it seems they live down the street."
                                       —*Chicago Tribune* (Editor's Choice)

"[Berg] has a gift for capturing the small, often sweet details of ordinary life."   —*Newsday*

"Berg's writing is to literature what Chopin's etudes are to music—measured, delicate, and impossible to walk away from."   —*Entertainment Weekly*

"Berg's great talent is knowing how to tell stories that touch the heart. . . . Reading an Elizabeth Berg novel is like lingering over coffee with a dear friend. It lets you know there are other people out there feeling the same way you sometimes do."
                                   —Charleston *Sunday Gazette-Mail*

"[Berg] specializes in illuminating little truths about women's lives, especially the nature of their relationships with men. . . . Berg's work also glows with a sensual appreciation of life's fine details: the cast of sunlight drifting through a window, the taste of food, the color of wood, the feel of rain."

—*Orlando Sentinel*

"We feel sympathy for these people, as much as we would for ourselves, which points up the success of Berg's gentle, but never bowdlerized, renderings of the hopes and desires of this rather large cast of every-day characters. . . . In the Winesburg, Ohio, tradition, [this is] a Middle Western book that focuses on time, vocation, family ties, hopes for love, and the loneliness that envelops almost everyone."

—Alan Cheuse, *Chicago Tribune*

"Zestfully wise . . . sublimely authentic . . . entertaining as well as enlightening . . . For everyone who has received an invitation to their high-school reunion and broken out in a cold, clammy sweat, Berg nails the experience." —*Booklist*

"Berg has gained a reputation for writing novels that fill the bill: smart, literate novels that offer opportunities for reflection and discussion. . . . [Her] latest work, is no exception. . . . Guaranteed to speak to women (and some men) of a certain age. . . . Berg's novel acknowledges the passage of time, grapples with it, and comes out on the other side hopeful and optimistic. Her fans will gladly join her on this journey."

—Bookreporter.com

"[Berg] zeroes in on an array of stereotypes—the hot girls, the jocks, the in crowd, the out crowd—and considers what makes each one tick. . . . Cleanly plotted, ably written, and sure to appeal to boomers staring down the barrel of their own fortieth reunions." —*Publishers Weekly*

"Rich with memories of the past and hopes for the future . . . [*The Last Time I Saw You*] will resonate with readers." —PioneerLocal.com

"A story about men and women who get a second chance...You will want to keep reading *The Last Time* to find out what happens to Candy and her all-too-human classmates. . . . Well done, Ms. Berg. Life painted large and small all at once." —*New York Journal of Books*

ALSO BY ELIZABETH BERG

the last time i saw you

the last time
i saw you

 A NOVEL

ELIZABETH
BERG

BALLANTINE BOOKS TRADE PAPERBACKS
NEW YORK

2010 Ballantine Books Trade Paperback Edition

Copyright © 2010 by Elizabeth Berg
Reading group guide copyright © 2010 by Random House, Inc.

Published in the United States by Ballantine Books, an imprint
of The Random House Publishing Group,
a division of Random House, Inc., New York.

BALLANTINE BOOKS and colophon are trademarks of Random House, Inc.
RANDOM HOUSE READER'S CIRCLE & Design is a
registered trademark of Random House, Inc.

Originally published in hardcover in the United States by Random House,
an imprint of The Random House Publishing Group,
a division of Random House, Inc., in 2009.

LIBRARY OF CONGRESS CATALOGING-IN-PUBLICATION DATA
Berg, Elizabeth.
The last time I saw you: a novel / Elizabeth Berg.
p. cm.
ISBN 978-0-345-51731-9
eBook ISBN 978-1-58836-892-8
1. Class reunions—Fiction. 2. Reminiscing—Fiction.
I. Title.
PS3552.E6996L37 2010
813'.54—dc22 2009040008

Printed in the United States of America

www.randomhousereaderscircle.com

2 4 6 8 9 7 5 3 1

Book design by Susan Turner

For Phyllis Florin
and
Marianne Quasha

High school, those are your prime suffering years.
You don't get better suffering than that.

—Uncle Frank (Steve Carell), *Little Miss Sunshine*

Every parting gives a foretaste of death
as every reunion a hint of the resurrection.

—Arthur Schopenhauer

Maybe one day I can have a reunion with myself.

—Sebastian Bach

the last time i saw you

ONE

Dorothy Shauman Ledbetter Shauman is standing in front of the bathroom mirror in her black half-slip and black push-up bra, auditioning a look. Her fortieth high school reunion, the last one, is one week away, and she's trying to decide whether or not to draw a beauty mark above her lip for the occasion. It wouldn't be entirely false; she does have a mole there, but it's faint, hard to see. She just wants to enhance what already exists, nothing wrong with that; it's de rigueur if you're a woman, and it's becoming more common in men, too. Wrong as that is. Dorothy would never have anything to do with a man who wore makeup or dyed his hair or carried a purse or wore support hose or cried or did any of those womanly things men are appropriating as though it's their god-given right. No. She prefers an all-American, red-blooded male who is not a jerk. They're hard to find, but she holds out hope that she will have some sort of meaningful relationship with one before she's six feet under.

She regards herself in the mirror, tilts her head this way and that. Yes, a beauty mark would be fun, kind of playful. She pencils in the mark gingerly, then steps back to regard herself. Not bad. Not bad at all. *Sexy.* Just like she wanted. *Helloooo,* Marilyn. She pictures Pete Decker looking up from his table full of jocks when she walks into the hotel ballroom and saying, *Va va va voom!* And then, *Dorothy?* Dorothy *Shauman?*

"Uh-huh," she will say, lightly, musically, and walk right past him. Though she will walk close enough to him for him to smell her perfume. Also new. One hundred and ten smackeroos. She got perfume, not cologne, even though her personal belief is that there is no difference. She'd asked the counter woman about that. She'd leaned in confidentially and said, "Now, come on. Tell me, *really.* If you were my best friend, would you tell me to get the perfume over the cologne?" And the woman had looked her right in the eye and said, "*Yes.*" Dorothy was a little miffed, because the woman had acted as though Dorothy had affronted her dignity or questioned her ethics or something. Like the time Dr. Strickland was telling Dorothy to get a certain ($418!!!) blood test and she'd said, "Would you tell your *wife* to get it?" And Dr. Strickland had drawn himself up and quietly said, "I would." Dorothy had been all set to give him an affectionate little punch and say, "Oh, come on, now; don't be so *prissy,*" but then Dr. Strickland had added, "If she were still alive," and that had just ruined everything. It wasn't *her* fault the woman had died! Dorothy had been going to refuse the test no matter what, but when he said his wife was dead, well, then she had to get it. Those dead people had more power than they thought.

Dorothy has never gone to a high school reunion. She'd been married when they had them before, and who wanted to bring *that* to a reunion. Now she is divorced, plus she saw that movie about saying yes to life. She steps closer to the mirror and raises her chin so her turkey neck disappears. She'll hold her head like this when she walks by Pete Decker. Later, when they're making out in his car, it will be dark, and she won't have to be so vigilant. Oh, she hopes he drives to the reunion; she happens to know he lives a mere three and a half hours away. She knows his exact address, in fact; and she Google-Earthed him, which was very exciting.

In high school, Pete had a four-on-the-floor metallic green GTO, and Dorothy always wanted to make out with him in that car. But she never even got to sit in it. She bets he has something like a red Lexus coupe now. And she bets that at the reunion he'll watch her for a while, then come up to her and say, "Hey, Dots. Want to take a walk?" And she'll say, all innocent, "Where?" And he'll get a little flustered and say something like "You know, just a *walk,* get some *air.*" She'll hesitate just for a second, just long enough to make him think she might refuse, and then she'll shrug prettily before she agrees to accompany him outside. They'll go right to his car and he'll open the passenger-side door and raise an eyebrow and she'll say, "*Pete!*" like she's offended at the very notion. But then she'll get in, will she ever. She likes this part of the fantasy best: She'll get in, he'll come around and get in on his side, and then, just before he lunges at her, he'll look at her with smoke practically coming out of his eyes. And in her eyes, a soft *Yes, I know. I, too, have wanted this for years.*

Dorothy does plan on being a little mean to Pete at first; she has finally learned it can be a good thing to be mean to men. Apparently they like it; it's supposed to appeal to their hunting instinct. That's why she's going to walk right by him when he first sees her and notices how attractive she is. Considering.

Her daughter, Hilly, is the one who told her about being mean to men. She said you do it just at the beginning and then every so often, just to keep up a level of intrigue, like immunization shots. And it works, too, because when Hilly started doing it, wasn't she *engaged* in what seemed like ten minutes! She's getting married in Costa Rica next month, and Dorothy thinks it's a wonderful idea, the destination wedding. Thank God Dorothy's ex will pay for everything. Poor he was not. She supposes he'll bring his new wife to the wedding, and pander to her every single second. Holding her hand, as though they were teenagers. Bringing her drinks, as though the woman is incapable of doing anything for herself. Staring into her eyes like the secret of the universe is written there. It's nauseating, the way they behave, anyone would say so. Hilly calls them the Magnets, though she might only do that to offer some kind of support to her mother, who lives alone now and must take out the garbage and figure out whom to call for repairs and check the locks at night and kill centipedes in the basement and everything else. Dorothy suspects the truth is, Hilly actually likes her stepmother. She hasn't said so directly, but she did say that she's happy for her dad, and wasn't that just like nails on a chalkboard. But Dorothy did the noble thing and said yes, she was, too. Uh-huh, yes, he did seem happy now, Dorothy said, and she just wanted to throw up.

Hilly's fiancé is a doctor. A proctologist, specializing in the wonderful world of buttholes and rectums, but still. Dorothy is working up to asking the question that—come on!—must occur to everyone to ask him: What exactly made you choose this line of work? When Dorothy tried to ask her daughter about it, all Hilly did was get mad. It is true Dorothy could have used a more sensitive approach—what she'd asked Hilly was "Why in the wide, wide world would you ever want to look up people's *heinies* all day?" Still, Dorothy doesn't see why Hilly had to take such offense. Her daughter had said something like perhaps Dorothy should consider the fact that preventing and treating cancer is a pretty noble goal. But that still didn't answer the *question,* did it?

Dorothy thinks it was a book her daughter read that taught her about being mean to men. Who knows, if Dorothy had been mean to Pete Decker in high school, they might have gotten married. They went out once—well, not a date technically, but they did spend some time together on the class trip to Washington, D.C., and Dorothy was *awfully* nice to Pete and then of course that was that, he never called her. But if they had gotten married, they probably would have gotten divorced, and then she wouldn't be looking forward so much to going to her high school reunion. Apart from her friends Linda Studemann and Judy Holt, she's really only going to see him. And, to be honest, to show off her recent weight loss. That was the one nice thing about her divorce: During the grief part, before she realized how much better off she was without her husband, she lost twenty-three pounds. She bets she'll look better than the cheerleaders, and even better than Candy Sullivan, who had been queen of everything. Not that Candy Sullivan is coming. According to Pam Pottsman, who is the contact person for this year's reunion, Candy came to the five-year reunion and hasn't come to any since. "Is she dead?" Dorothy asked, ready to offer an impromptu eulogy praising Candy's good points, even though Candy never gave Dorothy the time of day. But Pam said no, Candy wasn't dead, apparently she just thought she was too good to come, and then they both started talking about what a snob Candy always was, and she wasn't even really all that hot. "Did you know she stuffed her bra?" Pam said, and Dorothy said, "*Really?*" and felt that delicious rush, and Pam said, "Yup, I sat across from her in Mr. Simon's psychology class and I saw Kleenex coming out of the top of her blouse one day and I whispered to her that it was showing and she got all embarrassed and stuffed it back in and wouldn't look at me."

"But wait a minute," Dorothy said. "I saw her naked in gym class, and she didn't need any Kleenex."

"What year?"

"Senior. And she did not need Kleenex."

"Well, that psychology class was sophomore year," Pam said, and she sounded a little disappointed that Candy Sullivan had outgrown her need for bra stuffing. But then she told Dorothy how a lot more people were coming this year than ever before, probably because it was the last reunion their class was going to have; and she named several of their classmates who had signed up. Dorothy thinks it will be fun to see poor Mary Alice Mayhew, who is coming for her very first reunion, just as Dorothy is. Though there the similarity ends, thank you very much. Such a little mouse Mary Alice was, walking down the hall and looking at the floor, all hunched over her schoolbooks. She wore awful plaid dresses, and she never wore nylons, just thin white ankle socks, not even kneesocks. And loafers that were *not* Weejuns, you could tell. From a mile away, you could tell. Poor thing. And wait, didn't she put *pennies* in them? There's always one of them, and in their school, it was Mary Alice Mayhew.

Oh, and Lester Hessenpfeffer, who was screwed the moment he was christened. Lester's uncle, who was present at his birth, had just changed his own last name to Hess, and he suggested that Lester's father do the same for the sake of his newborn son. Lester's father reportedly screamed, "Change our name! Change our *name*? Why should we change our name? Let the rest of the world change *their* names!" Lester had told that story once when someone teased him about his name. You had to give Lester this: he was always an affable guy who didn't ever seem to take things personally.

Poor Lester. Never dated. He had such a cute face, but he was too much of a brain, and too sensitive. He probably ended up in computers. Maybe he got rich, like that homely Microsoft guy. And if so, you can bet your boots that Dorothy will be saying hello to him, too.

If Mary Alice Mayhew really comes to the reunion, Dorothy will make a point of being nice to her. Yes she will. She'll buy her a drink; oh, what a hoot to think of buying Mary Alice Mayhew a drink. So odd to think that they're *old* enough to drink now.

Mary Alice had silver cat-eye glasses with rhinestones on them and her hair always looked like she'd taken the rollers out and not brushed it. Dorothy has heard plenty of stories about how ugly ducklings come to their high school reunions as swans, but she'd bet money that Mary Alice looks much the same, only with wrinkles. She wouldn't be the Botox type. Dorothy's position on Botox is *Thank God*. Who cares if you can't move your eyebrows around like caterpillars on a plate?

"Is Pete Decker coming?" Dorothy asked Pam.

"He is."

"And his wife, too?"

"He only registered himself. You know Pete. Oh, I can hardly wait to see him again. What a dreamboat he was."

"Oh, did you think so?" Dorothy studied her nails casually, as though she and Pam were talking in person. If you wanted to sound a certain way, even on the telephone, it was good to act a certain way—the feeling crept into your voice. You were supposed to smile when you were talking on the phone if you wanted to sound friendly. A lot of the people who made recordings for telephone prompts seemed to do that, though such recordings always make Dorothy want to bang the phone against the wall until the wires fall out.

"I thought Pete Decker was the most handsome boy in the school!" Pam said. "Didn't you?"

"I don't know. I guess a lot of people found him attractive." Dorothy sniffed then, and changed the subject. No need for Pam to know of Dorothy's designs on Pete; Pam was quicker than Twitter at spreading things around.

Dorothy turns and views herself from the side: not bad. The bra, bought yesterday on her final stop for putting together a killer outfit, is doing what it promised; her breasts are hiked up and perky, rather than hanging down so low they appear to be engaging in conversation with her belly button. Eighty-five dollars for a bra! At least it's French. Dorothy always likes it when things are French. In the dressing room, she'd sniffed the bra to see if it smelled like Chanel or something, but no, it smelled like rubber. Not for long. Dorothy will have *everything* perfumed when she goes to that reunion, even her you-know-what. But she'll have to remember to *pat* it on down there; last time she sprayed, she gave herself a urinary tract infection and, oh, does she hate cranberry juice.

She steps back from the mirror, then leans in to darken the beauty mark. Perfect. She should take a picture of herself to remember to do it just like this on Saturday night. They're having a Saturday night dinner followed by a dance, complete with a DJ who's supposed to be really good and not tacky, and then there's a Sunday brunch. Two times for a final try at glory.

Dorothy's stomach growls, and she puts her hand over it and says aloud, "*No.*"

TWO

LESTER HESSENPFEFFER AWAKENS ON A BATH RUG STUFFED into the corner of a gigantic cage and stares into the open eyes of the bull mastiff. The dog wags his tail once, twice, and Lester feels his chest tighten with joy. Just before he fell asleep, he'd been preparing a speech for the dog's owners about how he'd done his best, how he'd tried everything, but . . . Samson had ingested a few Legos the day before, which the owners' great-grandchildren had left lying about. One had perforated his intestine. By the time he was brought to Lester's clinic, the dog was in shock and the prospects for saving him were almost nil. Lester had slept in the cage with him to provide comfort not so much to the dog as to himself. He'd known Samson since he was a puppy, and he was very fond of the owners, an elderly couple who thought Samson hung the moon. They'd wanted to spend the night at the clinic, but after Lester told them he'd be literally right beside the dog, they reluctantly went home. Lester had hoped they'd get some sleep, so that they could more easily bear the news he was pretty certain he'd have to deliver in the morning.

This is always the worst part of his job, telling people their pet has died. Sometimes they know it, at least empirically; on more than one occasion someone has brought a dead animal into the office hoping against hope that Lester can revive it. And when he can't, he must say those awful words: *I'm so sorry.* He's noticed a certain posture many people assume on hearing those words. They step back and cross their arms, as though guarding themselves against any more pain, or as though holding one more time the animal they loved as truly as any other family member, if not more. Oftentimes, they nod, too, their heads saying yes to what their hearts cannot yet accept.

But here Samson is, alive and well enough to give Lester's face a good washing with a tongue the size of a giant oven mitt. "Hey, pal," Lester says. "You made it! Let's have a look at that dressing." He rises to his knees and very gently turns the dog slightly onto his side. Samson whimpers and holds overly still, in the way that dogs often do when they're frightened. There's a lot of drainage, but nothing leaking through. He'll give Samson something for pain and then call Stan and Betty. By the time he's done talking to them—he can anticipate at least a few of the questions they'll have—he'll be able to change the dressing without causing the dog undue distress. He thinks Samson will be able to stand and move about a little this afternoon, and imagines him lifting his leg with great dignity against the portable fireplug his staff uses for cage-bound male dogs (the girls get Astroturf). The portable bathrooms had been Jeanine's idea; she was always coming up with good ideas. She had the idea for Pet Airways before they came up with Pet Airways, although her suggestion was that pets and owners fly together—cages would be installed next to seats so that an owner could reach down and scratch behind an ear, or speak reassuringly, or offer a snack. This was a much better idea for alleviating the stress caused to animals when they fly, and Lester advised Jeanine to write to Pet Airways suggesting it. She said she'd rather keep the idea for herself because she wanted to start Dog Airways, as it is her belief that only dogs *really* care when their owners are gone. She is by her own admission a dog chauvinist, but she's good to all the animals who come to the clinic, even the hamster whose hysterical owner brought her in because she was gobbling up her babies as soon as she gave birth to them.

Jeanine also had the idea that Lester should attend his high school reunion. When the invitation had come to the clinic, Jeanine had opened it, and then immediately begun a campaign to get her boss to go. Lester knew what she had in mind—she wanted him to find a woman.

When he was twenty-nine years old and had been married for only a year, Lester's four-months-pregnant wife, Kathleen, had been killed in a car accident. Since that time, not only has he not remarried but he has not dated. Oh, he has some women friends, and he's pretty sure some of them have had little crushes on him. But despite the charms of this woman or that, there's never been anyone who moved him the way his wife did. He had just opened the clinic when she was killed; Kathleen had worked as the receptionist for the grand total of four days before he lost her. It doesn't hurt the way it did at first—how could anyone survive such a thing?—but there is a place for Kathleen in his heart that leaves no room for anyone else. He is at peace with the idea of living the rest of his life alone, even if Jeanine isn't.

But he did finally agree to go to the reunion. It might be interesting to see all those people again, even though he'd never really been close to any of them. He'd pretty much kept to himself, for many reasons. He wonders if any of his classmates look anything like they used to, or if at the reunion they'll all walk around squinting at name tags, then looking up with ill-disguised disbelief into a person's face. He feels *he* still somewhat resembles the boy he used to be, but then he guesses that everyone does that, sees in the mirror a mercifully edited version of themselves different from what everyone else sees.

Lester was very pleased to see that, on check-in at the reunion, he would be given a box lunch. He feels about the words "box lunch" the way Henry James felt about the words "summer afternoon"—that they are the most beautiful words in the English language.

But mostly Lester agreed to go to the reunion so that he could get Jeanine off his back. He'd even asked her if she'd like to accompany him. Jeanine is married, seemingly happily so, but Lester thought she might get a kick out of going. He'd told her her husband could come, too; they'd find a way to sneak him in. Or maybe they wouldn't have to sneak him at all—anyone who looked to be in their late fifties would probably be able to walk right in, once people deserted their posts at the registration table. "That's true," Jeanine had said. "I used to think sometimes about crashing high school reunions, walking around asking people, 'Do you remember me? You remember *me,* don't you?' just to see what they'd say. But no, you need to go alone or you'll never meet someone. Not a wife, just someone to go to the movies with. It's your *last reunion*!" What she had not said, but what Lester heard, is, "You're getting old, now. It's not funny. You're going to *need* someone."

"All *right,*" he'd finally said. "I'll *go.*" And Jeanine had clapped her hands together and asked if she could pick out what he should wear and he'd said no, thank you. She'd asked if she could refer him to a good hairstylist, and he'd said all right because he actually did need to find someone new to cut his hair—his barber's cataracts had gotten so bad, Lester always came out of the shop looking a little electrocuted.

As soon as Lester agreed to go to the reunion, he'd actually started looking forward to it. Not because he was thinking of meeting someone he could go to the movies with, no. He doesn't need anyone to go to the movies with, he likes going alone, in fact. He likes sitting there with his popcorn and small Coke ("small" being roughly the size of a silo) and watching movies and thinking about them on his walk home. He likes putting in a garden every spring, nourishing it every summer, and putting it to bed every fall. He likes traveling to Europe every October. He loves reading, mostly history or biography, but classics, too; he never tires of rereading Proust or Dickens or Tolstoy or Flaubert. He also likes sitting in the living room of his small, well-tended two-bedroom house, listening to jazz while he enjoys a little scotch. He likes the way Rosaria changes his sheets every Thursday, the way the bed always smells so good then. He'd asked her once what she did to make the sheets smell so good and she'd put her hand up over her mouth, over her gold-filled teeth, and giggled. "Nothing especial; is detergent only, Doctor," she'd said. And he'd said no, it was something more, it must be that she had magical powers, yes, that must be it, and she had giggled again.

Rosaria had worked for him for many years, and occasionally he accepted one of her frequent invitations to have dinner at her house—both she and her husband, Ernesto, were inspired cooks, and Lester also enjoyed the company of their ever-expanding family, especially the black-eyed grandchildren who crawled all over him and brought him their stuffed animals to examine and treat. Rosaria had tried for a while to fix him up with various single women she knew—she would invite women to dinner on the nights he came, all kinds of women—but he never felt drawn to pursuing a relationship.

Over and over, it seems, he has to explain that his life is fine. He has his work and his friends and the beauty of the rotating earth. He does not feel he lacks anything, and he certainly does not think going to a high school reunion will put him on the path for finding a replacement for Kathleen. No, he's going to the reunion because there is something about it being the last one; and he also wants to go because, after he spoke to Pam Pottsman, he learned that Don Summers had become a vet, too. He wants to talk shop in a way he feels he couldn't do otherwise—surely a high school reunion permits a kind of honesty one does not often encounter in one's adult life. A high school classmate might be the equivalent of family in terms of offering an intimate access, as well as a lowering of the usual defenses. Lester imagines leaning against a makeshift bar and talking to Don about a lot of things: The ethics of chemo for extending the lives of suffering animals. The increase in aggressive behavior in dogs—is it from them being put in cages and left alone for so long? How many immunizations are now proven to be carcinogenic? Lester also wants to ask Don if he doesn't feel a little like a bullshit artist when he advocates brushing pets' teeth. Especially under anesthesia. Lester himself can't recommend it. Give a dog a marrow bone, give a cat a break.

If he were going to be completely truthful, Lester would have to admit that there is one other person he is interested in seeing at the reunion, one he's not thought about since he left high school, but now that he has been reminded of her, he wants very much to see what kind of woman she became. He hopes she shows up, but he'll keep it to himself, that kind of hope.

In his office, Lester dials the number for Stan and Betty Kruger. It rings several times and then Betty answers in an uncharacteristically soft voice.

"Betty?"

"Oh, God," she says.

"No, it's *good* news," Lester says, and Betty begins to cry.

"STAN!" she yells. "He MADE it! Samson's OKAY!" To Lester, she says, "We're coming right now. I'm in my robe and pajamas. Don't look."

After Lester hangs up, he sits back in his chair, his hands clasped behind his head. He thinks about a man he met on a train in France last year. The man, Hugo, asked him what the saddest experience he ever had as a vet was, and Lester said it was the day he had to tell someone whose son had died of cancer that the son's dog, whom the father had adopted, had developed the exact same disease. It happened more often than people knew, that dogs developed the same illnesses as their owners: diabetes, adrenal diseases, cancers. It was one of those mysterious things.

"And the happiest experience?" Hugo asked, and Lester said the happiest came after one of the saddest: he'd made a house call to put down a fourteen-year-old tricolor collie named Mike whom Lester had often seen standing with the family's kids at the end of the driveway while they waited for the school bus. Their mother had told Lester that Mike would go to the same spot and wait for the kids to come home in the afternoon, always at pre- cisely the right time. "We never tell him the kids are coming," she'd said. "He just knows. He'll go to the door and bark to be let out, and the kids will arrive right afterward, without fail." One Easter, the family had gotten a duckling, and he and the dog had become best friends—they'd slept together every night until the duck died, and Mike often visited the duck's grave, his tail wagging on the way there, hanging low on the way back. On the day Lester came to put the dog down, the family had Mike lying on a quilt and had just offered him beef tips, which the dog had refused. Four months later, the owners had returned to Lester's clinic with a new puppy, a beautiful female tricolor.

"So. This is life, eh?" Hugo said. "We lose something here, we get something there. The trick is to stop looking in the old place to find the new thing."

Lester nodded, and then he stared out the window of the train at the countryside as they traveled through it. Sometimes it was hilly; sometimes it was flat; always, in one way or another, it was beautiful.

THREE

MARY ALICE MAYHEW PUTS THE SOFT-BOILED EGG INTO the bright blue porcelain holder she bought at the thrift shop yesterday. Presentation is all. If Einer Olson finds his breakfast good-looking, maybe he'll eat it. She adds a bud vase with a half-opened yellow rose, though this is more for her benefit than for his. Einer is indifferent to flowers. He says all they do is die.

She carries the breakfast tray into his fusty-smelling bedroom. He insists on eating in his bedroom, sitting in an armchair next to the window where he can look out onto the street below. She places his meal on the TV tray before him, and cracks open the window. "It's beautiful out there today," she says.

"Is it?"

"Seventy-six degrees, no humidity. None. Perfect September day."

"Huh." He picks up his spoon, taps it against the egg. "I don't think I can eat this. Why don't you have it?"

"I already had an egg for breakfast. It was delicious. That one's for you." She moves over to his bed to make it. It appears he had a restless night: the sheets are twisted, the pillows flung onto the floor.

"I can't get it out of the shell."

She smiles over at him. "Sure you can."

He sits staring at the egg. Then, after a few tries, he slices off the top, dips the spoon in, and takes a bite. "That's enough." He pushes the tray away.

Mary Alice comes over to stand before him. "One more bite, and a half slice of the toast. It's Swedish rye, from Uppman's Bakery. You love their bread."

He looks up at her, his eyes magnified hugely by his glasses. It seems hard for him to breathe today: through the thin fabric of his shirt, she can see the muscles in his shoulders moving to help him. And has he gotten paler overnight? She feels a rush of anxiety, and it comes to her that Einer is her best friend. She doesn't want to think about what life will be like without him. She pushes his tray closer to him and speaks gently. "Eat just a little more. Then we can go out on the porch and read the newspaper and you can gripe."

He looks out the window, considering. "No more egg. A bite of toast. One bite."

"Two bites of toast, and a big drink of orange juice."

"You drive a hard bargain," he says. But then he mutters, "Deal."

Einer is ninety-two years old and Mary Alice's next-door neighbor. Two years ago, when Mary Alice moved back to town and into her parents' vacant house, he'd hired her for caregiving services, though he claimed he didn't really need help with anything except weeding the garden. She'd worked for him for a few weeks, then moved on to another job. Einer has a full-time caregiver named Rita Essinger now, but Mary Alice still comes over at least once a week to help out. While she takes care of Einer, Rita runs errands or just takes some time for herself. She always thanks Mary Alice profusely, but the truth is, Mary Alice offers relief for a selfish reason. She doesn't want Rita to burn out and quit. It's important that Einer have the right kind of person caring for him, and Mary Alice doesn't want to have to go through another round of seemingly endless interviews on his behalf anytime soon.

Mary Alice had been working as a research assistant in a laboratory in Cincinnati when the economy went bonkers in 2008. After a few months of trying unsuccessfully to find another job in that city, she had moved back to Clear Springs. It only made sense—she could live in her parents' house rent free, and besides, someone needed to take care of the place. Mary Alice's mother had died only a few weeks after Einer's wife had—Einer said it was because the two of them just *had* to have their coffee klatch every day, and if it meant Mary Alice's mother dying in order to continue that, well, so be it. "They're up there in heaven, sitting with their mugs and stollen and not letting God get a word in edgewise," he'd told her.

After Mary Alice's mother's death, the house had sat empty for months. It was only partly because of the real estate crisis that had accompanied the country's economic collapse. The house had problems. Not structural ones—it was a beautiful American foursquare, built at a time when there was a lot of integrity in both materials and contractors, and it had been well maintained. But it was reportedly haunted, and in a small town like this, word had spread; even the realtor had said she had a legal obligation to disclose this odd fact to potential buyers who hadn't already heard the rumor. In addition to that, the interior had not been remodeled since it was built in the thirties; the one bathroom had a chain used for flushing the toilet, its tank up high against the wall. The kitchen had no dishwasher, no fancy stove and refrigerator, no granite counters. Mary Alice liked it that way. She especially liked the large walk-in pantry with the cabbage-rose-flowered drape that she and her sister used to make into a theater curtain when they put on shows. And she liked the ghost. All it did was occasionally make walking sounds on the creaky floors—it was like a roommate who kept you company but didn't run up the grocery bill. So she came back to live in this house she'd grown up in, a place full of memories.

Sometimes when Mary Alice lies in bed in what used to be her parents' bedroom, she thinks about the day her father died. It happened on a cold winter day, when she was a junior in high school. She'd gone to the auditorium for band practice after school. The sky had been dark and menacing all day, and she'd been watching through the high, dirty windows for the predicted snow to start falling. She'd been worrying about her mother having to come to school to pick her up—her mother was a terrible driver under the best of circumstances. But then the office secretary had come and spoken quietly to the music teacher, who told Mary Alice she needed to go to the principal's office for a message. She remembers the other kids in the band falling silent to watch her walk off the stage and then across the polished floor, her footsteps echoing, her clarinet case bumping into her knee. Someone had whispered, "*What's* her name?" and she had felt a shameful blip of hope that now she might finally be known for something.

She had suspected that the principal was going to deliver bad news, but she'd never anticipated how bad. Mr. Spurry told her there'd been an emergency involving her father and he'd been asked to give her a ride home. "Okay," she'd said immediately, and then immediately regretted it, as though her easy acceptance of the fact made it more true than she wanted it to be.

Mr. Spurry had accompanied Mary Alice to her locker to get her coat and her books. Then he'd walked with her out to the teachers' parking lot. He'd opened his car's passenger door for her, which had embarrassed her. She'd sat stiffly upright in the front seat, her hands folded on her knees, her knees pressed tightly together, afraid that anything more casual might be seen as rude, or inappropriate; or that it might bring bad luck. She'd kept silent, and so had he. She'd listened to the music that played low on the radio, thinking that she didn't want to know this much about Mr. Spurry: what he drove, what station he listened to, how his car smelled slightly of something like hamburger grease.

When she'd come into the house, her older sister, Sarah Jane, and her mother had been sitting at the kitchen table. Her sister wouldn't stop crying and her mother was starkly dry-eyed, and each had seemed to Mary Alice to be equally bad. After Mary Alice found out what had happened to her father—an aortic aneurysm had burst; he'd never had a chance—she'd gone into her parents' bedroom and sat for a while on her father's side of the bed. She'd held his pillow and sat looking out the window as the sky abruptly lightened—the storm had never come. Later, she'd made fried egg sandwiches for the three of them for dinner. It was when her mother was washing the dishes from that dinner that she'd finally started to cry. She'd stood in her apron, her head bowed over the sink, her hands dripping at her sides, and she'd said, "Oh, *Ger*ald," as though her husband had grievously disappointed her, and then she'd cried and cried. Mary Alice had put her arms around her mother and rocked her in place. Her sister had sat bent over in her kitchen chair watching them, her hands shoved between her knees, and she was rocking, too, moving in that same universal rhythm. Mary Alice had looked at the bent heads of her mother and her sister and a thought had come to her: *You'll have to be the father, now.* So she had not cried. Not then, not that night, and not for many days afterward. The day after the funeral, her mother had gotten a job at the dime store, and the girls had helped out with babysitting and paper route money, so they were able to keep the house.

And here Mary Alice was again. The first day she worked for Einer, she'd told him she was glad to be back, she'd always liked Clear Springs.

Einer hadn't quite believed her. He said it had seemed to him that she'd led an awfully lonely life, sitting out there on the porch steps with her book and her glass of red Kool-Aid almost every summer afternoon when all the other kids, including her sister, were at the pool, or the movies, or hanging around downtown. And later, when she grew older, spending most Saturday nights at home with her mom instead of going out with some fellow.

"You know what, Einer?" she told him. "I had a very happy childhood." And when he frowned, deepening his already deep wrinkles, she said, "I did!"

Oh, it's true that Mary Alice had had her moments, growing up; sometimes she sat outside Sarah Jane's bedroom door listening to her gab on the phone and wondering if anyone would ever call her and inspire her to talk in that excited, girlfriendy way, full of gasps and exclamations; or in that low, seductive voice Sarah Jane used when she talked to boys.

As it happened, no one did call her. "Well, why don't *you* call someone?" her mother used to ask, and Mary Alice couldn't explain why not. It was . . . It was that something had to happen *before* you called, and that something had simply never happened to Mary Alice. So she learned—and came to like, really—a certain self-reliance. The world engaged and excited her; she looked forward to each day despite the injustices she endured in high school. She had been lucky to have a friend in her ninth-grade English teacher, a gay man, she realizes now, who'd told her that high school was good for getting a ticket into college, and that was all. Unless you counted the macaroni and cheese this school's cafeteria served twice a month. That was good, too. Otherwise, put everything in perspective, he'd told her. Life is long; you'll be fine, he'd said, and she was.

Mary Alice now works at a day-care center, in the toddler room. Her specialty is kids who bite—she somehow gets them not to. If a child bites someone, she takes them into the corner and talks to them in a very quiet voice and they almost never bite again. The other workers call her the Toddler Whisperer.

She has a way with children in general, she's discovered; she, more than anyone else at the center, can make them laugh, and there is no tonic like the sound of children laughing. No pleasure quite so pure. She doesn't make much money, but she's happy surrounded by children and glue and blunt-nosed scissors and fat crayons and Play-Doh. She likes the stuffed animals, the colorful balls, the blocks. In the reading corner are an oversize rocking chair and kids' books galore—the illustrations are marvelous, and the stories more intriguing than one might suspect. She likes watching children press their small hands against the sides of the day care's gigantic aquarium and talk earnestly to the fish; and she likes watching them play in the housekeeping corner, roughly dressing and undressing dolls and adorning themselves with costume jewelry and making dinners of plastic peas and pork chops. And if you smack your lips and tell them you like their cooking, oh, how *pleased* they are!

She is heartened by the way the children care for one another: the bending down of one toddler to stare solicitously into the face of another, the outright expessions of concern: *Do you feel sad? Are you going to cry? Do you want a hug?* She likes the art projects, the finger paintings and Popsicle stick sculptures, the Mother's and Father's Day cards so loaded with glue and glitter they flop over in the hand. She likes when the children use cotton balls to make Santa's beard and it looks instead like an odd kind of acne—invariably, the children are as sparing with cotton balls as they are generous with glitter.

She likes taking children for a walk on any kind of day: even a dreary, rainy day offers distinct pleasures, if only in displaying rainbows in oily puddles. She never would have considered working in day care if she hadn't been let go from her job in Cincinnati; now she's glad she did get fired. She has learned from the inside out the meaning of small pleasures, and she keeps her needs small, too.

Mary Alice used to long for a husband; she used to date a little bit and dream, dream a little bit and date; she had a list of names she would have bestowed upon her children, had she been lucky enough to have them, and had her husband agreed with her choices. Moselle had been her favorite for a girl, after the river. For a boy, she had liked Amos best; she thought it was an awfully friendly name. But the longing for a family of her own has stopped. In the gentlest and most good-natured of ways, she has given up on the prospect of being married or even living with a man. She did get one proposal, on her thirty-ninth birthday, but it was from a widower with four children under six. She felt bad for him, but they didn't love each other, not by a long shot. In fact, the night he proposed, they were at the Wagon Wheel Steakhouse, and he couldn't keep his eyes off their waitress, a buxom blonde with a sexy cigarette voice who had no interest in him other than knowing what kind of salad dressing he preferred.

Mary Alice has a body pillow named David. Her sister, Sarah Jane, gave it to her for Christmas many years ago as a kind of jokey imperative, but now she says she's jealous of Mary Alice for getting to sleep with a body pillow rather than a real live man like her husband, who is guilty of every bed-partner crime known to man. Forever encroaching on her side. Farting. Drooling on the lacy pillowcases. Snoring so loudly Sarah Jane can sometimes hear him from the guest room, where she retreats at least two nights a week so that she can get some rest. She says her husband has violent dreams that sometimes have him kicking her. And eating crackers in bed, he actually does that. He eats crackers with cheese and red onion and horseradish mustard.

Last Sunday afternoon, Sarah Jane had driven the thirty miles from her house in Dayton to visit Mary Alice. While Mary Alice claimed her old place on the top porch step, Sarah Jane sat gently rocking herself on the porch swing, embroidering a face on David, giving him eyelashes to die for. She also brought over some lovely plaid pajamas she'd made for him. She included long sleeves that had been filled with cotton batting, in case Mary Alice wanted the feel of "arms" around her. Mary Alice mostly uses David to back up against and has no use for arms at all, but she didn't tell her sister that. She told her it was a very good idea.

Mary Alice wonders sometimes if Sarah Jane doesn't waste far too much time worrying about her; it makes Mary Alice worry about Sarah Jane. "You don't need to keep coming *up* with things for me," she wants to tell her sister. "You don't have to bore your husband at the dinner table with your concerns about your old maid sister." But in the way of most families, Mary Alice only accepts with gratitude the inappropriate gifts Sarah Jane gives her, aware of the fact that she undoubtedly gives Sarah Jane things her sister would happily do without.

While Sarah Jane sat working on David's face, Mary Alice told her about receiving the invitation to the high school reunion. Her sister stopped rocking, stopped sewing. "God help us," she said.

Mary Alice knew her sister had not enjoyed her own experience at their high school. Sarah Jane was five years older than Mary Alice, so they'd not been at that school at the same time, but they'd had many of the same teachers and knew many of the same people. Sarah Jane had been more popular than Mary Alice—she'd been blessed with better looks, and she knew better than Mary Alice how to behave in various situations. But to say she had been more popular than her sister was not to say she'd been popular per se. She'd been accepted, but she'd not been *in*.

Sarah Jane was the kind of girl who was allowed to sit at the popular kids' table because she would go and get more catsup for them or take individual blame for what was a group infraction. She would spend hours decorating the gym for dances where the elite were honored and from which she was often excluded, for lack of a date.

When she was in high school, Mary Alice had occasionally confided in Sarah Jane about the kind of treatment she endured—the way she was mostly ignored except when she was teased. Once, on Valentine's Day, she'd found fake dog shit put into a candy box and left in her locker. Mary Alice had thought that was kind of funny. It was actually almost flattering, because it was the kind of weird thing some of the popular kids did to each other. She didn't tell Sarah Jane that, though. It used to make Sarah Jane crazy that Mary Alice was so unperturbed about the way kids treated her. Sarah Jane tried to help Mary Alice by offering makeovers or trips to the mall to enliven her wardrobe, but it was no use. Mary Alice made a fair amount of money delivering newspapers, but she would never use any of it on clothes or makeup. At first, she spent it on supplies for her microscope: slide covers and probes and fixatives—Mary Alice had from the age of nine been a card-carrying member of the Junior Scientists of America Club. By the time she was in high school, she spent all her money on record albums and on paperback books—she couldn't get enough of either. Why moon about not being invited to a party when you could listen to Bob Dylan? What date could compete with *Nine Stories*? She held out hope that, when she got to college, she'd be appreciated, and in some respects, she was right: she was appreciated when she was in college. She wasn't popular, but she was appreciated.

"So are you going?" Sarah Jane asked. She kept her voice light, but Mary Alice figured her sister's blood was boiling.

"I thought I might."

There was a thick silence until Mary Alice finally sighed and said, "What."

Sarah Jane looked up. "What? I didn't say anything!"

"Exactly."

"Well, Mary Alice, I mean . . . What can you possibly *gain*?"

"I don't know. These are people I used to know, so long ago! I'm curious to see how they turned out."

"I can tell you how they turned out. They were assholes then, and they'll be assholes now."

"Oh come on. People grow up."

Sarah Jane sniffed. "Some people do." She stabbed at the fabric with her needle. Then she gasped and looked wide-eyed at Mary Alice. "You aren't going there to see some secret *crush,* are you?"

"No," Mary Alice said. "Not at all. No."

"Oh, my God. You are, too! You're going to see *Pete Decker,* aren't you? That guy whose pictures from the newspaper you had up on your bedroom wall. Pete Decker, right? The football player, the prom king, president of the student council."

"Vice president," Mary Alice said. "Tom Gunderson was president."

"Mary Alice, listen to me, for once in your life. Believe me when I tell you: It is not a good idea to go to this thing. Everybody thinks things will be different at a reunion, but they're not: everybody just gets right back into their old roles from high school. It's awful. Those people won't want to see you now any more than they did then. They won't give you a second chance, believe me."

"You went to your fifth- and tenth-year reunions," Mary Alice said, and Sarah Jane said, a little too loudly, "Right! So I know what it's like! I was an idiot to go twice. A *masochist*! I should have brought Richard, because all I did both times—*both times!*—was sit at a table and eat maraschino cherries from watered-down drinks. I'll probably get cancer from all the red dye I consumed at those reunions."

Mary Alice spoke gently. "It's the *fortieth* reunion, Sarah Jane. And it's the last. It will be my only chance to ever go to a high school reunion. However imperfect it might have been, that time in high school is part of my life. I want to go and somehow revisit it. And I think it *will* be different."

Sarah Jane waved her arm. "Fine. Go, then. I'm just thinking of you. I don't want you to get hurt again."

"Oh, they never hurt me."

Sarah Jane stared at her until finally Mary Alice said, "Look. I appreciate your concern. I really do. But I'll be fine."

"Do you want me to go with you?"

Mary Alice laughed. "No, that's okay."

"Well, are you bringing Marion at least? You'll need an ally, Mary Alice. You'll need someone from your life now who really cares about you. You'll need someone who can defend you if . . . something happens."

Marion, a tall, pleasant-looking Polish man, is the owner of a construction company the next town over. He likes Mary Alice a lot, and occasionally they go out to eat or to a movie. But Marion doesn't speak much English. They mostly communicate with smiles and gestures, which actually suits Mary Alice fine. It seems graceful and kind, the way they talk. It seems *of the essence,* somehow. But she told her sister, "No. I'm going alone." Even as she said this, though, a little doubt crept in and she began to wonder. *Was* it so bad to go alone? *Should* someone go with her, just in case? But just in case *what*? What could possibly happen that would be so harmful?

Her sister is set on not believing it, but Mary Alice feels both secure and happy. She thinks she was born content, and she's grateful for that. She's not an insensitive person, but she has learned not to let hurt take up residence inside her. Everyone is entitled to their own opinion, but she learned long ago that she doesn't have to buy into what someone else says or thinks about her.

So yes, she is going to the reunion. She has narrowed her choices for what to wear down to two outfits: either a charcoal gray suit with a silvery blue blouse, a pearl necklace, and matching stud earrings, or a long black skirt with silver stars on it—she bought that skirt at a recycled clothing shop on a day she was feeling a little wild. It would be worn with a three-quarter-sleeved black V-necked top, the top quite low. Mary Alice hunched over to hide her breasts in high school, but now she does not hide them because they are beautiful—she blushes every time she thinks of Marion telling her that one night when they were making out in his construction truck. Just a little, they were making out. Each seemed afraid of going very far physically, though not *afraid* afraid. It was more like a don't-let's-break-this-thing-that's-not-broken fear. But that night Marion had kissed her breasts so sweetly and then looked up at her and sighed. He'd sat up and made a cupped-hand, up-and-down motion and said, "Beautiful. Still on high." When she got home, she'd stood naked before her bathroom mirror and thought, *He's right*. And she'd experienced a small rush of surprise, of delight, as if she'd walked into her bedroom and found a gift on her pillow.

"Well . . . *thank* you," she'd told Marion. What *does* one say in a situation like that? Mary Alice had never understood combining talking with sex. Do whatever you're doing and *then* talk, is what she thinks. Otherwise, it's like trying to listen to two conversations at once. In college, she once watched a porn movie with a couple of her dorm mates. One scene showed a woman lying beneath a man saying, "Oh, do it to me, do it to me, fuck me *hard*," and Mary Alice had no idea why the man didn't rear up and say, "I *am*!"

Mary Alice stares out Einer's bedroom window and decides that she'll wear the low-cut top and the starry skirt, and she thinks with it she'll wear big silver hoop earrings and many silver bangle bracelets. But then she worries how her glasses will look with that. Oh, enough! She'll decide what to wear on the night she's getting ready for the reunion: an answer will come to her.

Einer has taken one more bite than she asked him to, and she rewards him with a kiss on the top of his head. Then she helps him out onto the porch and begins to read the newspaper's front-page stories to him—he can no longer see to read. She's barely gotten through a paragraph when he starts in: "Oh, what the hell is Congress *doing*? In my day, a man had a thing between his ears called a brain, and guess what? He used it!" He'll settle down by the time she gets to the advice columns. They like to talk about what advice they'd give before Mary Alice reads the answers the columnist actually wrote.

Today, when she gets to the advice columns, she makes up a question. She keeps her eyes on the newspaper, as though she is reading, and says, "I am a middle-aged woman who has been invited to a high school reunion. I was not very popular in school and was often picked on. Should I expect that I might have a good time anyway?" She lets the question hang in the air, then says, "Hmmm. What do you think?"

Einer scrunches forward. "Don't you even think about going. Don't give those bastards the pleasure of your company."

"That's what you'd tell her?"

"That's what I'm telling *you*."

She looks away, and he says, "Everything's shot but my mind. You of all people ought to know that. Don't forget my wife taught music at that high school. She knew what went on. She used to tell me about how those kids treated you and your sister.

So, they're having a reunion, are they? Coming back to the old hometown they couldn't wait to get away from. You're not going, are you?"

"Well, yes. I am."

He grunts, adjusts himself in his chair. Then he leans forward and says, "I'm going with you, then," and she laughs, though a part of her thinks, *Well, why not?* This could be exactly what she needs: an ally who won't get in the way of anything.

"When we're there, if anyone says one snide thing to you, you help me out of my chair and I'll give them what for."

"Okay, Einer."

"I'm serious about this. You think I'm kidding? I'm serious! Where is it, anyway? At the school?"

"No, it's at the Westmore Hotel, out on Thirty-three."

"That's not but ten, fifteen minutes away. Short drive."

"Right."

"When is it?"

"Next weekend."

"Well, if I'm still here, I'm going."

"You'll be here," she says, though she's aware that he might not be, actually.

He sits back in his chair. "Punks," he mutters.

"Some of them were nice," Mary Alice says. "A lot of them were."

"Yeah. We'll sit at *their* table. All two of them."

Rita, Einer's caregiver, pulls up to the curb, and Mary Alice goes to help her carry in groceries.

"You will not believe what happened at the grocery store," Rita says. "I met the nicest man, over by the lettuce; he was all confused about what kind to buy. I helped him out and then we just got to talking, you know? When I said I had to go, he asked for my number, and I gave it to him. Oh, I hope he calls. I hope he does! Do you know how long it's been since I went out with a man?"

Mary Alice doesn't answer, thinking the question is rhetorical, but then when Rita says, "*Do* you?" Mary Alice dutifully responds, "No. How long has it been?"

"Well, it's been seven *months,*" Rita says. "Isn't that ridiculous?"

Mary Alice does not find this ridiculous. But, "*Wow!*" she says. And then, "I'm sure he'll call you."

"Oh, I hope so. And if he does, promise me you'll stay with Einer? I don't want to turn him down on the first date; I want to say yes to any night he proposes. Will you promise?"

"I promise," Mary Alice says. It's a pretty safe bet she won't have any other plans.

FOUR

Pete Decker has just cheated on his mistress with his wife, Nora. Now he sits at her kitchen table, watching her scramble eggs for him. Her ass shakes in that unattractive way that used to practically nauseate him, but now he sees it as comforting. And this woman knows *how* to scramble eggs, as opposed to Sandy, the woman he's been living with for the last three and a half months. That one makes scrambled eggs that come out like hard little yellow balls. He dropped Sandy off at the day spa this morning so that she could have her *stress* relieved. Though what she has to be stressed about, he has no idea. All she does is read magazines and natter on to her girlfriends and watch *The Housewives* this and *The Housewives* that and shop. On his dime. What a terrible mistake he has made. His kids will hardly speak to him, his office mates talk behind his back, and he's having an increasingly hard time getting it up. Never thought it would happen to him. Never! Not so young, anyway—he's only fifty-nine! (Though he's told Sandy he's fifty.) His dad was sticking it to them when he was *eighty*—he got laid the day before he *died*!

Well, Pete's not taking those damn boner pills. One reason is, he heard those things don't always work; two, they can cause vision and hearing loss. Wouldn't that just be perfect: he'd take a pill to amp up his sex life and end up with the trifecta of turnoffs. He'd be a limp-dicked guy, squinting into somebody's face and yelling, "*WHAT'S that?*"

Another reason he's not taking those pills is that it turns out Sandy's not worth it. If only he'd known that she drew on her eyebrows and wore false eyelashes, that she went to bed with purple crap on her face every night, that the vacuousness he had initially found so charming—such a *relief*!—would so soon wear thin. He'd only been living with her for two weeks when she got lazy about her appearance. The truth is, Sandy is a slob and a slacker. If you suffer under the illusion that all women are natural-born housekeepers, well, just come over and have a look at their place. They'd probably get evicted if anyone ever saw the kitchen or the bathroom. Sandy is great-looking, no one can deny that. Built, too, oh, sweet Jesus, built! But a slob and a slacker and a bore. What a terrible mistake he has made.

Nora puts the eggs down in front of him, perfect, fluffy eggs accompanied by the kind of bread that's good for you but tastes good anyway, and a little bowl of fresh fruit all cut up nice. "Thanks," he says. "Sandy mostly gives me Pop-Tarts."

"Well," Nora says. "Her cooking is not why you moved in with her. And you know, you could try cooking yourself sometimes."

It frustrates Pete, the way Nora defends Sandy, frustrates and mystifies him. He supposes it's really a way of getting back at him, a way of saying *You made your bed.* But still, shouldn't a wife be bitter and outraged about a mistress? Nothing's working out the way he thought it would!

"How are the kids?" he asks. He can't look at her when he asks this. It hurts too much.

"Didn't Katie call you?"

"She might have; I haven't looked yet today to see if I have any cellphone messages." This is a lie; he has looked, he's always looking, but his kids never call. If he wants to talk to them, he has to be the one to place the call. And then, when they show him the great honor of picking up, which is about one third of the time he calls, they make it plain they can't wait to get off the phone. They treat him a little like he's nuts. Which he guesses he was. But he's not, anymore. He's back.

"Huh!" Nora says. "She said she was going to call you yesterday."

"Well, what *is* it? Is she okay? Is it something bad?"

"No, nothing bad," Nora says, and then she smiles. "It's really nice news, actually."

"Nora. What is it?"

"I think I should let her tell you."

"Is she . . ." Pete sits back in his chair. "She's pregnant, isn't she? Oh, man, is she *pregnant*?!" Their twenty-seven-year-old daughter has been trying to conceive for two years. Last Pete knew, she was going to wait a couple more months and then start in with a fertility doctor.

Again, Nora smiles, but says nothing.

"No kidding, she's going to have a baby! That's great news!" But then the fact of his daughter's pregnancy suddenly slams into his brain and he realizes that if she's a mother, he'll be a grandfather. Him, a grandfather! Is he ready for that? An uncle, okay, but a *grandfather*? Is Nora okay with it? Is she ready to be a grandmother? Judging by her soft, pleased expression, he guesses she is. He forces himself to smile and says, "I'm going send her the biggest bouquet of flowers they can make. All . . . pink and blue!"

"Wait for her to tell you," Nora says. "I don't want her to

think I betrayed her; she asked me not to say anything. She said she would tell you, and I'm sure she will, when she's ready."

Betray. He looks down at his eggs and takes another bite. "Thanks for making me breakfast, Nora. It's really good. You know?" His throat is tight. What, now he's going to *cry*? He bites down hard on his back molars, swallows away the feeling. "Thanks for everything." Now he looks into her face and smiles. The woman may be thirty-five years older than Sandy, but she has her own eyebrows, for Christ's sake. And her smile is still dynamite. And the sex he just had with her was almost like it was when they first started. What a mistake he has made.

"How are the boys?" he asks. Their older son, Pete Jr., is having problems with his wife, though he's assured his mother he wants to work it out. He and his wife, Karen, are in therapy together. Pete himself has often said he'd never go to marriage counseling. But guess what? He'll do it now. He'll sit there and listen to all the bullshit and promise the moon. And deliver it.

Their younger son, Cal, is trying yet again to start up a business: selling boats, this time, God help him. Cal doesn't know a thing about boats. But he says he'll learn. Cal's a happy, wildly optimistic soul; it takes a lot to make him feel bad or discouraged about anything. His wife, Sunny, is aptly named: she'll go along with anything Cal wants to do. And her family mints money: if worse comes to worst, they can always get a loan from them.

"The boys are okay," Nora says. "Pete and Karen are going to Paris."

"Wow. So their problems are over." Pete imagines his son and daughter-in-law cuddled together on a nighttime flight to Paris. *Business* class. Pete Jr. would no doubt fall for that upgrade bullshit when the truth is that an airplane seat is hell no matter where on the plane it is. Save your money for when you get where you're going, is what Pete would like to tell him. But Paris, that's nice, he guesses. Very romantic place, he's heard. He should have taken Nora there, she always used to talk about wanting to go to Paris. But then she just gave up.

"No, their problems aren't over," Nora says. "They're just trying really hard. They say they want to work it out, they want to try to stay together. It's hard. But Cal! Cal is *great*! You won't believe it, but in the last week, he got three orders for yachts. Big ones!"

"How in the hell did he do that?"

"Well, he's got his father's charm and he's also connected to a lot of people that Sunny's family knows. And you know how it is; even in a bad economy, the rich still spend money."

Pete wipes up the last of his scrambled eggs with the last bite of toast. Perfect breakfast. "How are you fixed for funds?"

"I'm fine."

"Why don't I leave you a couple hundred?"

"I'm *fine,* Pete." She leans in closer to him. "Pete? Listen, I . . . What we just did? I feel bad about it. And I think you need to tell Sandy that it happened."

"Ah, jeez."

"If you admit it—and I think it's only fair that you do—you'll get to some problems in your relationship that you obviously need to face up to. And I'm going to tell Fred, too."

"You're . . . Fred who?"

"Fred Preston."

Pete can hardly contain his outrage. "You're involved with *Fred Preston*?" The wimpy guy down the block. Widower. Always wearing a hat so he won't get *skin cancer.* Runs every day in *a jogging outfit.*

"Yes, I am. I've been wanting to tell you."

"Fred *Preston*? You are fucking shitting me!"

"Do you mind watching your language?"

"You're kidding me."

"He's actually a very interesting man."

Pete snorts. "Yeah, well, he'd better be. Not much else to recommend him."

Nora stands and starts clearing the dishes. "Not true. I think he's quite good-looking."

"Oh, *please*."

She turns from the sink to look over at him. "Well, you may not think so."

"Oh, come on, Nora. You're *attracted* to him?"

She raises an eyebrow, lifts one shoulder.

"And you're going to tell him we had sex."

"Yes, I am. I am interested in having a completely honest relationship, for a change. I'm going to say I had a little slip, but it won't happen again."

Pete lowers his voice to what he hopes is a sexy register. "Are you sure?" He wishes Nora would look at him. He has gorgeous turquoise eyes, god damn it.

She comes back to the table and sits down with him. "Pete. Listen to me. We're done. I want to finalize the divorce."

Her words actually take his breath away. They make for a deep pain right in the center of his chest.

He speaks rapidly. "But I'm getting out, Nora. I'm leaving her. I was just going to tell you that. You think I haven't been regretting what I've done since the day I left? What we did here today . . . I understand something now.

"I want to come back. I'll tell Sandy this afternoon and then, right afterward, I'll pack my bags and come home. Let me come home, Nora. Everything will be so different, you'll see. I didn't mean all those things I said the day I left. How could I have meant those things? I was just frustrated about . . . I don't know. About everything, I guess. But I didn't mean those things, Nora! Please! Do you believe me?"

"Yes. I believe you."

He closes his eyes, exhales. "Oh, God, thank you, honey. Thank you." He can't wait. He'll pack just a few . . . No. Fuck it. He'll leave everything in that crap condo Sandy couldn't live without. He never wants to go back there again. Let her have everything. All he wants is to have his family back, that's all he wants. Once again, he feels the burn of tears. "I want you to know, babe, that I—"

"Pete," she says. "*Don't.* I know you really meant what you just said. But I mean what I said, too. I'll be your friend, we'll co-parent the kids, but . . ." She shrugs. "It's over. Such a silly word for such a serious thing, it seems like such a cliché to say it, so Roy Orbison. But it's true. We've come to the end, there's no going forward for you and me. And I'm not even . . . I'm not hurt anymore. I'm not bitter or angry. The kids are, but they're working that out. And I'm trying to help them with it. This has been coming for a long time, Pete. I knew it was coming; you must have, too. I guess I had more time to get ready than I'd thought. In the back of my mind, I think I'd resigned myself long ago to our not staying together.

"Look, down the road, I can see us all having dinner together, you and Sandy, and me and Fred, and the kids . . . and the grand-kids! Things will all work out. But, Pete, you have to listen to me, now. You have to hear me. I don't want to live with you again. It wasn't good for me, as it turns out. I'm happier now." She sighs. "I'm sorry, pal."

"Aw, Christ. Don't call me '*pal.*'"

"I always call you that."

"Yeah, but now it means something different." He stares miserably at the table, where the sun has come through the window to illuminate his hands. They are clenched so tightly together his knuckles are white. He separates them and clears his throat. "Hey, Nora? Did you get the invitation to our fortieth high school reunion?"

"Yes. I threw it away."

"You're not going?"

"When have I ever gone to one of our reunions? I didn't RSVP, but Pam will figure it out. Not that she was the brightest girl. *Nice,* though. And always so cheerful! She always said hi to you every time she passed you in the hall, remember? 'Oh, *hi!*' in that real excited way, even if she'd *just seen* you. She'd say hi and wave. Once she started to wave to me and she dropped all her books. I helped her pick them up and we bumped heads and it really *hurt.* And then we couldn't stop laughing, we were just sitting on the floor and laughing and then we were late for class." Nora shakes her head, smiling. "God. Pam Pottsman. I haven't thought about her in years. Maybe I will call and tell her I'm not coming. I'll catch up with her a little bit."

"Don't call!" Pete says, so loudly that Nora jumps.

"Sorry," he says, and smashes down the hair at the back of his head, a nervous habit he hates. "Don't call her," he says again. "Or do call, but say you're coming. Say you're coming with me."

"But I'm not coming with you!"

"Will you? Please? It's the last one!"

"Pete. No."

He gets up and stands before her. He holds her familiar face in his hands—oh, God, look at her. "Nora. I fucked up big-time. I know it. I fucked up for years. I'm *sorry.* I *heard* you, when you said we were done, I heard you, okay?"

She starts to respond and he talks over her. "No. No. Listen to me. We were married for a long time, Nora. A long time, you know? Why don't you just think about going with me? That's all I'm asking. Just think about it. I know it wouldn't necessarily mean anything. But if you'd go with me, I'd be so—"

"Pete, I can't. Fred and I are going on a trip that weekend."

He can't speak. He stares at her and feels again that terrible ripping sensation in his chest.

"We're going to the Grand Canyon," she says.

Oh, for fuck's sake. The *Grand Canyon*. Which she's already seen, she went with a couple of girlfriends not two years ago!

"You know what, Nora? I'll take you to Paris. I will. No strings attached or anything. First class! You can have your own hotel room, if you want. If you need to. We can go—"

"Okay, Pete, enough. Listen, I made a mistake with you this morning, and I am fully prepared to take responsibility for it. I think you should do the same, though I recognize that it's not really my business anymore what you do. But now let's just move on. Let's not see each other for a while. If anything with the kids comes up, I'll tell you. Or, you know, anything else you really need to know about. But let's not see each other for a while. Let's look upon what happened today as a final goodbye, and get on with our lives. Okay?"

"Nora," he says. "I'll do whatever you want. I will. But let me just ask you something. And don't answer yet! Don't answer yet. I want to ask something very important." He sees her mouth tighten and he says, "I'm *going*, Nora, but I just need to ask you this one thing."

She crosses her arms, steps back. "What."

"I want you to consider moving your trip with Fred to another weekend and going to the reunion with me." If she does this, he'll still have a chance to get her back. If not, his goose is cooked.

She starts to speak, and he holds up his hand. "No! Please, don't answer yet! Come on, Nora, can't I even . . .

"It's just that it would mean so much to me. It really would. And also, I think if you do this for me . . . If you do this, then I can start letting you go. I know you want me to let you go. I just want us to end on a pleasant note. You know?" He shudders, then, an autonomic response that humiliates him. He looks away from Nora, and when he turns back to her, he sees tears in her eyes.

"Okay, so I'll take off," he says. From the corner of his eye, he sees a fork still on the table. He retrieves it and hands it to her. "Here you go."

"Thank you," she says softly.

"Finally helping with the dishes, huh?"

She smiles.

"Do you . . . The lawn's gotten long. Do you want me to mow it? I won't come in after or anything. Nothing like that."

"Pete," she says. "Go home."

I am home, he wants to say. But he's not, anymore.

He walks out to the car on feet that seem to have become numb. Now what? Get some Viagra, he supposes. Then go home and screw the living daylights out of Spa Girl. That's right. That will make him feel better. He climbs into his car, thinks about what he can try with Sandy that he hasn't done yet. Then he rests his head against the steering wheel and stares down at the stupid tasseled loafers she talked him into buying. Nora looked at them when he flung them off before they went to bed, but she didn't say anything. That's what she does when she doesn't like something. That's what she used to do, anyway. Now she speaks up, at least about the important things. Well, so will he. He'll call Pam Pottsman and he knows exactly what he'll say, he can all but see the lines like they're a script. He'll say, "Hey, Pammy, how you *doing,* sweets?" Then she'll *blah blah blah.* Then he'll say, "Listen, I'm going to need another ticket for the reunion. Put me down for two instead of one. A little surprise for Nora, so don't say a word." He bets Pam will think that's romantic. He bets she'll flirt with him on the phone, too, just like she did last time. Any girl in their class would flirt with him, if she had the opportunity. Somebody like Pam Pottsman, that could be a trial. You didn't want to be rude, but Jesus. Another kind of woman, though, that's another story. Couple of months ago he ran into Beth Hillman at the airport in *Detroit,* for Christ's sake, and she remembered him right away. He remembered her after a minute, too. Head cheerleader. They'd had a few sessions. Oh, yeah, they had. Bethie was a *real* blonde. At the airport, they'd gone to a bar and had a drink, had a real nice talk, too, no time for anything else, but if there had been time, he could have checked them into the adjoining hotel, no problem, he could tell; she was ready steady. "You know, you really haven't changed a bit, Pete," she'd said, and don't think he didn't know what that meant.

He heads out onto the freeway, and when the traffic slows, he regards himself in the rearview mirror. Game so not over, not for this boy. Not by a long fucking shot. He starts to smile, to check out his killer dimples, but his smile becomes a grimace. He grabs at his chest, his hand over his heart and grunts, *Unh! Unh! Unh!* He manages to pull into the breakdown lane, to put the car into park, call 911 and give an approximate location. Jesus, it's hard to talk, it's hard to talk! He snaps the phone shut, then slumps down, closes his eyes, and waits to die.

FIVE

DOROTHY CAN HARDLY DIAL THE PHONE FAST ENOUGH. When her friend Linda answers, Dorothy says, "You won't believe this! Candy Sullivan is coming to the reunion!"

"Get out," Linda says. "How do you know?"

"Pam Pottsman called me. Just this very minute."

"Does Judy know?"

"No, I called you first."

"Oh, my God. Let's have a conference call tonight. I'll send Judy an email and tell her. How's seven o'clock?"

Dorothy's favorite television show comes on at seven, but this is more important. She can always watch it with the sound down. She wishes she knew how to use the recording device on her television, but it's all she can do to turn it on and off. When her husband was moving out and asked if he could take the TV, she had hollered, "*No! No! No!* You don't take *one* thing from this house unless it belongs to *only you*." And he hadn't. He'd left quietly, with a great deal of dignity, Dorothy had to admit. She'd been a screaming banshee, but she is so much better now. Completely recovered. A new person, really.

Hilly said she'd teach her mother how to record shows; it's easy, she's said; but she hasn't shown Dorothy how yet. She hasn't done much of anything lately but talk about her wedding: Should she wear a necklace with her gown? Drop earrings or stud? Are take-home monogrammed cookies for the guests a charming or a tacky idea? Must the hand towels in the ladies' room be linen or is high-quality paper all right? Dorothy wants to help, but she's never been good at this kind of thing. And although she's never told Hilly this, she doesn't really like all the fuss made over weddings. She herself had the thinnest of affairs, and it was all she could do to get through *that*. So far as she is concerned, the whole industry is nothing but a rip-off. Nonetheless, when Hilly told her she was engaged and wanted a big, big wedding, Dorothy ran right over to the bookstore and purchased an armload of bride magazines. But looking at them only depressed her. So many decisions! You see a classic multilayered ivory fondant cake decorated with fresh flowers and wide bands of periwinkle blue ribbon and think, *Oh, that's the one!* Then you turn the page and see a tiered silver server loaded up with purposefully imperfect cupcakes and think, *Oh, but what fun this one is!*

It went on and on. Where to have the wedding? At what time of day? How many guests should be invited? What should the meal be? The music? Open or cash bar? And the choice in bridal gowns! Thank God Hilly pretty much knew what she wanted going in. In less than three hours, she chose a floor-length, strapless confection of a gown with a subtle pattern of seed pearls and other shimmering embellishments strewn across the bottom half of the skirt. She's wearing a full-length veil, too, a lacy one with the same kinds of embellishments as the dress. When Dorothy saw the price tag, she had to bite her tongue to keep from squawking in outrage. But she didn't say anything. She wasn't the one paying the bills, after all. And anyway, Hilly looked beautiful in that dress. She looked absolutely transformed. That was a moment, when Hilly tried the dress on, and their eyes met in the mirror. Dorothy stood behind her daughter, her purse clenched tight up against her middle, and blinked back tears, then let them freely flow. *Oh, my love,* she was thinking. *My little girl.* And so much more, she was overwhelmed with feelings, a curious mix of joy and sorrow. And even though Hilly laughed and made fun of her mother, Dorothy saw tears in Hilly's eyes, too.

Dorothy tells Linda, "A conference call! Great idea. Okay, call me at seven. I'll be right by the phone."

"Here's your assignment," Linda says. "Start remembering stories about Candy so we can have a really good session. Oh! I just remembered one now! I'm going to go write it down."

After Dorothy hangs up, she inspects herself in the mirror again. She's going to have lunch with her daughter, and Hilly can be very critical. Honest, she calls it, and it is honest, Dorothy supposes, but it's also barbed-wire critical.

It bothers Dorothy how much she wants Hilly to like her. She knows it's wrong, she knows you're not supposed to worry about your children liking you, you're just supposed to raise them right, but from the day Hilly was born, she has always wanted her daughter to like her. Not love her, although that, too, but actively *like* her. In the early years, it wasn't much of a problem. Hilly absolutely adored her. Oh, she went through her I-only-want-Daddy! phase when she was a toddler, but Dorothy knew she didn't really mean it. She came soon enough to the knowledge that Dorothy was the one to whom she should really be grateful.

All through Hilly's elementary and junior high school years, she and Dorothy had been like best friends. Hilly told her mother everything: what boy she was crazy over, how her breasts were infuriatingly small, how embarrassing it was when she burped during math class. And Dorothy told Hilly things she supposed she shouldn't: that she sometimes cried in the middle of the day and didn't know why. That she suspected their neighbor of having an affair with the FedEx deliveryman. That she feared she would be abandoned in her old age. She hadn't said all the mean things she wanted to say about Hilly's father; she knew how damaging it was for a child to hear one parent bad-mouthing the other, and besides that, it could backfire and make Hilly move closer to Team Daddy.

But then, right around age fifteen, Hilly had begun preferring her father to her mother. In every way. Since the divorce, which her father had instigated just after Hilly graduated from college because he found someone who *appreciated* him (God almighty, the woman looks like a *frog*, plus she's older than he is!), Hilly has been a bit nicer to her mother. But heaven forbid Dorothy even think a negative thought about her ex-husband. Pops, Hilly began calling him in her senior year of high school, and every time Dorothy hears it, she wants to roll her eyes.

Dorothy told Hilly about what she's wearing to the reunion: one of those extravagantly ruffled black blouses with sheer sleeves, a black pencil skirt, black nylons, and some heels that will probably necessitate her having back surgery after she wears them. But it's important that she look fabulous and not a victim of collapsing vertebral disks. After she described her outfit to Hilly, her daughter had said, "Hmm," and that's when Dorothy knew she'd done it all wrong. Well, there's plenty of time to get a replacement outfit. She'll see what Hilly suggests, if, as she suspects, she nixes her mother's first choice.

Dorothy hears the front door opening and then the sound of her daughter calling her. "In the kitchen!" she says, and she grabs her purse, a clutch her daughter gave her last Christmas, so she knows it's right.

She meets Hilly in the hallway, and they give each other a

quick embrace. Dorothy doesn't really like embracing people in this way, but you have to, these days. Everybody does that European kiss-kiss thing now, too, and Dorothy thinks it's so fake. Why must people *touch* one another so often? Look at all the germs you're spreading around for no reason. Oh, touching is fine when it's for a reason, but when you're just saying hello? Well, she'd better get used to it. She bets at the reunion they'll be double-kissing like crazy. She'll have to remember to get some of that nonsmear lipstick.

"So!" she says. "Where would you like to go for lunch? We can go anywhere you like!"

"I don't know, Ma," Hilly says. "You pick. I thought you had a place in mind."

"I thought it would be fun for you to choose."

"Fine, Bistro 102."

"Oh, great idea! They have such good food!"

"Not really, but it's close. I need to get over to the wedding coordinator's office by three; she's screwed everything up again."

"What's wrong?"

Hilly waves her hand. "Oh, a million things. For one thing, the videographer I wanted is moving overseas before the wedding, so now I have to choose another one. And there's a bunch of miscellaneous problems you don't want to hear about, believe me. *I* don't want to hear about them!"

"Do you need me to help?"

"No, Ma. Thanks."

"Okay," Dorothy says, "so we'll go eat, and then if we—"

"Didn't you want me to look at your outfit for the reunion?" Hilly says. "I thought you wanted me to come over here so I could look at your outfit!"

"Oh!" Dorothy says. "Right!" She puts her purse down on the hall bench and says, "Come upstairs with me, I'll try it on for you." She's excited; she wonders what Hilly will say.

"Can't you just show it to me?" Hilly looks at her watch.

For a moment, Dorothy thinks of saying, "You know what? Forget the whole thing. Just forget the whole damn thing! You ungrateful child! I used cloth diapers so you'd never get a rash! Everything I fed you I made from scratch! I stayed home to raise you and I played Candy Land with you over and over when other women were forging interesting careers. Who changed your sheets when you vomited all over them? *Pops?*" But she doesn't say that. She says, as evenly as she can, "You have time for me to try it on. You can't really tell me how it looks unless I have it on."

She walks ahead of her daughter up the stairs and hears Hilly say something. "What?"

"You have a *run* in your stocking," Hilly says. "You know, nobody even *wears* those things anymore, and that's *why.*"

And now Dorothy turns around to speak angrily to her daughter but collapses on the steps, just falls on her butt with her legs spread out like a man's so anyone who wants to can see up her skirt, as if. Then, to make matters worse, she starts to cry. Hilly's not the only one whose nerves are on edge. Dorothy has a lot to think about, too!

"Ma," Hilly says. "Jesus Christ."

"Just go!" Dorothy says. "I don't want to have lunch with you! And I don't care what you think of what I'm wearing!" She kicks her leg out angrily, like a toddler, and her shoe falls off.

Hilly retrieves it and sits beside her mother on the steps. She slides the shoe onto her mother's foot and then puts her arm around her shoulders. "Ma," she says, and her voice is softer now. She smells good. She's wearing a black-and-white blouse and black pants and many silver bracelets. Her hair is done in one of those half-up, half-down styles, and it looks very pretty. She has Chanel sunglasses perched atop her head. "Look," Hilly says. "I'm sorry. I am just a mess these days. I'm such a bitch I can hardly stand to be with myself, let alone other people. It's this wedding crap. All these details to decide, it just never stops, it's like Mickey Mouse in that movie with all the brooms and buckets. I swear, I don't even *want* to get married anymore."

"Don't say that!" Dorothy says, and hastily dries her eyes. He's a doctor, for God's sake, and Hilly is almost forty. This is no time to throw a good fish back into the ocean!

"I mean it, Ma. I don't want to. I don't see why I should. The only reason to get married these days is to have kids, and I don't think I want kids."

Dorothy looks at her. Blinks. "You don't?"

"No. I mean . . . I don't know."

"I think you should have children," Dorothy says. "Oh, Hilly, you can't know how wonderful it is. You never can know, until you're in it up to your eyeballs."

"At which point it's too late," Hilly says, ruefully. "What if you don't *like* it?"

"You'll like it," Dorothy said. Though even as she says it, she recognizes, as if for the first time, the possibility of it not being true. It reminds her of the glib reassurance she was given by a nail tech who talked her into getting those false fingernails. "You'll love them," the woman had said. But they were awful! It hurt when you got them put on, and you had to get them filled all the time and they made your real nails a fragile, peeling mess, and you could never keep them clean under there. Oh, how she cringes when she's handed food by people with nails so long they couldn't clench their fists if their lives depended on it. Those long nails with *things* all over them, like hieroglyphics. She herself finally had the false nails removed, and after a few months her own nails were back to normal. She'd only gotten those nails because she had been relentlessly schooled by her mother in what a girl was required to do: Maintain ten long painted nails at all times. Put your fork down after each bite, and make sure each bite is minuscule. Practice walking with a book on your head to ensure good posture. (Dorothy actually did that, up and down the hallway, over and over.) Sit with your knees pressed together and your legs slanted to the side. Cream your face, powder your feet, know when to use "who" and when to use "whom." Never let anyone see you in rollers; those women who went out with scarves on their heads weren't fooling anyone.

There were a million rules that Dorothy endeavored to follow and still her mother never seemed satisfied. Or her father. Dorothy's mother had been a bona fide beauty queen, Miss Ohio, and Dorothy had never lived up to her parents' expectations of her, she knew it. She would lie in bed at night vowing that the next day would be better, and it never was. She was the worst in dancing class. The ringlets her mother put in Dorothy's hair were ruined by cowlicks. She fell off her horse the first day she rode and many times thereafter. The one and only time she tried to kiss her parents goodnight, it went so badly, she never tried again. They were not big on touching in Dorothy's little family, which is to say they did not touch at all. They did not praise or say "I love you"; that was too effusive, utterly unnecessary. But one night when Dorothy was four, a summer night, the sky still blue at bedtime, she was overwhelmed with a desire to kiss her parents goodnight. Dorothy remembers every detail: her hair was put up in bobby pins, and she was wearing a new white nightgown, white ribbons and white lace, a ruffled bottom. She remembers how her mother sat stiffly, her hands clenched, when Dorothy embraced her, and how her father smiled indulgently and then pushed her away, saying, "Now, now." And Dorothy had felt full of shame. Full of it. She had understood that you do not do that, no matter how your heart may be calling for it. It was yet another mistake she had made. The only thing she is good at is inspiring a certain kind of friendship and loyalty in some people, and she still doesn't know how she makes that happen.

But children. She recalls a night when Hilly was maybe six years old and Dorothy was tucking her into bed. She pulled up Hilly's covers and kissed her forehead and said, "Now I'm going to make a magic sign so you will have wonderful dreams." She made a kind of swirling motion with her hand and Hilly watched solemn faced, believing absolutely in her mother's powers in the way that children do. Up to a certain age, anyway, after which they believe nothing you say, but never mind. That night, Dorothy had tucked a little blanket she'd made for Hilly's favorite stuffed animal—a bedraggled Snoopy dog, who at that point seemed held together purely by Hilly's love for him—around him. Then she'd kissed his nose and said, "Goodnight, Blackie," and Hilly had said, "Make a sign for Blackie's dreams, too," and Dorothy had; and at that point she'd kind of believed in her powers herself. Hilly had sighed and said, "You're a good mommy." And something had swelled inside Dorothy's chest, and she'd thought, *If I never have anything else, at least I had this.*

But now Dorothy tells Hilly, "You don't *have* to have kids, of course. You can enjoy other people's children. Or live a life that doesn't have much to do with children at all—what's important is that you're honest with yourself."

Well! She said that and immediately she wanted to lock herself in the bathroom and sit on the floor and think what it meant. What did that *mean,* to make your own decisions, independent of all the grabby influences in the world? How did it feel to say, "No, I don't think that's for me," and then simply *not do* what it seemed like everyone else was doing? She couldn't imagine. Yet here is her daughter clearly attempting to be in charge of her own life, to be aware that it is created by the choices she makes, and Dorothy wants to weep in gratitude. It is too late for Dorothy to live a conscious life. She never escaped her mother's iron hand, she had not even *tried* being a hippie except for one time when she didn't wear makeup or shave her legs. And even then, she returned quickly enough to her learned standards of hygiene. You did your hair and you shaved your legs and you put your face on, no matter what. But Hilly was out from under something huge. Hilly was able to look up and see the sky. And Dorothy had somehow been a part of making that happen.

"I don't know about kids," Hilly says. "But I will get married, I guess. I mean, I kind of have to."

"You mean because of the money?" Dorothy says. "Because we'll lose the deposits? Don't get married for *that* reason! Who *cares* about the money?" *Especially when it's your father's,* she thinks. But she feels certain Hilly's father would offer the same advice.

"No," Hilly says. "It's not because of the money we'd lose." She turns to face her mother. "It's just that . . . I don't think I'll find anyone better than Mark. If I'm going to get married, I guess he's the one. But all of a sudden, it feels so . . . I don't know. *Arbitrary. Dangerous.* I don't see how anyone can ever feel completely convinced that marrying someone is the right thing to do, I don't see how anyone can not be consumed by doubt. Did you feel absolutely sure about marrying Pops?"

Dorothy had felt absolutely sure about being pregnant, that's what she had felt. But Hilly doesn't know that. So she says, "Course I wasn't sure! I was full of doubt, too. I think almost everyone is. You have to be! Who can possibly subscribe to the notion that there's only one person in the world for you? No. But you find someone you care for, that you think you might be able to build a life with, and then you just go for it!"

"And then you get divorced," Hilly says bitterly.

Dorothy speaks carefully now. "No, now, Hilly, you know that's not true. Some people have very happy marriages. I think the biggest problem is people's expectations are so high. And so wrong! People think marriage is going to be so romantic and fulfilling. They think the other person is going to *complete* them. But that's not what happens. In a good marriage, you complete yourself while sharing a bathroom. You go through life with company, rather than alone, and humans seem to need company. And . . . You remember in *Carousel,* when the doctor tells the high school graduating class not to worry about others liking them, that they should just try to like others?"

"I love *Carousel,*" Hilly says, sighing. "I still love it. Everybody makes fun of me, but I still love it. We used to watch it and eat caramel corn and dill pickles."

"I know," Dorothy says. "But do you remember that part?"

"Of course."

"Well, that's it. That's what you need to do in your marriage. You need to *give* what you *want.* And don't expect so much. That only sets you up for disappointment. If you expect anything, expect that marriage will be hard, that it will be work. And expect that the pleasures will be erratic and often small, but they'll turn out to mean more than you know."

Dorothy's voice has thickened; there is a sizable lump in her throat. *Now* look what she has just said! What is she, Dr. Phil? Or whoever? She wishes someone had told *her* the things about marriage she just told her daughter. Her husband might still be with her instead of with Amphibian Face. It comes to her all at once the lack of generosity she showed her husband all the years they were together. The lack of simple kindness. The way she blamed him for everything.

"Where did you read that?" Hilly says. "I might buy the book."

"Oh, here and there," Dorothy says. "And of course I've had a little experience in learning what *not* to do. Not only in marriage, either." She inspects the tops of her knees. She stares intently at them as though trying to locate a tiny thing she just felt crawling on them.

Hilly speaks in a small voice, stripped of arrogance or defense. "So . . . do you think I'll be okay, then?"

Now Dorothy's heart warms and opens, and she turns to face her daughter. "Oh, sweetie, I think you'll be just fine. I think you'll be great. I think the two of you will have a wonderful marriage. All brides are nervous wrecks in the weeks before their marriage. It's good luck!" She doubts that this is true, really, but what the heck.

Hilly reaches over to hug her mother, and Dorothy hugs her back, and there, *that's* how a hug should be given.

"Let's see that outfit," Hilly says, standing and reaching out a hand to help pull her mother up.

"I don't know," Dorothy says. "Now we've had this emotional exchange, and maybe you won't quite tell me the truth. You'll think you have to spare my feelings."

"You know me; I'll tell you the truth," Hilly says, and so Dorothy gets up and goes into the bathroom and changes into her outfit, complete with beauty mark that she draws in above her lip. She talks to Hilly about Pete Decker through the closed door, how handsome he was, how popular, what a great car he had, how he'd seemed pretty interested in her at one point.

"So I want to just knock him out," Dorothy says. "I just want one more chance with him. And the first time he sees me needs to be really memorable." She opens the door. *"Ta dah!"*

Hilly widens her eyes and bites at her bottom lip. Nods.

"See?" Dorothy says. "You hate it but you won't say so."

"I don't *hate* it," Hilly says. "I think you should wear the blouse with jeans for the breakfast. But for Saturday night, may I make a suggestion? I saw a Stella McCartney the other day that would look terrific on you. Cobalt blue. You look really good in blue. And you've lost more weight, you'd look fabulous in it, you'd look absolutely cachectic."

"Oh, honey," Dorothy says. *"Thank* you."

"You're welcome." Hilly points to her own upper lip. "You've got something on your lip, right here."

"That's my beauty mark. I drew it in. I'm going to wear it to the reunion. Kind of fun."

"Oh."

"No?"

"It's your party, Ma."

"Okay, no." Dorothy rubs it off. But she will wear it at the reunion. Her daughter doesn't know everything. Beauty marks aren't from her time.

Hours later, Dorothy is in her bathrobe and seated on her sofa in front of the television, waiting for her friends to call. She's put egg white on her face—she's going to use a different kind of facial every night before the reunion, and her hairdresser told her raw egg whites work wonders. "It feels like a big glob of snot when you first put it on," she told Dorothy, "but then it tightens your skin like you wouldn't believe, and it gives it a wonderful glow." The egg has indeed begun to tighten her skin—she just saw herself in the mirror and she looks like she used to when she would pull a nylon down over her face for Halloween.

The phone rings, and Dorothy answers by saying, "Hi, it's Candy Sullivan, I can't come to the phone right now because I'm too busy admiring myself in one of my many gilt-framed mirrors." It just pops out. She guesses she's through being all wise and kind and generous in spirit. But she can't help it; gossip is so delicious and, anyway, Candy will never know.

She hears Judy and Linda laugh, and then Linda says, "Okay, I want to go first. Did you guys ever hear about Candy and George Keethler?"

"Nooooo," they say together.

"Well, I heard they were in his car and she was giving him oral sex—"

"No way!" Dorothy says, and sees that her fingers have inadvertently flown to her breastbone. She reminds herself to make an appointment for a manicure the day before the reunion, the last appointment of the day. "Candy Sullivan? She would never have done that!"

"Oh, yes, she did!" Linda says. "She gave BJs! The whole football team knew it! And she was giving one to George Keethler and the car's engine was on 'cause they needed the heater, and her head bumped into the gearshift and they started rolling and he sat up real fast and she *bit* it!"

Judy is laughing, but she says, "How do *you* know this?"

"The guys on the football team! George showed the bite mark to them! And Ross Duggan was a friend of my brother's and he told my brother, and my brother told me. It was when my brother was pissed off at Candy because she wouldn't go out with him because she had moved on to the college boys. He made me promise not to tell you guys, but I think we're past the statute of limitations."

Out of the corner of her eye, Dorothy is watching a scene on her television show. She reaches for the remote and turns the volume up, just a little. Oh, her life seems suddenly to be an embarrassment of riches. Her daughter and she seem to be getting closer, she's lost weight, she's got a beautiful dress in which to seduce Pete Decker, and she's about to hear more delicious stories about Candy Sullivan. The one she'll share isn't nearly as good. She had science class with Candy, and one day the teacher had asked the question "What is matter?" He had called on Candy even though her hand was not up. Dorothy knew the answer and her hand was up, but Mr. Templeton did not call on her. He asked Candy the question, and she answered, "Nothing." Mr. Templeton's forehead wrinkled and he said, *"Nothing?"*

"Right," Candy said. "Nothing." She was wearing a heather pink A-line skirt that day, Dorothy remembers because she loved that skirt, it had a matching cardigan sweater and Candy wore it that day with a floral-print, round-collared Villager blouse and the little cheerleading megaphone necklace that she always wore, all the cheerleaders did, God forbid anyone ever forgot for one moment that they were *cheerleaders,* and her hair had been all the way down that day, she had the most unbelievably thick blond hair that hung down past the middle of her back. Really beautiful hair.

Mr. Templeton frowned at Candy and looked over at Dorothy, still waving her hand in the air like she was trying to flag down roadside assistance. "All right, Dorothy," he said. "What is matter?" And she answered breathlessly, "Matter is anything that takes up space and has weight."

"Right," Mr. Templeton said, and then stared pointedly at Candy. She smiled that unbelievably beautiful smile and said, "Oh! I thought you said, 'What's *the* matter?'"

"I've got a story," Judy says, and Dorothy turns the sound back down on the television. They're showing a commercial for food, and Dorothy doesn't want to hear a word of it. She's starving to death but a girl can do anything for four more days.

SIX

"Cooper?" Candy Sullivan Armstrong says, softly. No answer.

"Coop?" She can tell from the sound of her husband's breathing that he's deep in sleep. She won't wake him. He won't be able to give her what she wants, anyway. What she wants is to say that she's scared, and for him to take her into his arms and simply hold her. But if she does say that, Coop will sigh and say, "Why are you *scared*? You don't even *know* anything yet. Go back to sleep." And then he will do precisely that.

The truth is, she does worry too much. On four separate occasions when awaiting medical test results, she diagnosed herself with terrible diseases; and then it turned out she was just fine. But this time is different, it really is. This time it feels as though something has come into her house and sat in her darkened living room, waiting for her to come upon it. And now that she has, it has said, *Ah. There you are. Don't be turning on the light, now.*

She pushes the bedclothes off and sits up, slides her feet into the slippers she keeps at her side of the bed. She reaches for her

robe, pulls it over her nightgown, and stands for a moment looking at the dim outlines of the furniture in her bedroom: the bed,
the night tables and lamps, the antique writing desk, the armoire,
the little French sofa and the table that sits before it. Her eyes follow the sweep of the draperies, the line of the velvet cushion on
the window seat. She can't make out the images in the various
paintings, but she knows full well what they are, and she loves
them, every one. Everything has become precious: the slippers on
her feet—her *feet*! She looks back at Coop, still sleeping soundly,
and tiptoes out of the bedroom.

When she was a girl, she thought of old age as a kind of insulting, almost humorous infirmity. You got gray and wrinkled,
you couldn't run or even walk fast, you couldn't see or hear very
well, you spoke in a voice that trembled and cracked, you rubbed
your aching knees with hands whose knuckles had gone knobby
and high. That was all. It astonishes her now to think how she
was so unaware of the smorgasbord of frightening diagnoses, or
the need for constant doctors' visits, or the mountains of pills required just to keep up the ever-deteriorating status quo. Her own
parents died young, in their late fifties, in a boating accident
when they were on vacation in the Bahamas, so she never saw
them deal with the trials of living a long life. Cooper's parents
also died relatively young. But she has seen her neighbors Harriet
and Arthur Gilbert begin to decline in terrible ways. They were in
their early sixties when she moved here, robustly healthy, very ac-
tive and happy people who went out often: to friends' houses for
dinner, to the symphony, to art exhibitions and county fairs.
They loved taking long walks around the neighborhood. Now
most of their outings are to doctors' offices. Last week Candy ran
into them as they returned home from the neurologist Harriet
has been seeing, and Candy asked how things were going. "We
didn't get the news we were hoping for," Harriet said. "Nothing
awful, but not the news we were hoping for."

"We decided we are entering the time of life where true courage is called for. True courage and a sense of humor!" Arthur said.

"And *faith*," Harriet said.

"Well," Arthur said. "One always needs that."

In the kitchen, Candy starts a pot of coffee. Then she'll go out to the front porch to see if the newspapers have been delivered yet. She and Cooper get three papers: *The New York Times, The Boston Globe,* and *The Wall Street Journal.* Coop looks at all three, but normally it's all Candy can do to get through the *Globe.* It's because she doesn't like to skim, as her husband does. If she's going to read a newspaper, she's going to *read* it.

She steps out onto the porch and shivers, pulls the edges of her robe closer together. It is still night-cool, a few stars remain in the sky, and the moon looks half erased. The papers are there, lying in a jumbled pile, and she gathers them up with a kind of relief. Today she will read all of them in order to have something to do before she goes to the doctor's office. Her appointment is for nine-thirty. She and Coop are going together to hear the Report. Coop thinks it's unnecessary for him to come along. He said if it were bad news, the doctor would have *told* her to bring her husband along, wouldn't he? But Dr. Johnston hadn't said a word about Coop. He'd just said that there were some things he needed to talk to her about. "He probably just wants to put you on some new medication," Coop said. But in the end, he reluctantly agreed to come along. And Candy thanked him.

Candy can hardly believe the way husbands go with their pregnant wives to routine OB visits these days. Coop and Candy didn't have children, but she bets if they had, Coop wouldn't have gone with her to the doctor for such visits. Of course, back in the day when she would have been pregnant, not many men did. Back then, they were just starting to let husbands witness the birth. She had really wanted children, but Coop hadn't. He'd made it plain on their first date that he didn't want them, and her initial thought was, *That's the end of* this *relationship!* But she was so attracted to Coop, and she kept going out with him, and finally she thought, *Well, it's all right if we don't have children. We'll have each other.* She has so often recalled the day that she told Coop those very words. It was fall of their junior year, and they'd been sitting on a blanket beside the Charles. Coop was a rower for Harvard, and when he wasn't on the river, he liked to be by it. He was dancing around the idea of marriage and when she told him she didn't need children, he squeezed her hand and said, "Well, finally. A girl almost as smart as she is pretty. We'll be married next June." And she thought, *What do you mean, "finally"? How many women have you proposed to?*

The last time Candy went for her routine physical, she sat on a narrow table in her doctor's office in a blue paper gown that had ripped when she put it on. Over her left breast was a wide opening that looked oddly suggestive, and she kept lightly touching the edges as though this would magically repair the tear.

She hates paper gowns, and she always wears a nice pair of earrings and a bracelet whenever she has a doctor's appointment, so she won't look so horrible in them. She also ties the thin plastic belt tightly around her still enviable waist, and has on occasion even rolled up the sleeves a turn or two—she doesn't like the way the sleeves fall to a neither-here-nor-there place on her arm.

Candy doesn't understand why people being examined by their doctors don't just get naked and lie under a sheet. What, doctors have never seen a naked body before? And wouldn't it be easier than the false modesty offered by gowns that only get pulled far down, or pushed to the side, or lifted way up anyway? Or, if you're going to make patients wear gowns, why not have them be made of bamboo fabric in pale pastels, so they'd be pretty to look at, soft against the skin, and ecofriendly to boot? Candy has a lot of ideas about how medicine should be practiced. She'd gone to Boston University to become a nurse but had never worked as one. Coop didn't want his wife working. He made enough as a trial lawyer to support five wives. Candy had volunteered at Mass General until the advent of AIDS, and then Coop ordered her to stop, lest she bring home the deadly disease those godforsaken pervs, as he called them, were responsible for creating. She tried arguing with him, but it got her nowhere; not for nothing was he a lawyer who almost never lost a case.

While Candy sat in the examining room listening to the sonorous tones of her doctor talking to a patient in the room next door (a patient who kept *laughing*—oh, how wonderful to hear *that* sound in a doctor's office!), she leafed through a gossip magazine someone had left behind. She felt sorry for the movie stars who were featured. She stared into the eyes of this beautiful person and that, thinking their rise to stardom may have been awfully exhilarating at first—all that excitement, all that money, all that attention; but now look. Now they couldn't even go out to an ice cream stand on a hot summer night, and what was a hot summer night without an ice cream stand? They couldn't even take a walk! No one would ever just nod hello to them and say, "Nice out, huh?" and be done with it. People always *wanted* something from movie stars. They acted foolish around them, too, and Candy thought it must be a lonely feeling to have people act foolish around you all the time.

When her doctor came into the exam room, Candy said, "Boy, *someone's* in a good mood!" And when he looked confused, she said, "I heard you through the walls. I heard your patient laughing. I wondered why in the world he was so happy! Want to know my fantasy?"

Candy finds Dr. Richard Johnston, whom she calls Dick, an inordinately kind man. He has been Candy's internist for over thirty-five years. He's an elegant dresser, and he wears a bow tie with no sense of irony. She used to have a little crush on him, he's very handsome; and she thought he maybe had a crush on her, too, until the day he told her he was gay. That had been both a comfort and a disappointment to her. Naturally she didn't tell Coop when she found out Dick was gay; she enjoyed the irony.

Dick had his back to her, washing his hands; and she went ahead and told him what she'd imagined about the patient she'd heard laughing. "I decided it was someone going on a fabulous trip to some exotic place; and he came here today to get his shots. And he's so excited, he just keeps laughing."

Dick turned around and gave her one of those raised chin, closed mouth smiles and she realized that it was none of her business. She looked into her lap, embarrassed.

"Not quite that," he said, and asked her to lie down. Then, as though to mitigate her embarrassment, he shared a little information. "That patient's been living with a terminal disease for a while, and has learned some terrific coping mechanisms. He's a pleasure to be around, he's always cheering everyone else up."

"Oh," Candy said, "that's wonderful." But now she felt even worse. She felt as though she'd come onstage to audition after someone really, really good had just performed. Not that this was an *audition,* but didn't one always want to be one's doctor's favorite patient?

Dick asked her to lie down and proceeded to examine her. When he pressed on her abdomen, she felt a sudden, deep pain. "*Ouch!*" she said, then, "Sorry, that just kind of hurt a little."

Dick looked over the top of his bifocals at her. "It *hurt?*"

"No, I guess . . . not really." She waved her hand. "I'm sorry. I think you just surprised me." He pressed again, a little more deeply this time, and she gasped and reflexively pushed his hand away. "What's *under* there?" she said.

"Your ovary, among other things." He spoke in the same soothing voice he always used, but wrinkles appeared between his eyebrows and he began pushing again, here, there; and Candy clenched her fists and didn't make another sound. At one point he looked at her and said, "Is this still hurting?" and she nodded and looked at the wall. He ordered some blood tests and an ultrasound and an MRI. And she had them all done, praying to the blessed Virgin before and after each one.

About a week later, just after Candy had finished eating lunch, her doctor's office called to say she should come in on Friday morning to get the results. Candy leaned against the kitchen counter and said, "Is it bad?" She looked at the sandwich crust she'd left on the plate, and thought, *I should have eaten it.*

"We'd just like you to come in," the receptionist said. "It's pretty standard procedure."

Pretty standard. "But is it bad?"

"You know, you'll have to talk to Dr. Johnston about the results. I don't even have all the information here. I'm just calling to make an appointment."

"So it's bad," Candy said, and her kitchen suddenly seemed vastly bigger. She made the appointment and then washed her lunch plate and started thinking about what problem she might have that wasn't *so* bad. In the back of her brain, someone stood clanging a big bell, and the bell did not peal but rather spoke, and what it said was *It's very hard to survive ovarian cancer.* It said, *Gilda's fame and fortune couldn't help her one bit.* At that moment, Candy wanted a sibling more than ever before, and she had spent plenty of her growing up years wanting a sister or a brother. She wanted a sibling or her parents. Or a child. But her only family is Cooper. Who has grown tired of her. To put it mildly. Oh, not that he has cheated on her, not to her knowledge. But they've not had sex in years. And for many more years, he has not complimented her, or rushed to tell her anything, or listened with any interest to anything she has to say.

They get along, she supposes she would have to say. They have their routines: Breakfast out every Saturday morning. The

Sunday morning news shows. Plays, the symphony. Trips to Europe twice a year. Candy focuses on the house and garden, her visits to various art museums in the city, her donations to this charity and that, and their bulldog, Esther. Cooper works long hours, and then comes home to their huge Wellesley colonial, eats dinner, and watches television until he falls asleep in front of it. When there are terrible headlines, or terrible storms, or something awful happens to someone they know, they talk then. They come together almost like in the old days, then. What a strange way to find intimacy in a marriage, she always thinks.

Candy doesn't have girlfriends to talk to. Most women don't like her. Men always did. Boys always did. At first it was because she was so pretty—she was awfully pretty for a very long time. But when they got used to the prettiness, as always happened, then they would like her because she was actually a very nice person. But she is no longer beautiful and Cooper is not particularly gratified by his wife's being nice. "What's *that*, being *nice*?" he'd once said, when they were having one of those arguments where she felt compelled to defend her attributes. "How about *interesting*, how about that?" he'd said. "How about *intelligent*?" Well. Maybe he won't have to endure her vacuity for much longer.

She pours herself a cup of coffee and snaps open the *Times* and starts reading the front-page stories. When, after about half an hour, she hears Cooper coming down the stairs, she can't help it, she feels glad. She folds the *Times* back up and puts it on his side of the table.

He comes into the kitchen, pours himself a cup of coffee, and sits heavily at the table with her. "Damn, that coffeemaker's loud," he says.

Her mouth tightens. *Not today, Coop,* she thinks. *Today* you're *taking care of* me. And yet she hears herself saying, "I'm sorry. Did I wake you up?"

"Well, Candy, what do you think?" He opens the newspaper.

"Do you want some breakfast?"

"Yeah, in a minute, let me wake up." He wipes at something under his nose. "Get me a tissue, would you?" he asks, and she does.

She moves to the center island to begin chopping onions and peppers for an omelet.

"What time did you get up, anyway?" he asks.

"I didn't even look. The sun was just starting to come up. It was two pink clouds after a star." She figures he'll turn around and say, "*What?*" and she'll say, "You know, like two minutes after five, *two clouds after a star.*" But he doesn't turn around. He doesn't do anything.

When she puts his omelet in front of him, he says, "Smells good." So, you know. She sits down. She salts her omelet. She eats it. When she has finished, she will put on one of the beautiful St. John suits he insists she wear. After the appointment, no matter what the news is, she'll tell Cooper that she's going to her high school reunion this weekend. When she got the invitation and asked if he'd like to go, he'd said, "Good God, no. *Clear Springs?* No. Thank you." She waited a day or two, then called the airlines to make a reservation for herself and her dog, and then called Pam Pottsman to say she'd be coming, alone except for her bulldog; and Pam was so excited. "Are you still unbelievably gorgeous?" Pam said, and Candy said, "No, Pam, I am not." Pam said, "Oh, yes you are!" and they both laughed. And it was fun, that moment on the phone. It lifted her heart to hear Pam's voice and to be suddenly enriched by a rush of memories. She saw the wide steps of the high school, smelled that janitorial waxy smell you always noticed when you first came into the building, saw the lit trophy case out in the hall with the photos of outstanding athletes. She saw the crowds of students walking down the hall, the teachers standing at the fronts of their classrooms. She saw the gymnasium at night, decorated for a dance, felt the pressure of a crown being put on her head as she sat on a plywood throne that had been painted gold. After Candy hung up, she went to look at herself in the mirror, and for the first time in a long time she saw how her blond hair was still thick and lovely (if chemically enhanced), how her wide eyes were still a clear green, how her expensive night creams had kept wrinkles at bay. She thought, *I am still kind of gorgeous.*

She's going to that reunion tomorrow, no matter what. Before, she just kind of wanted to. Now, she needs to. Now, she would go in jeans and a sweatshirt and a shower cap and no makeup, just to sit at a table and be surrounded by people she used to know, just to be near someone familiar in the old way. Someone from before.

SEVEN

LESTER, ON LUNCH BREAK FROM HIS VETERINARY CLINIC, takes the mini Lop from his nine-year-old neighbor, Miranda. He holds the rabbit tight up against his stomach, facing out. "When you examine a bunny," he says, "the thing to do is to hold it like this." The bunny begins to kick wildly. "And when they kick, which they usually do, you rub your hand slowly over their tummies, which sort of hypnotizes them." He demonstrates, and the rabbit does indeed calm down. Lester uses one hand to support the rabbit's bottom and turns him to face his owner.

"Yup. He looks pretty happy, now," Miranda says.

"What did you decide to name him?"

"Custard."

"Ah."

"Because he's gooshy like custard. You're the one who told me to name an animal because of how it *is*." Miranda pulls her T-shirt away from her neck and blows down on herself. It's a warm afternoon. She and Lester have just had lunch, as is their custom on Friday afternoons. Lester does scheduled surgeries on Friday mornings, and most times there's a couple hours' window before he needs to be back at the clinic for routine appointments. Miranda, who comes home from school for lunch, began eating with Lester on Friday when she was seven, and they alternate preparing the food. Today was Miranda's turn, and she brought a sophisticated roll-up: lemon hummus, lettuce, tomato, onion, and kalamata olives, which were inconsistently pitted.

The little girl is set on becoming a veterinarian herself, and thus far Lester has given her a stethoscope, an otoscope, a white lab coat, a thermometer, empty vaccine bottles, and syringe barrels minus the needles. She brings a notebook on the days they have lunch, and she writes down the things she learns. She has a cat, a dog, and a parakeet, and she taught the bird to retrieve quarters she rolls across a table, something Lester frankly doubted a parakeet could do until he saw it with his own eyes. Just yesterday, she and her parents rescued the rabbit from the humane society. The people who surrendered him had him for only four days before giving him up, saying he had destroyed all the downstairs electrical cords. "Do you think it's really true he did that?" Miranda asked Lester when she first showed him her new pet. And Lester told her that the only thing rabbits like better than electrical cords is birdseed. "Really?" Miranda said, and Lester said yup, that for rabbits, birdseed is like candy. You shouldn't give them too much, though, just like people. A little went a long way. The girl considered this, then asked, "Do *you* like birdseed?" Lester allowed that he had never tasted it. "Should we?" Miranda asked, and Lester said he thought he'd rather have the sandwiches Miranda had brought. "That's not all," she said and showed him the red apples, the entire roll of Oreos, and the napkins she had decorated with rainbow stickers.

Now she lays Custard in her lap and pets him. "Aren't they so luxurious, rabbits?" she says. "They're like you have a mink coat but you don't have to kill anything." She looked up at him. "I have something to ask you."

"What's that?"

"Tomorrow night? There's a play at seven o'clock in Mr. and Mrs. Pichiotti's basement. This kid Eddie Sandman wrote it. He's twelve. It's about a vampire, and guess who the vampire is?"

Lester strokes his chin. "Hmmmmm. Would it be Custard?"

Miranda giggles. "No!"

"Would it be Eddie Sandman?"

"No, he's the *director*!"

"Hmmmm," Lester says. "Give me a minute. . . ."

"It's *me*!" Miranda says.

"You're *kidding*."

"No!"

"You can *act*, too?"

"Yes! Can you come? I get to suck blood two times. And we have strawberry jelly hidden in a Baggie in my cape and I secretly smear it on and it looks exactly like real."

Lester sits back in his chair and reaches over to pinch off a dying leaf from one of the plants on the windowsill next to the table. He's got a series of glass shelves in lieu of curtains, and they're full of flowering plants. It had been his wife's idea; the window got lots of sun. "I can't come tomorrow night. I'll be out of town."

"Where are you going?"

"I'm going to a high school reunion. You know what a reunion is, right?"

Miranda scratches a mosquito bite at the side of her neck with apparent satisfaction; it makes her mouth draw over to one side. "Yeah, it's really good friends who all come from all over to see each other again."

"Right," Lester says. Though to himself, he thinks, *Well, really good* friends . . .

"What all are you going to do?" Miranda asks.

"We're having a dinner and dance and then brunch the next morning."

"You can *dance*?"

"Why, yes, Miranda, I can."

"I never saw you dance!"

"I never saw you dance, either."

"Well, I can."

"And so can I. For your information, I took ballroom dancing as a young man." Not that it did much good, actually. Lester was an awful dancer. But at least he knew how the steps were *supposed* to go. The fox-trot. The waltz. The cha-cha; oh, how he had hated doing the cha-cha. He had wanted to murder his mother every time he did the cha-cha. There was simply no good way for a guy to hold his hands when he did the cha-cha.

"What *is* ballroom dancing?" Miranda asks.

"Well, literally, it's dancing in a really big room made for dancing. But if it's a class called ballroom dancing, it kind of teaches you everything you need to know. I mean, the basics, anyway."

"Who are you going with?"

"Nobody. I asked Jeanine and her husband to come, but they can't."

Miranda studies his face as though it's a palm she's reading. She worries about him, has told him on numerous occasions that he needs a girlfriend, and has made recommendations ranging from Miley Cyrus to the cashier at BuyLow who told Miranda she loves animals, too. "I can go with you. If you want."

"That's very nice of you. But what about the play?"

She slaps the top of her head. "Oh, yeah!"

Lester looks up at the wall clock and tells Miranda he's got to get back to the clinic, and she back to school.

"Do we have time for Three Things?" she says.

Every week, Miranda is told three things about various animals. Parakeets have about a teaspoon of circulating blood volume; elephants grieve; horses can get sunburned on their noses; dogs sweat through the pads of their feet—that sort of thing. "Well, you have one thing already," Lester tells her. "Rabbits like birdseed." Miranda dutifully writes it down. He notices that she has moved into an elaborate cursive and he's happy to see it. He's heard that many schools aren't teaching cursive anymore, and it makes him unaccountably sad. He still remembers Mrs. Lord in her blue crepe dress and enormous pearl clip-ons, standing over him in elementary school, trying to impress on him that good penmanship was a sign of good character and civility. She used to wear entirely too much perfume, Mrs. Lord, a heavy, spicy scent that reminded Lester of carnations. She wore rhinestone pins on her shoulder every day, and her ankles seemed to spill over her low pumps in what Lester knows now was a sign of congestive heart failure but at the time believed was a kind of *decision* she had made—flesh as accessory—and he wasn't quite sure how he felt about it. He used to look at his mother's slender ankles and wonder if she wasn't lacking somehow.

"What's another thing?" Miranda asks.

"Well, let's see . . . ," Lester says. "How about a cow one? We haven't done a cow one for a long time."

"I've decided I'm not going to be in large animal practice," Miranda says. "I don't want to be driving around all over to farms and to hell and back."

"I see," Lester says.

"Can I *ask* two things?" Miranda says.

"Of course."

"Is it true that dogs can't see colors?"

"No," Lester says. "They can see colors. Just not like you. They see gray, and they see the colors of the world as basically yellow and blue. You know, a lot of people don't know that dogs don't actually see all that well, period. They rely more on scent and hearing. For some sounds, they hear hundreds of times better than people."

"They are always better than people."

"Well," Lester says.

"It's true! There are hardly any people as good as dogs, you have to admit. Name me one person you ever met who was as good as a dog."

"Oh, I've met a few."

"Who?"

"My wife, for one. And you, Miranda Bryson, if you must know. You are as good as a dog."

"I am?"

"You are."

"If I *think* about it, I guess you are, too."

"Thank you. But listen, we have to go. Hurry and ask me your second question."

"Okay. Okay, it is . . . Oh! Custard keeps rubbing his face on me. Why?"

Lester puts their plates in the dishwasher. "Well, that's for a good reason. He's marking you. Rabbits have scent glands under their chins, and they secrete something from there that only other rabbits can smell. It's totally odorless and only a little bit damp, so you might not have noticed. But he's saying you belong to him. That behavior is called 'chinning.' "

Miranda smiles. "That's a good one."

"I thought you'd like that."

They go out the front door onto the porch, where Lester's dog, Mason, is sleeping in the shade. "Let's go, buddy," Lester says, and the dog leaps up and heads for Lester's truck.

Lester is backing out of the driveway when he hears Miranda calling his name. He leans his head out the window. *"What?"*

"You should wear something *blue* to the renewion!"

He nods, waves, and as he drives toward the clinic, he thinks, *Maybe I will.* His wife used to like him in blue, and since she died, he's purposefully not worn it much. But maybe it's time. *Renewion.* He looks into the rearview mirror, at Miranda fading away in the distance. There was a period in his late thirties when he seriously considered adopting a child, but he worried about whether he'd be able to adequately care for a son or daughter as a single parent. Now it's too late, and in quiet moments, he sometimes feels a profound regret about not having gone through with it. It could have worked. He could have hired someone to help him. It might not have been ideal, but he would have had the experience of raising a child, something he thinks he would have enjoyed for all kinds of reasons. The day after his wife told him about her pregnancy, she'd given him a miniature fishing rod and tackle box. It's still in the back of his closet, and sometimes he takes the little metal box out and looks at all the lures Kathleen had chosen. Their child would have loved it, he's certain.

He supposes, too, that it would have been nice, at this point in his life, when retirement is not so very far away, to think that he belonged to someone, and they to him—to chin and be chinned.

He shifts the truck into third and catches a glimpse of himself in the rearview mirror. There are a few years on him, yes, but he's in pretty good shape. He wonders if Candy Sullivan's coming to the reunion. He used to think about her in a certain way, though he knew it was useless. He used to sit at his desk doing homework and then stop and look out the window and think of her. Maybe he'll have a drink and tell her that.

He walks into his clinic, thinking about how fast time goes by, one's whole life. When Jeanine sees him, she slams down the phone and stands up behind the reception desk. "I was just trying to call you. Samson's back. He's in trouble; his temp and heart rate are sky-high. He's in room one."

EIGHT

"*D*AMN IT!" COOP SAYS. "I JUST CAN'T *BELIEVE* THIS!" IT'S eleven o'clock, and Candy and he have just come back to the car after having met with Dr. Johnston. Coop sits slumped behind the steering wheel, his car door open to let out some of the heat that has accumulated—he'd parked the car in the sun, thinking they wouldn't be longer than fifteen or twenty minutes. Candy's door is not open. She doesn't feel the heat. She doesn't feel much of anything but a need to get home and get out of this suit, out of these heels.

Coop looks over at her. "Fuck. I don't know if I can *drive*."

"I'll drive," Candy says and starts to get out of the car.

Coop grabs her arm. "I'll do it." He holds on to her for a moment longer, then closes his eyes tightly and Candy can see he's trying not to cry. "Just give me a minute." She waits, staring out the windshield at the line of cars parked before her, wondering how many other people will walk to their cars feeling weirdly shaken. She wonders if she wins for worst diagnosis for the day.

"Candy, I . . . I'm so sorry for all—"

"Don't," she says. "You don't need to do that. Let's not do that. Let's just go home."

He sighs, puts the key into the ignition, and turns on the engine, the air conditioner. He shakes his head. "I really can't believe it. Can you?"

She shrugs.

Coop puts the car into reverse and begins backing out. "Well, we're not going to listen to that and just assume it's right. We're going to get a second opinion, maybe a third. Let's just see what happens after that. Let's see what *they* say."

"Yes, all right."

"I mean, I literally cannot believe this! You haven't even felt sick!"

She laughs, a small sound.

"What," he says. "What's funny."

"I don't know. Nothing."

They drive in silence for a while, and then Coop says, "He's not that good a doctor, anyway. I don't know why you insist on going to him. Is he even board certified?"

"Coop."

"What?"

"I knew something was wrong."

Now he laughs. "You always think something is wrong! And it never is!" He pulls out onto the freeway and sits back farther in his seat, more relaxed, now. "It's not going to be anything this time, either. It's a mistake, it's got to be. You'll see. They make *mistakes*."

"Okay, Coop."

He looks over at her. "Okay?"

"Yes."

He looks at his watch. "We'll go somewhere nice for lunch."

"I want to go home."

"I'll take you anywhere you want to go."

"I want to go *home*, Coop." In his face, she sees a quick flicker of . . . what? *Annoyance?* Coop doesn't like it when she doesn't take him up on his offers for things he thinks she should like. Once, he told her such refusals reflected her self-loathing.

Remembering this confirms her decision to tell Coop about the reunion tomorrow. She will say that she is going, and that he is not going with her. He might say he'll come now, but she'll say no. She'll say she'll be fine, it's just a weekend. Nothing has changed, except that they've heard some words, a first opinion.

When they pull into the driveway, their neighbor Arthur is outside moving slowly toward his house, carrying what looks to be a heavy bag of groceries. Candy tells Coop to go and help him. When he starts to argue, she says, "I'm fine. Go and help him, please."

Coop gets out of the car and calls to Arthur, saying, "Hey there, need a little help?" For a moment, Candy worries that Arthur might be offended by the offer, but no, his face lights up and he hands his bag to Coop. She hears him say, "Tell you what, there are three more bags in the car. Thanks a million, awfully neighborly of you. It's those big tin cans that'll kill you! Those crushed tomatoes!"

Candy goes into the house and does not acknowledge Esther, though the bulldog greets her at the door and begins snorting and spinning in happy circles. She picks up the mail from the vestibule floor, sorts it by size, and lays it on the table. When she walks into the kitchen, she realizes she has no memory of who sent the mail she just picked up. But what does it matter.

She goes upstairs and into the bathroom and starts water running in the tub. Then she goes to the bedroom and takes off her clothes and puts on her softest bathrobe, the blue one she's had for so many years now. She goes back down to the kitchen and pours herself a glass of Pinot Grigio and gets out a tray on which she arranges fancy cheeses, crackers, a bunch of grapes, and a bar of Vosges chocolate that features a combination of sweet, salty, and hot, her favorite. She adds a rose from the arrangement at the center of the dining room table and carries the tray up to the bathroom, where she balances it on the wide edge of the tub and turns off the taps. The tub is deliciously full, overfull, and wisps of steam rise and twist enticingly.

Esther has not left her mistress's side, and now Candy pats the top of the dog's head. "Did I ignore you?" she says. "Did I? I'm sorry." She gives Esther a bite of cheese and watches as she swallows it without chewing, then lies down, her chin on her crossed paws.

From downstairs, Candy hears Coop call her name.

"In the bathroom," she calls. *Back to the womb,* she thinks. She has always taken baths when she feels bad, seeking out—and finding—an elemental comfort.

There is an unopened bottle of scented oil on the wide ledge of the tub that Candy's been saving for a special occasion. She opens it now and adds it to the water, then steps in. She looks down at her dear, familiar body, her pale skin and the cheerful scattering of freckles across her chest, down her arms. She lowers herself slowly—the water is wonderfully hot—and feels a dull pain in her knees. She leans against the back of the tub, takes a sip of wine, and sighs. When did she start feeling it in her knees when she bends down this way? Will she never again in her life do a cartwheel? When *was* the last one?

She hears Coop coming up the stairs and then he knocks at the door and speaks through it. "You're taking a *bath*?"

"Yes." Another sip of wine. Very good.

"Didn't you take a shower this morning?"

"Yes, Coop."

"Can I come in?"

She looks again at her body, seeing it in a different way, now.

Having no affection for it at all, and feeling embarrassed by her sagging breasts, her soft belly, the blueness of the veins that run close to the surface.

"Candy?"

"Come in."

He opens the door, and she sees him take in the tray, her blue robe, Esther, then: her, though he looks quickly away from her body and fixes his gaze on her face.

He sits awkwardly at the side of the tub. "So . . . Are you comfortable in there?"

"Yup."

"Need anything?"

"Nope." She looks into his eyes and it is as though she hasn't seen him for a long time. He's a very handsome man, beautiful gray eyes, high cheekbones, and a strong chin. Silvery temples on an otherwise black head of hair. She says, "You know what I was just thinking? I was in a department store the other day and I used the restroom, and there was a receptacle for tampons in the stall. And I thought, *What do they need that for?* You know? I thought that because *I* no longer use tampons, there was no need for a receptacle."

Coop stares at her. He doesn't understand.

Candy sits up and the water makes a sloshing sound. "I mean that I've become so incredibly self-centered that I—"

"You're not self-centered," Coop says. "Arthur was just telling me how you're always running next door to ask them if they need anything, that you bring them turnovers from the bakery and pick up their library books and shovel their snow and everything else."

Candy nods. She wants her husband to listen to what she is saying. She wants him to understand what she *means* by what she says. She may have an opportunity to try to explain herself now in a way she would not have been able to before. "But I am, Coop. And I've cut myself off from others, from important things, really important things!"

He makes the smallest gesture of impatience, but he does not speak.

She moves closer to him, tries to hold his eyes with her own. "You know, you get a diagnosis like this, and it's like there's a seismic shift or something. A very personal seismic shift. All I could think, after Dick gave me the odds, was, *Oh my God, what I haven't* done! It's as though . . . It's like all around a person, the world goes on, all the time, all the goodness and all the evil. All the living and the dying and we always seem to forget that our time for dying will come, too. We walk in cemeteries and feel sorry for the people who are buried there. Like it will never happen to us! And yet now that I've been told I'll die—"

"That's not what he said!"

She looks at him.

"It's *not*! He gave you some statistics. That's all. And we don't even know if he's right. He could be wrong!"

"Well," she says. "Anyway." She smiles at him. "I'm fine, Coop. Really I am."

"So . . . you want to just stay here for a while?"

She nods.

"Do you want me to read to you or something?"

He used to do that. In the early years, knowing that she loved to be read to, he would ask her now and then if she would like him to read to her. Always, she said yes. But it's been years. It's been a lifetime, truly. She could accept this gift he's offering. But what she really wants right now is solitude. And for once, her needs are going to be honored over his. She says, "Oh, that's sweet of you. But no. Not now. I'd like to just be in here and . . . I want to think. The warm water feels good. And doesn't it smell nice?"

"Yeah."

She doubts he's noticed the smell at all, even now, when she's pointed it out to him. But that's all right. It's for her, and she smells it just fine.

"Want me to bring you anything else?"

"No, I've got everything I need."

"Well . . . Don't you want me to just sit here with you? So you're not alone?"

"I'm okay. You go and do whatever you want. I'd actually like to be alone."

He stands and she can see him trying hard not to look relieved. "All right, so I'll just go and work on the computer. Call me if you need anything."

"Okay. Coop?"

He turns around. "Yeah?"

"I'm going to my high school reunion tomorrow. I really want to. But you don't have to come."

"Well, I will, now."

"I don't want you to."

He stands there, and she says, "What I mean is, I don't *need* you to go. You said you didn't want to when I asked you before, and that's fine. But I want to go. I've got the tickets. I just need you to give me a ride to the airport, and pick me up when I come back. Or I can take a cab."

He puts his hands in his pockets and nods. It's all she can do not to get out of the tub and embrace him. She thinks of how her wet body would imprint on his dry clothes.

Two hours later, he knocks on the door again. "You okay?"

"I'm fine."

"You don't need anything?"

"No."

"Can I . . . do you still want to be alone?"

"Yes. But take Esther out, will you? She needs a good walk."

Many hours after that, Coop comes to the door and says, "I'm starving. You?"

"I'm not getting out quite yet, Coop. You'll have to make your own dinner."

"Well . . . What have we got?"

She almost laughs. "Why don't you *look*?"

Twenty minutes later, he comes into the bathroom with toasted cheese and tomato sandwiches. "Coop!" she says.

"Dinner. I *made* these."

"I know."

"Wasn't that hard, really."

"I know that, too."

"It wasn't *easy*, either."

She looks at him.

"The damn tomatoes were slippery."

"Well. It looks very good."

"But *taste* it."

She takes a bite. "Yes. Very good."

"I used two kinds of cheese."

"Uh-huh."

"Kind of fancy."

"Yes, it is. It's very good, Coop."

They eat their sandwiches and talk a bit, and Coop does not ask again if she wouldn't like to come out of the tub. It's as though she lives there now, like a fish. He brings her a book she asks for, a gardening magazine, sets a radio on the floor and tunes it to the classical station she requests.

Candy lets her mind roam. She thinks about how she wanted to be a horse when she was a little girl. She thinks of a tangerine-colored scarf she wore under a brown leather jacket when she was in college. She thinks of a time when she and Cooper were on vacation. They were staying at an inn on the water in Connecticut, and she had awakened early and taken a walk alone across a causeway. On the way, she saw two swans sleeping, rocked by the water, their long necks wrapped around their bodies so that their heads could be supported on top of their folded wings. She spoke softly to them, asking them, absurdly, if they were asleep, though she could plainly see that their eyes were closed. It is Candy's habit to speak to almost every animal she comes in contact with; she has a deeply grounded affection for animals similar to that which she has for young children, and she thinks it's for the same reason: they are unapologetically themselves, and their default setting seems to be for happiness. On that same walk, she remembers, she saw a seagull flapping its wings against a strong wind, struggling hard just to stay in one place, and the image now has particular poignancy.

She thinks about how she went into a coffee shop yesterday and sat at a table next to one where an old woman and her daughter were sitting. The old woman was a mess: her hair long and stringy, her face thin and ravaged-looking. She looked homeless, but Candy didn't think she was, not with her daughter sitting there with her official-looking papers. The daughter was dressed in a stained black top and loose-fitting black pants, Clark Kent–style glasses. She was overweight, her hair greasy, and there was a distinct smell of body odor coming from her. The daughter was giving her mother some sort of test, checking for Alzheimer's or something, Candy thought, for she said, "Okay. Concrete is *hard,* or concrete is *soft*?" She repeated the question, and repeated it yet again, with no pause in between. Then, *"Mother!"* she said.

"Concrete is hard or concrete is soft," the mother said quickly. Obediently.

"No, but which *is* it?" the daughter said. "Concrete is *hard* or concrete is *soft*?" And again she repeated the question two more times.

"Concrete is soft," the mother said.

Her daughter sighed. Then she said, "Okay, that's kind of a trick question. Because concrete is soft when they first pour it, isn't it? But *then* it gets hard."

Yes, Candy thought. *One for the mother. Why don't you ask her if a* sidewalk *is hard or soft?*

"Next question," the daughter said. "Mother? Mother, pay attention, listen *carefully.*"

Listen carefully? Candy thought. *The espresso maker is making such loud noises, people keep coming in the door and going out of it, there are conversations going on at every table—how can she concentrate? Take her home, to her own kitchen table. Give her a chance.*

"Okay, next question," the daughter said. "You keep money in a wall or you keep money in a wallet, you keep money in a wall or you keep money in a wallet, you keep money in a wall or you keep money in a wallet?"

I'm going to scream, Candy thought.

"I'm so hungry," the mother said.

"Well, Mother, so am I," the daughter said. "Okay? Now pay attention. Listen carefully. You keep money in a wall or you keep money in a wallet?"

If you say something over and over again, it begins to lose its meaning, Candy thought. *Say anything enough times and it becomes gibberish.* Then she thought, *You could keep money in either a wall or a wallet. You could have a safe.*

The mother said, "You keep money in a . . . ," and Candy didn't move a muscle, waiting to hear the woman's answer, praying that she would get it right, that she would have this small triumph.

"In a wall!" she said, and then, "Oh. No. Did you say . . . ? It's *wallet!*"

"Right!" the daughter said. "Very good! Now listen to the

next question: A *banana* is round, or a *coconut* is round?" She repeated it, repeated it again.

"A banana is round," the mother said, and the daughter said, "*No*, Ma. *Concentrate.*"

But a banana is *round!* Candy thought. *Depending on where you look at it! A banana slice! What about a banana slice?*

"I'm so hungry," the mother said.

Candy went up to the counter to order a piece of coffee cake for the mother. She would give it to her with a flourish and say, "You can share it with your daughter, if you want." But she ended up ordering two pieces of coffee cake, and two twenty-dollar gift cards, and asked the counter person to wait for her to leave the store before she delivered it all to the women. She thought, *Everyone's in the same boat. Pass the coffee cake.*

At around ten-thirty that night, Candy awakens from having fallen asleep. She shivers; the water has grown cold. She thinks about adding more hot water yet again but decides not to. Instead, she climbs out of the tub, dries off, applies a luxuriously thick orange- and ginger-scented lotion, and pads into the bedroom. She sees that Coop has fallen asleep on top of the bedcovers, legal papers in his hand, the light on. She turns out the light and puts the papers on the floor, then lies down beside him. He turns and pulls her close to him, then closer. It is so unfamiliar now, the feel of him pressed up against her. She has been missing this, yearning for it for so long, yet now she finds it claustrophobic. Still, it's nice. It's a kind of home. Or like revisiting a home she used to love. Neither of them speak. She remembers reading an essay in the newspaper that a woman hospitalized with a terminal illness had written about her ex-husband. Their divorce ten years earlier had been exceptionally acrimonious, and each had felt vastly relieved to be rid of the other. But when the woman was admitted to the hospital for that final time, her ex sent her a lavish bouquet and a letter, the contents of which she did not disclose. But she did say she'd pressed the letter to her heart for some time before saving it in a zippered compartment of her purse, because she didn't trust keeping it in the hospital nightstand. She said she wanted it for as long as she could have it; and then she wanted her children to have it. She also wrote, "It came to me that the experience of dying didn't necessarily have to be all bad. That parts of it could be glorious."

Candy feels tears slide down her face, and she makes no move to wipe them away. They are a miracle of composition, tears, and they provide a vital and intimate service without ever being asked. She moves her left toes, then her right. They are still working. *Miles to go,* she thinks. *Miles to go before I sleep.* She recalls the earnestness of Mr. Little's face when he tried to show his freshman English class the elegance of the construction of those last two lines of the poem "Stopping by Woods on a Snowy Evening."

"Why does Frost say the line twice?" he asked the class, and they all sat still before him. "Well, why do you *think*?" he said, his pale blue eyes pleading. Finally a boy raised his hand to answer. It had been Lester Hessenpfeffer, who always knew the answer to everything but liked to give others a chance, so he would wait before he raised his hand. Lester answered the question, saying, "Well, one is specific, and one is general. He's talking about getting home and going to bed that night, but he's also talking about dying."

"Very good," Mr. Little said, with obvious relief. And Candy remembers thinking, *That's what I thought! I should have answered; that's what I thought!* She'd smiled at Lester, and he'd blushed and looked down at his desk. His shoes were weird, she remembers, his shoes and his clothes; but he was cute, that Lester. She wonders if he's coming to the reunion. She wonders if Buddy and Nance Dunsmore are coming; they'd had to get mar-

ried; she wonders if they stayed together. She begins remembering more names: Annie Denato, who had such a terrible reputation for being easy; Karen Erickson, who once fainted in home ec
class at the sight of raw liver and banged her head and the am-
bulance had to come and take her to the hospital; Marjorie
Dunn, who won a big prize for writing an essay none of them understood—something about a white bird with one black feather
and a black bird with one white feather. None of the kids had any
idea what it meant but the English teachers were all very pleased.
Tommy Metito was on the swim team and looked like Arnold
Schwarzenegger and this was before steroids, or at least she
thinks it was. Lou Kressel wore an *ascot*; she wonders if he's out
as gay now. She gets more and more excited and then it's like she
runs right into a wall, because she remembers what the doctor
told her this morning. Extraordinary that she forgot, but then the
world is full of surprises. She would like to see some more of
them.

The last thing she thinks of before she falls asleep is a time she
was a little girl outside playing on a summer night. She was the
first to be called in, and she resented it: the sky was violet and
the clouds were pink; the fireflies were just coming out; the taste
of sweat at the bend in her elbow was delectable; and the earth
had given up its heat to the coolness of evening, making the grass
so pleasant to lie in. She complained bitterly to her group of
friends about having to go in, and Mary Nix said, "We'll all have
to go in in a few minutes, anyway. You're just the first." That
made it better. Then, when she got inside, there were clean sheets,
and the light on at her bedside, and the covers turned down, and
the little statue of the Virgin to whom Candy prayed every night
and who Candy believed knew her best. Knew everything, in
fact, and just kept quiet about it.

*Death is a beginning or death is an end? Death is a beginning
or death is an end? Death is a beginning or death is an end?*

NINE

ON FRIDAY EVENING, MARY ALICE AND EINER ARE IN downtown Clear Springs at Styletique dress shop. Late that afternoon, Mary Alice had shown Einer the choices for what she was going to wear to the reunion dinner and dance tomorrow, and he had shaken his head and said, "Absolutely not." Half an hour later, they were here. On the way over, Einer had told her that he himself intends to wear a medium-weight gray suit and an electric blue tie to the reunion. Might be nice if she would coordinate with him and wear a pretty blue dress. Men like dresses, he said, and men like blue. He said, "You ask any man, what's your favorite color, and he won't hesitate. Blue."

Well, Mary Alice likes red. She likes a red so deep it's almost black, and as soon as they walked in the store, she saw a dress in that very color, a kind of satiny number with a crisscross bodice and a full skirt with rhinestone belt buckle, and she likes it very much. When she modeled it for Einer, he only sat still, staring at her, which she took to be a compliment. But apparently not, for he finally said, "Inappropriate. Now try on the blue." For Einer's benefit, she tried on the midnight blue dress he liked. It is nothing like what she would normally wear. For one thing, it's awfully close fitting. Also, it has cap sleeves, a risky thing for a woman her age. And it's so plain, not a rhinestone or ruffle to be found! But, "Yup, that's the ticket," Einer said, nodding. "Didn't I tell you? Wear that one."

She wants to follow Einer's advice and wear what he picked out; she could always wear a dressy little cardigan with it. She understands that telling her what to wear makes him feel important and gives him something to do. But she so loves the red! How to disagree with him tactfully? He's already crabby; he usually eats at five o'clock and now it's a little after six. Not that he'll eat much, but the man likes his routine.

Maureen Jernoff, the owner of the store, comes back to the dressing room area. "Have you decided yet?" She has managed to keep the impatience from her voice, but her arms are crossed a little too tightly beneath her bosom. It's past closing time. She's probably hungry, too.

"Well, I'm leaning toward the red," Mary Alice says, hoping Maureen will enthusiastically endorse her choice. But no such luck. "The blue was much better on you, you ought to get that one," she says. "Up to you, of course. But hey, listen; are you going to pay cash or charge?"

"I'll charge it," Mary Alice says and reluctantly starts to put the red dress back on the rack. But then she says, "You know what, Maureen? I'll take them both." To Einer, she says, "The red one I can wear another time."

"I thought I'd get the chicken pot pie," Einer says, and Mary Alice guesses he misheard her. Never mind. She's getting both dresses. And she's getting the chicken pot pie, too.

At the Tick Tock diner, Mary Alice is amazed at the amount of food Einer puts away. He eats almost half of a very generous serving of chicken pot pie, and he says he could eat more, but he's leaving room for pie, as he has been advised to do both by the bold print at the top of the menu and by—especially by—their waitress, Desiree. "You leave room for pie, now," she told him. And then, leaning over so that her considerable cleavage was exposed and the scent of her heavy perfume more apparent, she said, "That way we'll have more time together. Won't that be nice?"

"Yes, it will," Einer said, and glanced quickly over at Mary Alice, who looked pointedly off into the distance. Desiree is a sexily overweight black-haired woman in her late forties who wears wildly colored tights—hot pink or turquoise or fire engine yellow or multistriped or paisley print—with her uniform. She has very pretty and very clear porcelain skin, and she wears deep red lipstick. She *looks* like a Desiree. Mary Alice has a sneaking suspicion the woman has given herself that name, and why not? If Mary Alice were to pick a name for herself, it sure wouldn't be Mary Alice. It would be . . . what? Maybe initials. Initials beg a question, they're inherently mysterious, and she thinks they suggest a certain authority, too. K.C., she might be. She imagines herself at the reunion, someone saying, "Hey, aren't you Mary Alice Mayhew?" and her responding, "It's K.C. now." She wonders how many people go to reunions just to try on another way of being, confident that they'll be able to sustain the ruse for that short amount of time.

Desiree knows both Mary Alice and Einer well, but she pays attention only to the old man. Mary Alice doesn't mind. It's nice to see him engaged in conversation with a woman who is not checking on his bowel status or asking if he would like his pills mixed with applesauce, and it gives Mary Alice time to think her own thoughts.

She hadn't really believed Einer would go with her to the reunion. She thought he'd forget about it, or lose interest, or that some medical ailment—*minor!* she'd imagined, *minor!*—would develop and he would be unable to go. But no. Rita's man friend had asked her out for this Saturday and so Mary Alice is going to honor her promise and stay with Einer—it just won't be in his house. And Einer's thrilled. He's begun to act like it's *his* reunion, talking about people he remembers from his own senior class. Peggy McClure, who used to slip him brazen love notes in the hallway. Cecil McIntyre, who bore a strong resemblance to the actor Johnny Weissmuller and whose nickname, in fact, was Tarzan. How he went down in a plane crash in World War II a week before he was supposed to go home. Priscilla Embert, in the class behind him, who went to New York City and became a Rockette. Ned Connady, who started out his bitter enemy and ended up his best friend—they'd had a double wedding. Oh, he'd had some times in high school, he said, and he's begun to tell her more and more stories, and to become more and more animated while doing so. Frankly, Mary Alice is beginning to resent it. She wants to think her own thoughts about her high school experiences, imperfect though they might have been. In fact, once one gets older, there's a kind of pride in having survived a bad high school experience; it certainly makes for more interesting conversation when a group of people are comparing notes. What would be the follow-up question, after all, to "I didn't have *any* problems in high school!"? Though she wonders now if anyone ever would say that, if even the most popular kids weren't full of doubt and self-loathing, if they weren't victimized by the same take-no-hostage hormones that plagued everyone else.

Mary Alice also wants to think about how she'd like to approach the man she's going to the reunion to see. Even if nothing happens, it will be interesting to see him. How he has turned out. If his personality is still kind of the same. If he has a huge beer belly or is still fit and trim.

When Einer pays the check (which he insisted on doing—and after Mary Alice saw the size tip he left Desiree, she understood why), he says, "You'd better get me home; I've got to get my beauty sleep. Now, tomorrow's just registration and then the dinner at seven, right?"

"That's right," Mary Alice says.

"I don't suppose I'd need to go to the registration."

"No. Considering the fact that you're not registered."

He looks sharply at her. "Well, I know that. I guess I know that. Take me out in the backyard and shoot me if I don't know that! But what I was thinking is, do you *need* me to come?"

Mary Alice is suddenly and unexpectedly touched, both by Einer's interest in protecting her and by his excitement at getting out, to go to the reunion with her. She knows this magnanimous feeling probably has to do with the fact that she's about to drop him off at his house and back into the care of his homemaker. Still. "I'll be fine, Einer," she says. "If anyone messes with me, I'll tell you, and then at the dinner you can clean their clock for me."

"I'll rabbit punch them," Einer says. "That'll take any man down."

"What if a woman offends me?"

"Well, I'll rabbit punch her, too. You all want equality, by golly, I'll give it to you." He straightens himself in the booth. "What are we having for dinner, anyway?"

"Surf and turf."

Einer is quiet.

"Do you like that?" Mary Alice says. "I thought it might be good to get two things. You know, more choice, since we have to share."

"Well, to be honest, I'd have preferred the chicken, there must have been a chicken dish. Seems like people always have chicken."

"I'll see if I can change it," Mary Alice says. She likes chicken, too. She just hopes there's no garlic in it.

After Mary Alice gets home, she plays back the two messages

on her answering machine. The first one is from Pam Pottsman, saying that there's a problem with dinner on Saturday night. There aren't going to be enough surf and turfs, the hotel just called; somebody screwed up on the ordering. Would Mary Alice mind very much having the chicken instead? Pam herself was going to have to change her order; there just wasn't enough surf and turf, but oh well. She would assume it was okay with Mary Alice unless she heard otherwise, and she can't *wait* to see her tomorrow night, she is so *excited,* isn't Mary Alice?

Perfect, Mary Alice thinks. And perhaps a sign, too, of how well things are going to go generally? Maybe all she'll have to do is sit back and good things will happen of their own accord.

The second message is from Marion, asking her if she'd like to go with him to the Olde Warsaw Buffet next Saturday night. Of course she would. Unless there's someone new in her life by then. Who knows, there could be. There really *could* be! She had done a little research. She knows what he does, where he lives. No reason they couldn't have a relationship with some miles between them. Why not take a little road trip to visit a special friend? Who might become more than that? Though even just a friendship would be fine; Mary Alice needs more friends, as Einer is always quick to point out.

She goes upstairs and into her closet and finds her senior yearbook. She turns to the page he's on and looks into his eyes, assesses for the billionth time his open smile. A man at peace with the world, and in love with it, and she'll bet anything he's still like that. As is she. "Hey," she says softly to the picture. "It's Mary Alice Mayhew. Remember me?"

That's what she'll really say, and now she runs through possible responses. A blank—though kind—look, mixed with a mild curiosity. Or a blank look followed by sudden recognition and a friendly hug. *Immediate* recognition followed by a warm hug, and him saying, "Well, of course I remember you!" Finally, her favorite: grateful recognition, followed by a lingering hug and him saying low in her ear, "Gosh, I'm so glad you came! I was hoping you'd come!" Then he'd step back a bit from her and look into her eyes and say, "The last time I saw you, you were walking out of the gymnasium on graduation day. Where'd you go, anyway? Why didn't you come to the party?" This last, she knows, is a bit unlikely, but she plays it out in her mind anyway. She feels pretty certain that, when they talk, he will ask her what she's up to now, and she will answer by saying she has just moved back to Clear Springs. She won't reveal that she knows where he lives. She'll just say, "How about you?" And he'll tell her where he lives and she'll say, "Really. Well, that's not so far. We ought to get together sometime." She knows about his wife, and that he's single, now.

Before she goes to bed, Mary Alice tries on both dresses again. Here at home, in different light, she decides that Einer is right—the blue brings out her eyes and doesn't fight so much with her glasses. It isn't so much plain as elegant. She turns to the side, then grabs a hand mirror to inspect the rear view. Yes. The blue. She leaves the dress hanging in the bathroom, as though to discourage herself from changing her mind, and then lays out on a chair in her bedroom the outfit she'll wear to register in: black pants, a white blouse, a string of pearls her mother wore on her wedding day. Simple, but pretty. And surprise: red shoes, with four-inch heels. She might not see him there, but she'll see somebody. And they'll see her. "Mary *Alice*?" they'll say.

When she gets into bed, she closes her eyes and for a moment she wonders about the meaning of this sudden . . . silliness. She is being so silly! But silliness is in everyone; so far as Mary Alice is concerned, it's a pleasant common denominator. She remembers once meeting a distinguished professor of Asian studies on an airplane; a woman whose eyes held such fierce intelligence. And what did they talk about? Gregory Peck's unending appeal, and laundry detergent. For some reason, Mary Alice jokingly (if truthfully) told the woman that she herself used a brand of detergent Tim Gunn from *Project Runway* recommended, and the woman asked why, and then asked many more questions and finally pulled out a Mont Blanc to write down "Tide Totalcare. Renewing Rain scent."

Mostly, Mary Alice thinks, her silliness is Einer's fault. The way he's after her all the time to enrich her life. "Get out there!" he says. "Do things while you still can! Blink a couple of times and you'll be an old fart like me, with memories your only entertainment. You think I'm kidding? I'm not kidding! You'd better *make* some memories before it's too late!"

As angry as he has made her, picking away at her like this, now she is grateful to him. It isn't too late for some things. It isn't! She may have gray hair and a few brown spots and her memory may not be quite as excellent as it once was, but the taste of a good vanilla ice cream cone or the sound of church bells on a Sunday morning or the sight of a red sky still thrills her. And in those moments of appreciation she, like all people, becomes ageless.

TEN

"I THINK I CAN MAKE YOU FEEL A WEENSY BIT BETTER, BABY." IT'S
ten-thirty on Saturday morning, the day of the reunion, and
Sandy is talking in the pooched-lip baby voice that Pete used to
like so much. Now she reaches under the sheet for his penis.

He pushes her hand away. "Cut it out," he says. "This is a
hospital."

But it's not because he's in a hospital that he doesn't want her
to touch him. It's because his heart is breaking—again, and in the
more painful way, having nothing to do with a myocardial in-
farction, which is why he's here. He'd had a heart attack. A *heart
attack*, a man like him! After he was stabilized in the emergency
room and the doctor told him the news, Pete had yelled "*What
the fuck!*" before he could stop himself, and his doctor—a female, not bad looking, Indian chick—had pressed his chart to her
bosom and stepped back.

"Sorry," he'd said, and she'd given him one of those tight-ass
smiles and nodded. He saw right away he wouldn't have any fun
with this one; with this one, he'd have to play by the rules.

"Sorry," he'd said again, and then listened dutifully as she explained what the EKG had shown, the cardiac enzymes. She'd given him some stupid pamphlet called "You and Your Heart." He'd listened, he'd promised to read the pamphlet, but mostly he was thinking, *This is bullshit. I'm fine. I don't need anything except to get the hell out of here. This was a fluke, that's all.* The doctor had told him about how he'd need more tests, how he'd be on this medication and that medication. Jesus Christ. She'd told him he'd have to be in the hospital for at least a week, and when he got out, he'd need to wear one of those weird MedicAlert bracelets, what a babe magnet that was. Not that he gives a shit about babes anymore, but still.

Earlier this morning, his wife came to visit him. His kids, too. Nothing like a near-death experience to make everybody suddenly get along. Katie left after only a few minutes—she'd had to go to a birthday party—and the boys left soon afterward. Still, when the kids were there, they were loving and kind. Forgiving. Cal put his hand on Pete's shoulder and invited him to dinner next Sunday. Pete Jr. told him about some tickets he scored for a baseball game and invited him to go along. It made Pete think having a heart attack wasn't all bad. The MedicAlert bracelet will be a continual reminder to everyone that he is vulnerable, even if he doesn't seem like it.

After the kids left and Pete was alone with Nora, he said, "Listen, I can't go to the reunion today. They won't let me out until Monday. But I'd like to ask you to go for me. Would you, Nora? Please. I signed us both up, it's all paid for, all set."

She looked into his face with a kind of gentle weariness. "Oh, Pete. Why would you want me to go without you?"

Because he wanted her to think about him in the old way, that's why. He wanted her to be among their classmates, who knew them both back in the day. He thought this might provide the tiniest chink in the wall, a way for him to begin the arduous process of trying to make his way back into her life. He's determined to get back what he has lost, a woman whose honesty and character he admires, someone who from day one saw through his bullshit to the good that lives inside him, and helped make him a better person than he is able be on his own. Nora was so pretty when he first started dating her, a raven-haired girl with big brown eyes, a heart-shaped face with deep dimples, a cute little figure. It is true that she is no longer a head turner. But her spirit. Her soul. He wants what he has come to see matters most. Which is not Sandy, though, God bless her, she's knocked herself out trying to look hot today. And has succeeded. Sprayed-on jeans would look like elephant skin compared to what that girl has slithered into today. The orderly nearly had a heart attack himself when he came in and saw her, he couldn't keep his eyes off her ass. And Sandy, in her inimitable way, made it possible for him to get a good look the whole time he was in there, leaning over Pete to adjust his sheet when it needed no adjustment, standing with her back to the guy to read the couple of cards taped to the wall, even though she had sent both of them.

"I just really wanted to go to that reunion," Pete told Nora. "I wanted to see what happened to all our classmates. Wouldn't you like to see that?"

She shrugged. "I don't know. Not really. The only people I'm interested in are the ones I've kept up with anyway."

"But . . . Lester Hessenpfeffer!" Pete said, and then he started madly thinking of whatever names he could remember. "Trudy Lebbing! Tommy Metito! Aren't you even a little curious?"

She didn't have to answer. He saw it in her eyes. She picked up her purse, stopped short of sliding the strap over her arm. "*Any*way . . ."

He tried one more time. He shifted himself as though he were really uncomfortable but bravely trying to hide it from her. He made his voice just the tiniest bit pinched. "Nora," he said. "It's one night in your life. A few hours! And it's the last reunion!"

"Well, you *know*, Pete, you never wanted me to go before."

"Everything's different now, Nora." He considered getting a little short of breath here, then dismissed it for being too over the top. But he did try another idea, a brilliant one, he thought, that had suddenly come to him. "Ah, never mind," he said. "I'm being a selfish prick again, aren't I? Of course you don't need to go, just to tell me what everybody's up to. I'm sorry for asking. You don't have to put yourself through that."

She stood silent for a moment, thinking, and then, by God, it worked. She said, "Oh, all right, I'll go! Just for tonight's dinner, though, I'm not doing the whole thing. I'll go just to the dinner and that's all; I'm not even going to stay for the dance."

Yes, she will, he thought. Never mind, he still knows her. She'll get to talking, and she'll end up staying, if for no other reason than to talk some more. And all the girls—well, women, now, he supposes—will be asking her if Pete is still so handsome, if he's still so much fun. Which he is.

He mocked grateful surprise. "Aw, honey—*sorry!*—I mean, *Nora*. Thank you. Oh, man, that's so nice of you. Thank you. Fly United, and use my miles for the ticket; I've got more miles than I know what to do with. You know my password. And if you have any problem at all, just put it on my card. There's a flight that leaves in two hours, that's the one I was on, you can make it."

"It's less than a four-hour drive. And I really like to take road trips, as you know. And so does Fred."

Pete's smile froze. "What?"

"I'm going to bring Fred. You registered for two, right?"

"Well . . . Yes, but—"

"I don't want to go alone, Pete. I'm bringing Fred. End of discussion. I'll call you tomorrow and let you know how everybody was." She kissed his forehead. "I'm sorry. Feel better. I've got to go."

"*Petey?*" Sandy says, and Pete snaps back into the ugly present.

"What."

"I *said,* do you want me to bring you something special for dinner?"

He looks up at her, her big hoop earrings, her drawn-on eyebrows. "Listen, I need you to do something for me."

She blinks once, twice. Then she smiles and moves her face closer to his. "*Sure.* What'll it be, baby?"

He looks around her to be certain there's no one in the hall, and lowers his voice. "Get me my clothes. I'll watch to make sure nobody's coming while you get my things out of the closet and put them in the bathroom. I'll go in there and change while you stand guard, and then we'll make a break for it."

Her eyes widen. "You can't do that!"

"Sssh!" he says, then whispers, "Yes, I can. They're just keeping me for observation. I'm not even wired anymore. I can observe myself."

"If you leave a hospital before you're supposed to, you have to sign something. When Uncle Tony left after his hernia repair, he had to do that. It's an ANA form."

"What's that?"

"It's a form you have to sign if you leave before you're supposed to."

"I *know,* but what does ANA stand for?"

She consults the ceiling. "I think it's . . . *against* something?"

"Oh," he says. "Right. I know. AMA. Against medical advice."

"That's it. That's right. So anyway, you can't go without signing that."

He sits up, swings his legs over the side of the bed. "Watch me."

"Pete, I can't—"

"Just get the clothes and put them in the bathroom," he says. "I'll watch to make sure nobody sees. You can leave after that, leave before me, and nobody will know you did a thing."

"No, but I . . . What I'm trying to tell you is that you don't have any clothes here!"

He sits there. Stares at her. Then he says, "Why not? Where are my clothes? What happened to them?"

"I'm washing them."

"You're *wash*ing them?"

She scratches her arm, and her bangle bracelets jingle. "Well, not this very minute. But I'm going to. I'm going to wash them for you so you can have all clean clothes to come home in."

He looks off to the side, nodding. "All right. All right. Just bring me some other clothes. Pack me a bag with a casual outfit and a nice suit, some pajamas, my toiletries."

"Where are we going?"

"Not we. Me. I've got a business meeting. Very important. How soon can you get the stuff over here?"

"Well, I don't know. I have a therapist's appointment this af- ternoon; I could get them for you after that."

"You have a *therapist's* appointment?"

She shrugs.

"What the hell are you seeing a *therapist* for?" She doesn't have enough of a brain to be picked!

She shakes her finger at him. "Now, see? That's where I draw my boundary line. It's not your business. It's my business. It be- longs to me, and I'm not telling you."

"What are you seeing a therapist for?"

"Self-esteem issues."

He shakes his head. Sighs. "Well, cancel it, and go to the

condo and pack my bag and bring it back here. Don't bring the suitcase in the hospital, just bring my clothes to change into. Please."

"I can't cancel my appointment this late; she'll charge me!"

She'll. Couple of women sitting around man-bashing, one of them getting paid big bucks for it.

"I'll pay for it," he says.

And to his amazement, Sandy says, "No."

"Sandy."

"No! I'm doing this for me and I will pay for it myself. And also you can't bully me. Not anymore."

Fuck! He makes his tone soft, placating, sexy. "Come on, baby."

"I have to go now," she says, and damned if she doesn't leave. *Click, click, click* on her white high heels, right out the door.

Pete looks at his watch. If he leaves right now and gets out to the airport, he can make his flight and be at the reunion ahead of Nora and Fred. He can register himself and Nora and then, so sorry, no room for Fred. Oh, he'll be perfectly cordial to Fred—Have a few drinks on me in the hotel bar, pal; Nora will be back later. He'll tell Nora the doctor sprang him after all, and he decided to surprise her. He looks down at himself. He's wearing surgical scrubs, thanks to the kindness of one of the nurses who went for him big-time. None of those ridiculous tie gowns for a guy like him.

He goes over to the door and peers out into the hallway. No one in sight. In the little metal locker at the side of the room, he finds his trench coat—thank God it had been a cool morning when he went to see Nora. He slips on his socks and loafers, puts on his coat, collects his wallet from the little bedside table. He wonders for one second where his car keys are before he remembers that Pete Jr. has his car.

Again he checks the hall. The elevator is some distance away, but the exit to the stairway is two doors down. He walks rapidly to it and starts down the steps. He forces himself to go slowly, which isn't hard, because he's kind of dizzy.

Credit card, driver's license, he's thinking. Twenty minutes to the airport. Boarding pass at the kiosk in the walkway from the garage to the terminal. He'll buy an outfit to wear on the plane at the pro shop—there's a golf store at the airport. He can get a razor and toothbrush and comb at the hotel.

Right outside the hospital is a line of cabs. *Piece of cake,* he thinks, and climbs in the one in front.

"Airport," he says.

The cab pulls away from the curb and the driver looks at him in the rearview mirror. "Where you off to, Doc?"

The scrubs, Pete supposes. "Going to visit my parents," he says. Then, warming to the situation, he says, "They're having their sixtieth wedding anniversary." That's what he and Nora will have.

"That right?" the cabbie says. "Wow, that's something special. What all you going to do for them?"

"Oh, the works," Pete says, and then, "I gotta tell you, I'm beat. Don't mind me if I keep quiet. I've been up all night—just finished with a major operation."

The driver looks again in the rearview. "Oh yeah? What kind, if you don't mind my asking."

"Brain surgery," Pete says. "Tough case, but the guy's out of the woods now."

"Good for you," the cabbie says. "Okay, you take it easy. Sleep, if you want. I'll wake you up when we're at the airport."

"Yeah, good. Thanks." Pete closes his eyes and feels his pulse racing. *Calm down.* He takes in a deep breath, and imagines Nora in his arms, dancing with him, falling in love with him all over again in spite of herself. She'd say that very thing: "Oh, Pete, I'm falling in love with you all over again in spite of myself."

And if she does say that, he'll pull her closer. He'll say, "Nora, I'm a changed man."

He'll be so tender to her, all night. So kind. So *listen-y*. And when they go back to the hotel room, he'll make love to her like she's never seen. Like *he's* never seen. At some point, she'll remember Fred, and he'll say, "I'll take care of it, sweetheart." And Nora will say, "Don't be *mean*," and he'll say, "I won't," and he won't be, because he will have won.

The cab has been sitting still for too long. Pete opens his eyes and sees a long line of cars stalled behind what appears to be an accident. He starts to get angry, but then doesn't. Nothing really great has ever come to him without *some* effort. Plus, what if him getting all upset blows a gasket or something? He wishes he'd brought that pamphlet about the heart. He'll look up some stuff on the hotel computer, everything's on the computer now. He closes his eyes, unclenches his fists. By God, relaxes. He *is* a changed man. The cab begins to move again. Pete closes his eyes, but he's never been so wide awake.

ELEVEN

Dorothy Shauman sent four bouquets of flowers to herself at the Westmore Hotel, and now she goes around checking them before she unpacks. You have to watch these people, to be sure they don't send out some second-rate bouquet and think you won't do a thing about it, but Dorothy will, you'd better believe it. But the flower company has done right by her: each bouquet is just fine. They're not big bouquets, but they're pretty, and there are no wilted carnations or yellowing baby's breath or those awful supermarket alstroemeria snuck in there. She doesn't want supermarket flowers, no. As she always explains when she orders flowers, if she wanted supermarket flowers, she'd buy them herself from the supermarket, duh. She doesn't say it that meanly. She makes a little joke of it, and usually the people laugh back. Not the gay men, but gay men never like her. And she doesn't know why because she likes *them*.

The hotel has put all four bouquets on the desk in the corner, and now she happily distributes them: the pink one to the bathroom, the white one to the nightstand, the yellow one she puts on the little table with the lamp stationed near the door, and the blue one she leaves on the desk. Next, she opens the sheer curtains to see what her view is. Well, it's the parking lot, but never mind. Could be interesting to see who all is coming and going.

She's left word for Judy and Linda, who are sharing a room, to call her when they arrive; until then, she'll unpack and eat her box lunch: tuna sandwich and red grapes and peanut butter cookies. She suspects some of the people will get together to eat their lunch, but she wants to save herself. Besides that, she has a lot to do to get ready. She and her girlfriends have booked themselves a hot stone massage at the hotel spa, and then they're getting their hair done at the adjoining salon. Dorothy has availed herself of the salon's makeup service, too, which provides partial false eyelashes, which Hilly has told her are all the rage. She's a little worried she won't like it and then what? But if that happens, she'll just take it all off and do her makeup herself. Judy and Linda said they would never pay to have makeup put on, but they'd stay with her while she did it. Well, here's what Dorothy knows: if she looks good when she's done, Judy and Linda will fall all over themselves getting it done, too; and then she'll have to wait for them. She's glad she made the appointments for early in the afternoon; she wants no rushing as she prepares to see Pete.

A dark cloud comes onto her psychic horizon: what if Pete's wife is there after all? When Dorothy checked in, she'd quietly asked Pam Pottsman if Pete had arrived yet, and Pam had told her in her nine-billion-decibel voice that, yes, he'd arrived—alone, even though he'd registered for both himself and Nora. "I am going right up to him tonight and asking for a dance," Pam had said. "It's my very last chance, and I'm doing it!" That had made Dorothy kind of mad, and nervous, too. Not because Pam was any kind of competition—please—but because she'd take time away from Dorothy and Pete, and Dorothy had a lot of work to do in a short amount of time, especially if she went according to plan and ignored Pete at first.

If Nora comes, everything will be harder. That damn Nora, she'd been popular and pretty and smart, all three. And she'd never liked Dorothy, Dorothy knew it, even if Nora never said it. Whenever Dorothy tried to talk to her, Nora just acted tired. Surely Pete wouldn't bring her, he's just not the type, he's never been the type, and even if he does, well, he's *Pete Decker.* He would never turn down a ripe peach. So to speak. Especially at a last high school reunion, where *everything* is almost *required,* isn't it?

She didn't see anyone else when she was registering. It was just Pam Pottsman, with her three chins and badly dyed red (??) hair, acting like she was the queen bee just because she organized this whole thing. Which *was* something, Dorothy supposed. Credit where credit's due. Once everyone's registered, though, Pam will be left in the dust, just like in high school, when she used to organize all the dances and then not be invited to go to any of them. But you couldn't ever discourage that girl! She loved life! She loved everything! And she doesn't seem to have changed one whit, sitting there behind the registration table smiling and laughing and acting like everyone she sees is her long-lost friend.

In a way, Dorothy is glad there weren't a lot of people registering when she arrived. She never looks very good after a plane ride; she needs time to rehydrate and rest after a flight. She did pass Ben Small on her way to the elevator. Ben was in the drama club and everyone thought he'd be a great actor but no; when Dorothy asked him about it, he laughed and told her that what he did was sell products for people who were incontinent. Imagine having to say that over and over again tonight! If Dorothy were Ben, she'd say she was in the medical supply business and let it go at that. Ben always did share too much; he was needy that way. You'd say, "How's it going, Ben?" and he'd *tell* you!

As she was heading down the hall to the elevator, she saw Nance and Buddy Dunsmore—they'd hardly changed at all! Thank God they didn't see her. They were the Cute Couple in high school; everyone liked them. Nance was a cheerleader who wasn't all that pretty, and Buddy was the football player that nobody got all that excited about. They were just *cute*, like Karen and Cubby in the Mouseketeers. And they'd been together forever, since fourth grade, everyone knew. Buddy used to walk Nance slowly to every class, which made him late for his own, but the teachers all tolerated it because they were *Nance and Buddy*.

In the winter of her senior year, Dorothy was at a party and went into the bedroom to get her coat to go home, and there Buddy and Nance were, she resting back on her elbows at the end of the bed, her skirt shoved up and her garters revealed, and he kneeling before her with his face shoved between her thighs. . . . Well, you can just imagine how it felt to walk in on *that*. Dorothy had never seen such a thing; it gave her a sick and vaguely discouraged feeling, like when she saw dogs' red penises sticking out, and she did what she had to: she told the boy hosting the party that there was lewd behavior going on between Buddy Dunsmore and Nancy Greene right in his parents' bedroom. Plus, okay, she told a few other people. She thought it was indecent! She thought people needed to know so that they could leave, too! Word spread quickly and someone must have alerted Nance and Buddy because, very soon afterward, they came out of the bedroom, hastily rearranging their clothes, Nance all shamefaced and crying, as well she should have been, Dorothy had thought. But Buddy was mad. He'd come rushing up toward Dorothy and scared her so that she reached out and slapped him preemptively and also inadvertently scratched him. It was a bad scratch, he bled a lot and later there was a scar on his cheek, and she was horrified at what she'd done. She was sorry, too, that she

hadn't just gotten her coat and said nothing to anyone and quietly gone home. But she remembers thinking, *If your neighbor's
house is on fire, you tell him!* There Nance and Buddy were, de-
filing the party, behaving in what she believed at the time was an
immoral way that, really, affected everyone else who was there.
Everyone was guilty by association! Dorothy had wanted no part
of it, and she'd assumed that, if the others knew, they'd want no
part of it, either. She'd imagined, in fact, that everyone would
leave, talking about how they were so grateful that Dorothy had
walked in on Nance and Buddy, because otherwise there they
would have been with *that* going on not twenty feet away. But afterward, all the kids stayed at the party anyway, and they were
mad at Dorothy, as though she'd been the one behaving in such a
disgusting way. Which of course was true.

If only people were given the opportunity to behave differently at certain times in their lives! That party would be a time
that Dorothy would revisit. Never mind the popular sentiment
you heard every five minutes these days: *Everything that's happened in your life has helped to make you who you* are! No,
Dorothy would like to be back at that party, and she would open
the door to the bedroom, and she would see Nance and Buddy,
and she would quietly close the door. She would wait until they
came out of the bedroom to get her coat, and then she would go
home without having said a word to anyone about what she had
seen. Not because she thought what they did was all right, but
because it was none of her business.

Not long after that party, Nance got pregnant (the night of a
church social, of all things, Dorothy had heard). The whole
school knew about how she had lain in bed crying night after
night when her period didn't come, and how she'd then tried to
solicit advice for how to get rid of it. Lynn Donnelly told her to
take hot, hot baths. Debbie Goodman said to drink vinegar three
times a day. Joyce Ulrich told her to stick a chopstick up there,

and Nance had reportedly started to, but then she got scared and ended up telling Buddy she was going to have the baby. And he'd said, well, they'd just get married, then; and he'd get a job after graduation and take care of her, no problem. He said that, even though he had gotten a football scholarship and was all set to go to college. He just kept on loving her, and he treated her even *better* after he knew she was pregnant, like glass! Nance had come to graduation with that bump showing, wearing her wedding ring with the microscopic chip of a diamond, everybody trying to act like it was okay, but it was not, not in those days.

Buddy got a job bagging groceries at SaveMore and had to wear a white shirt and black pants and a red bow tie and a green apron. He'd always looked so sexy in his letter jacket, moving down the hall with the other jocks and carrying his books at his hip. And then there he was, looking like a little Christmas elf or something. Dorothy saw him in the store a few times before she left for college and she was just mortified on his behalf. He didn't seem much different, though, still the same smiling, affable guy, but, oh how sorry Dorothy felt for him. To be married at eighteen! Surely he felt a terrible shame! And how could a marriage like that ever last? How? And yet there they were, still together and holding hands, for goodness' sake! And they were still very nice-looking people, just the tiniest bit overweight.

Dorothy ran into Karen Erickson when Karen was getting off the elevator, and they chatted for a while. Karen reminded her that they were in chorus together, though Dorothy had no memory of that, not at all. She would look Karen up in the yearbook later; she had brought along the yearbook for just such things. Karen Erickson was Karen Slater now. Her husband was not there, but Karen made sure she let Dorothy know that he was an orthodontist, and Dorothy raised her chin and said *"Oooh!"* appreciatively, even though who the hell cared.

Karen asked if Dorothy had seen anybody else yet, and

Dorothy said she'd talked to Ben Small, and she'd caught a glimpse of Buddy and Nance but hadn't spoken to them. "Oh?" Karen said. "Well, I've kept in touch with Nance. She and Buddy own a few Subway franchises and they have five children, can you imagine? They're a very close and happy family. Two of their children, a daughter and a son, work at NASA. One is an English professor and one is an actor on a soap opera, very successful. And the youngest has just become an executive chef at some fancy hotel in Milwaukee, where they live."

Dorothy said, "Huh," and her spirits sagged a bit. Other people's happiness could do that, put a pin to your balloon, you'd think people could keep good news to themselves instead of acting like those god-awful trumpeting Christmas letters: *Look at US!* But never mind. Buddy and Nance had their happiness; Dorothy was about to enjoy her own. Dorothy said she'd see Karen later, and she got into the elevator and quick punched the button so she wouldn't have to talk to anyone else, she had a lot to do.

In her room, Dorothy opens her suitcase and starts unpacking. When she goes into the bathroom, she catches a glimpse of herself in the mirror and is actually shocked to see herself as a fifty-eight-year-old woman. She'd been thinking of herself as that high school girl in her plaid skirt and kneesocks and circle pin, but no, *here* is who she is. Fifty-eight years old. She really can't believe it. Oh, she believes the changes in herself physically, but inside she still feels like a girl. She does! Aaron Spelling's wife, Candy, feels that way, too; Dorothy heard that, in some interview, she described herself as a child who happens to be sixty-something. Dorothy could probably be friends with Candy Spelling, because she feels exactly the same way. She wonders if they were friends, if Candy would pay for everything all the time—she's so rich!—even though Dorothy *would* offer to pay for herself.

Dorothy leans in closer to the mirror and looks deep into her own eyes. She experiences a sudden descent into what feels like the center of herself. She is aware of a lonely regret: she isn't that high school girl any longer; and she can't do a single thing in her life over again—though she wonders if, given the opportunity, she really *would* do anything over. One is given one's own particular box of tools; one does what one must at various points in one's life. She supposes she might have been a little kinder in high school. She wasn't very kind, then. Though who was, in those days? What adolescent could be described as being *kind*? An aberrant one, that's who. Well. Nothing for it but to make the best of what one has, at the moment. Which is exactly why she's here.

On the shower rod, Dorothy hangs all the clothes that she'll wear tonight and to the breakfast tomorrow: the steam from her bath will make the few wrinkles fall right out. On the counter go all the things for personal hygiene, including the new bottle of Chanel No. 5 she bought that had necessitated her checking her bag. Checking her suitcase had made her very nervous—what if it got lost?—but she had sat by the window and watched as the bags got loaded into the plane, and there was her suitcase on the conveyor belt, the handle tied with a hot pink ribbon you couldn't miss. She leaned back against the seat after that, relieved, and refused the offer of peanut M&M's from her seatmate, even though she was dying for some. There would be time enough for peanut M&M's after the reunion, unless she was still seeing Pete, in which case she would still be dieting, but it would so be worth it. She wonders what Hilly would think of Pete, wonders if her Mom Stock wouldn't go up if her daughter saw her with such a handsome man. It could be their time, Dorothy and Pete's. Reunions are breeding grounds for just that sort of thing. Divorces happen all the time in the wake of reunions. She wonders if you can get divorced online; it seems to her that you can do everything online, these days. Soon no one will venture out of their house for anything, ever.

The phone rings and Dorothy actually jumps, then laughs at herself. She's so nervous! Or *excited,* or something! It's Linda and Judy calling from their room. They want to know if Dorothy has eaten her box lunch yet, it actually looks pretty good. They suggest coming up to Dorothy's room and they'll all have lunch together. And then she has to come with them to look at the ballroom—it's decorated so cute, in their high school colors, all burgundy and white! There are Kleenex carnations at every table, felt pennants. On the wall there are blowups of photos that had been in the senior yearbook. There's a cheerleader outfit and a football uniform hung up there, too; and there are posters made to look like the ones that used to hang in the halls when people ran for things.

"Never mind all that," Dorothy says. Those damn cheerleaders; would their glory *never* fade? They'd be in a *nursing* home and everyone would still be fawning over them because they were *cheerleaders.* "We're due at the spa in less than half an hour."

"It's right here at the hotel," Linda says. "We'll have plenty of time. Relax!"

But Dorothy says, "We can't be late. Why don't you guys eat and then come and get me and we'll all go over together. I'll see the ballroom tonight. I'd rather see it tonight anyway, it will be more romantic."

Judy says, "It's hardly romantic! There are plastic *horses* on every table, for the Mustangs. And the crepe paper is twisted and hung up all swoopy, you've got to see it."

"We don't have time," Dorothy says. And since she remains the boss of their little group, the women agree, and Dorothy finishes making ready her room. She puts her pajamas in the bureau drawer, sprays her pillowcases lightly with Chanel, removes the dust from the window ledge. Those maids. All they do is watch soap operas and begrudge you extra bottles of lotion.

When her friends come, Dorothy knows they'll comment on all the flowers in her room, and she isn't sure she should tell them she sent them to herself. Then she decides she will admit to it; she might as well get back into the habit of telling them everything, because if she gets her way, she'll have plenty more to tell them. Not for nothing did she opt out of staying with them, and get a single. It had been fun to think about making out in Pete's car, and they still might, some, but for the grand finale, no. A bed, please, they probably both have joint issues.

She pulls the blackout curtain, then lies on the bed to practice her Kegels. No one can tell when you're doing that, they say you can even do it when you're sitting at your desk, but still. She lies in the exact center of the bed, closes her eyes, and squeezes, releases, squeezes, releases. Dorothy could never do this sitting at her desk. For heaven's sake! It gets you hot! If she gets to be intimate with Pete, she's got to remember not to get on top no matter what. All the loose skin on her face will fall forward like ice cream sliding off a plate. And besides, when she lies flat her belly looks . . . containable.

After a few minutes, Dorothy hears a knock at the door. She gets off the bed and opens the curtains, then opens the door, and there they are, Linda and Judy, squealing *Hi!* and *Oh, my God!* and *Can you believe it?* They are wearing bright orange feather boas, and after they come into Dorothy's room they offer one to her. Which she takes and wraps gaily around her neck, then immediately removes and lays on the table. No boas. Next they'll be suggesting red hats. No.

"Who are all the *flowers* from?" Judy asks, and Dorothy admits that she sent them to herself. Judy and Linda have a good laugh about that, though Dorothy doesn't know why—she doesn't think it's so astounding that a woman would send flowers to herself, she thinks it shows a kind of spunk.

Linda sits on the edge of the bed and says, "Guess who *we* just saw?"

Dorothy presses her lips together and tries to contain her emotions. "Pete Decker?"

"*Yes!*" Judy and Linda squeal, together. "He was going into his room and no one was with him! He's three doors down from us!"

"Oh, my God," Dorothy says. "Is he still handsome?"

"He is *so* handsome!" Linda says, and she shakes her hands like she just burned them. Linda is still cute, Dorothy realizes, blond, petite, her big blue eyes still huge in her face and no lines around them, thank you Mr. Botox. Judy's not bad-looking, either, tall and slender, with front teeth crossed in an endearing way, brunette hair still long and thick, and those great boobs that are now and always were 100 percent natural. Dorothy hopes her friends have no interest in Pete.

"He was wearing doctor pants," Linda says. "Did he become a doctor?"

"No," Dorothy says. "He's a stockbroker." Facebook.

"Well, he's wearing scrubs."

"It's probably some cool fad or something," Judy says. "He was always starting fads; whatever Pete did, a whole bunch of other guys did."

"I'm going to hit on him," Dorothy says.

Linda rolls her eyes. "We *know.*"

"So don't either of you."

"We're *not,*" Linda says, but Judy says, "I might." When Dorothy's mouth drops, she says, "Just kidding. I do think I might hit on Buddy Dunsmore, though."

"He's still married to Nance, and she's here with him!" Dorothy says, and Judy shrugs and says, "It's a reunion. That's what these things are *for*. Although I also just saw Lester Hessenpfeffer. And he is *really* hot. But he's, you know, Lester *Hessenpfeffer*. Ew."

They all laugh, and then Dorothy looks at her watch and says it's time to go to the spa. When she walks down the hallway toward the elevator, she feels oddly outside herself. Here it comes, the reunion is here, it's all starting to happen! This is the *before* before the *after*.

When they get off the elevator, they start heading toward the spa. But then Judy suddenly stops in her tracks. "Look!" she says, pointing toward the registration table down the hall.

Dorothy gasps. "Is that . . . ?"

"Oh, my God," Judy says.

"Mary Alice Mayhew," Linda says. "I can't believe it. Why would *she* ever want to come back and see any of *us*?"

They watch as Mary Alice chats with Pam, then fills out two name tags.

"She's bringing someone," Judy says.

"Where is he?" Dorothy asks.

"I'll bet it's not a he. I'll bet she's a lesbian," Linda says. "I'll bet her partner is unloading the car and that they brought sex toys. A feather and a dildo!"

"Stop that!" Dorothy says, and then they start laughing.

"Damn, I wish she hadn't come," Linda says. "I was going to put her name on a tag and pretend to be her!"

Dorothy stops walking. "You still can! In fact, why don't you change tags with her?"

"Nah," Linda says. "She wouldn't do it."

"She might," Judy says. "People change."

"Here's one thing I'd stake my life on," Linda says. "Mary Alice Mayhew has not changed. Not one bit. People like that? They don't change. Even if they change. Put Mary Alice Mayhew in red stilettos and she's still Mary Alice Mayhew. To us, anyway, because we knew her when."

They reach the door to the spa, a frosted door with elegant silver script on it, and all the women quiet down. They want to get in the mood.

Dorothy opens the door and gestures to her friends to go ahead of her. *"Après vous,"* she says, in an accent she's sure their high school French teacher, Mademoiselle Florin, would have appreciated.

"Hello, ladies," the receptionist says, and Dorothy wants to smack her. *Ladies,* that condescending catchall greeting used for women of a certain age. She wants to say to the receptionist, "You think you'll never get old, but you will." Instead, she joins her friends in a weak chorus of *"Hiiiii."* It is almost like a question, the way they say it. It is almost as though they're asking for permission for something. As they kind of are, Dorothy thinks. Really, they kind of are.

TWELVE

LESTER SITS ON THE SIDE OF HIS HOTEL BED, THINKING, HIS unpacked suitcase beside him. He checks for messages again, even though his cellphone has not rung. No messages. Samson had developed a massive infection after his abdominal surgery; but his wound has been debrided, he's been resutured, he's been given an antibiotic bolus intravenously and now is getting oral doses every four hours. He's staying in the clinic a couple of days for close observation. He should be fine.

Dumb dog. Rolling in fertilizer when his belly had just begun to heal. Lester imagines him in the cage in the back room, his chin on his favorite stuffed animal, his brown eyes shifting left and right, watching what little activity occurs there. He should be fine. Still, Lester calls his clinic, and when Jeanine answers, he says, "I'm coming back."

"*No!*" There are three loud banging sounds and then Jeanine says, "Did you hear that? That was the sound of my head hitting my desk."

"That was not your head."

"It might as well have been."

"Listen, Jeanine. It's not important that I be here. It's important that Samson be monitored very carefully, and I'm—"

"How long have I been working for you?" She sounds angry now; she's speaking in the cool, clipped tone she uses on the phone with her husband when they're fighting.

"I'm not saying a thing against you and your complete and utter competence," Lester says. "It's just that I'll be thinking of him the whole time, anyway, so I might as well—"

"Dr. Hessenpfeffer. Lester. You're *an hour* away!"

"Ninety minutes," Lester says. "Without traffic."

"Samson is just fine. He's afebrile. His heart rate and blood pressure are perfect. His dressing is dry. He's alert. I had to give him a squeaky toy because he's *bored*."

Lester sits still on the bed, stops his knee from bouncing.

"*And:* Miranda said she'd sleep with him tonight."

Well, yes. That's what Lester wants, is for someone to sleep with Samson. But he can't have Miranda in the cage with the dog. Insurance and whatnot. But before he can voice his objections, Jeanine says, "I'll make up a cot for her right outside his cage. And I'll make up one for me, too. We'll *both* be there. He'll be fine. And I promise you, if the least little thing happens— a whimper!—I'll call you right away. You need to learn to take some time for yourself."

"I take time! Every year!"

Jeanine sighs. "You know what I mean. Now, will you promise me that you'll stay there?"

"All right. Fine. I *promise*. But put him on the phone."

"Who, Samson?"

"Right."

"Hold on."

She puts Lester on hold and then he hears her voice sounding a bit far off, saying, "Okay, you're on speakerphone, go ahead."

"Hey, Samson!" Lester says.

"He's wagging his tail and cocking his head," Jeanine says. "Aw."

"You hang in there, buddy, and I'll see you tomorrow."

"Now he's trying to get *up*!" Jeanine says. "Lie down, Samson, Doctor's not here. Lie down, buddy. Good boy! Stay, okay? Stay there. *Good* boy." To Lester, she says, "Don't you say anything else, you're getting him all excited and he needs to keep still. He's all right. I just irrigated his incision and it's clean as can be. You go and enjoy yourself."

Lester stands to look out the window. There's a striking blonde crossing the parking lot, pulling her luggage behind her. Candy Sullivan? He squints to see better. Yes, it's Candy all right. And she's still . . . Candy Sullivan.

"Call me if there's *anything*," he tells Jeanine.

"I will."

"Any other news?"

"Nothing. Routine shots today. Oh, and Pia is pregnant again."

Lester sighs. "They need to spay that dog."

"Duh. But you know, she throws the cutest puppies. I might even take one this time."

"Then you're just encouraging them."

"I know, but remember the last litter? The runt that looked like he came off the set of *The Little Rascals*? I want one like that. I want to name it Spanky."

"Go down to the shelter and you'll find a *bunch* of Spankys." He looks outside to see what door Candy is headed toward. "All right, I'll call you later."

"Dr. Hessenpfeffer?"

"Yes?"

"*I'll* call *you* if I *need* you. If you call me, I'll quit. I swear to God, I will flat-out quit."

"You'll never quit."

"I know, but *don't call me.*"

Candy disappears into the hotel door closest to the registration table. She'll be there in just a few seconds. No one is with her. He grabs his box lunch and heads for the elevator. He'll see if she'd like to have lunch and catch up. He supposes he'll have to tell her who he is. Which is fine.

But by the time he gets to the ground floor and then to the registration table, there is no sign of Candy Sullivan. There's only Pam Pottsman, sitting at the table and looking at her watch, and some other woman sitting on a chair in a conversational grouping of furniture a little ways down the hall. She must be a classmate; she's eating her box lunch.

He approaches Pam and asks quietly, "Did Candy Sullivan register?"

Pam laughs, then bellows, "Good grief! She's *still* the most *popular girl*! Yes, she just went up to her room."

"Did she take her lunch?" Lester asks, then immediately regrets asking.

"No, she said she wasn't hungry. Do you want it?"

Actually, he would like it. He's hungry, and the lunch doesn't appear to be all that big. "Sure," he says. "I'll take it. Thanks."

Pam reaches into a large bag and pulls out a lunch. There is only one more box left in the bag. Almost everyone has come, then. She hands him the box, then points to the woman eating alone. "You remember Mary Alice Mayhew?"

He remembers the *name*. And then, looking over at the woman, well, of course he remembers Mary Alice. One of the uncool nerds, like him. Kids used to be pretty mean to her. He remembers a time a group of jocks made catcalls after her as she walked down the hall. He'd wanted to defend her—what was the *point* in that kind of cruelty?—but hesitated out of fear of being attacked himself. But then he saw that she didn't seem in need of being defended: she'd held her head high and walked steadily on, seemingly impervious to their taunting. And there that knot of thick-necked boys stood: utterly ignored, suddenly looking sort of foolish.

Mary Alice still has the same hairdo: mid-neck length, but salt and pepper now. It's styled more attractively now, not sort of lumpy like it always used to be. She's gotten to be rather nice looking; she seems to have grown into herself. Her glasses are certainly better. As are his.

He walks over and smiles at her, holds out his hand. "Hey, Mary Alice. I'm Lester Hessenpfeffer. Do you remember me?"

Her mouth is full and she smiles apologetically, holds her index finger up, swallows. Then, "Hi, Lester," she says. "Of course I remember you. The last time I saw you, you were giving the valedictorian speech. *To creating our destinies!*"

Lester nods. "My Sally Field Oscar moment," he says. "Ah well. All I meant to say—"

"Oh, no," Mary Alice says. "I loved what you said. The idea that you could create your destiny, that you weren't imprisoned by some preordained set of circumstances. It was a wonderful speech, Lester."

They regard each other, each of them doing their own *then* and *now,* Lester supposes. Then Mary Alice says, "I see you have your lunch. Want to join me?"

"Well. Lunch*es,*" Lester says.

"If one's good, two is better," Mary Alice says. "And it actually is good."

He sits in the chair next to her and opens one of the little boxes. There on top, a folded paper napkin, red-and-white-checked. "I love these things," he says. Then, looking over at Mary Alice. "Box lunches."

"Me, too," Mary Alice says. "I always think I know who made them."

"A grandmotherly type with a drooping apron top who takes her time folding the napkin?" Lester asks and Mary Alice laughs and says, "Exactly!"

Her laugh is clear and genuine, a nice sound.

"The only thing we're missing is a train ride," she says.

"Okay, let's be on a train. Where are we going?"

Mary Alice tilts her head. "Where are we going. . . . Hmmm. I don't know! Where do you want to go?"

"Along the Mississippi, I should think."

"The West Coast being too obvious?"

"Exactly." Lester bites into his sandwich. One slice of bread is white; one is whole wheat. Something for everyone. And there's a crosshatched peanut butter cookie and fruit. If the sandwich were wrapped in wax paper instead of plastic wrap, his happiness would be complete. He looks over at Mary Alice and smiles. She has the kind of brown eyes that seem lit by little golden lamps. She has dimples at the corners of her mouth, he'd never noticed that.

"Are you here with someone?" he asks.

"Not really. I'll be bringing a friend with me tonight. An older gentleman I work with sometimes. He's taking a nap, and then I'm going to go and pick him up for the dinner and as much of the dance as he can stay awake for."

"He lives here in Clear Springs?"

"Yes. I do, too."

Lester talks around a bite of sandwich. "You stayed, then."

"No, I left. But I came back. I like it here. I like small towns." She points to the corner of her own mouth, and Lester wipes off a crumb of bread from his.

"I'm not far away," Lester says. "I live over in Hopkins. I have a veterinary practice there."

"That figures. You were the one who was so utterly respect-ful whenever we had to do dissections in science class. Remember how the other guys would fool around with things, how a couple of them took that fetal pig and switched around all the organs? But it always seemed kind of *sacred* to you."

Lester looks at her. "Yes."

"You were right."

Two people walk up to the table and Lester hears Pam say, "Just in time! I was just going to give up on anyone else coming. Now, who are you guys?"

The man points to himself and says, "I'm just a friend." He puts his arm around the woman. "This is Nora Decker."

"Nora Hagman Decker," Nora says.

Pam squeals and leaps up. "Nora! Oh my God, I can't believe I didn't recognize you!" She shakes her finger at Fred. "It was you who threw me off." She comes around the table and hugs Nora, then tells Fred, "Co-captain of the cheerleading squad, did you know that?"

"I did not know that," Fred says, in a terrible, terrible Johnny Carson imitation, and Nora looks down. "Fred," she says.

"Well, welcome!" Pam says and hands them a box lunch. "Gosh, you just missed Pete."

Nora and Fred exchange glances and Pam frowns. "No?" she says. "Uh-oh."

Lester looks over at Mary Alice, who shrugs.

"*Hmmm*," Lester says quietly. And then, looking out the window at the beautiful warm day, "You feel like a walk, Mary Alice Mayhew? *Is* it still Mary Alice Mayhew?"

Mary Alice smiles. "It is. And I know a great place to walk, red-winged blackbirds so thick you think you might have to beat them off with a stick. But we'd have to go a ways to get there."

Lester finishes his cookie, stands. "I'm all yours."

Mary Alice's face grows serious. Almost shyly, she says, "I'll have to walk barefoot. These are not good walking shoes."

"Barefoot girl and a box lunch. You can't get much better than that."

Mary Alice smiles. "I'll just have to get back in time to get ready for dinner."

"Me, too," Lester says. Candy Sullivan is *in* the building. Doing what, he wonders. Maybe napping. He thinks of her lying on her side, her yellow hair spread out against the pillow. He thinks of how beautiful women look when they lie like that, and some sleeping thing inside him opens one eye.

THIRTEEN

CANDY SULLIVAN LETS ESTHER OUT OF HER LITTLE CARRY-on, and the dog runs excitedly around the room, sniffing deeply at this place and that. Candy and Cooper once watched a documentary on hotel cleanliness—or lack thereof—and Coop said, "You see why I don't like to travel?" But it wasn't true that he didn't like to travel—he relished his getaways with his male friends. It was traveling with her that gave him pause. She had figured that out, finally, and only last year went to Paris alone, which at first scared the hell out of her, but then she actually enjoyed it quite a bit. To linger before a painting in the Musée d'Orsay or over a platter of cheese at an outdoor café, to watch the waters of the Fontaine d'Agam or sit in the stained-glass-colored light of a cathedral, without worrying about someone else's level of tolerance for such things! To take in a sunset while sitting beside the Seine and allow it to be the religious experience that it was, to come to tears over the astonishing beauty in a totally uninhibited way! She ate three croissants with raspberry jam for breakfast one day, and had no breakfast at all the next.

She deliberated over a little painting for sale at a gallery on Rue des Beaux-Arts, worrying and worrying about the cost of just under two thousand dollars, but then got it anyway, and after she brought it back to her hotel room and propped it up so that she could see it from the bed, she decided it was worth three times what she'd paid for it. It was of a rolling field of lavender in late afternoon, the sun a deep gold wash, and she wanted to be buried with it, she told Coop on the phone the next day, when she called to check in. That was when the idea of being buried was still an abstraction.

He'd said at that time that he missed her, that he was eager for her to come home, but then when she came home, he didn't seem so glad after all. The first thing he said to her after she cleared customs was, "Christ, what *took* you so long?" When they got home and she showed him the painting, he said, "Huh. *How* much was that?" Later, he just seemed sad—sighing over his dinner, seeming to avoid her by planting himself in front of the television and then his computer, and when finally she called him on it, he said, "Oh, for fuck's sake, here we go again. Don't blame your moodiness on me!"

She considered not responding, but then she said, "I'm only asking you to tell me what's going on. You seem upset. Or sad, or something. If I'm wrong, you can tell me. You don't have to get mad."

"*You're* the one who's *mad*!" he said.

She stared at him, her stomach aching, then said, "And yet you're the one who's yelling."

He shook his head wearily, his eyelids at half-mast. Then he lowered his voice to a chilling level and said, "I'm not *yelling,* Candy." He stood back from her, put his hands on his hips, and shouted at the top of his lungs, "*THIS IS YELLING! See the dif-ference?*"

She walked away, and—how to say it?—feared for her back

as she did so. She walked away and straightened some things in her desk drawer. She sat at the edge of the bed and contemplated her knees. She took a bath. She went to bed.

There is a knock at the door. For one second, she thinks it might be Coop, and she looks around the hotel room with his eyes, thinking about how he'll disapprove of the tacky artwork, the floral bedspread. She straightens her suit jacket and skirt and goes to the peephole to look out. It's someone from the hotel, an awkward-looking young man in a uniform that's way too big for him, and he's holding a massive bouquet of flowers. Candy sighs, presses her forehead against the door, and then opens it. "My goodness!" she says. "Aren't they lovely!"

The man—boy, really—holding the flowers seems barely aware of them. After Candy exclaims over them, he gives them a quick look, then smiles at her. "Yeah, these are for you," he says. "You're Candy Armstrong, right?"

"Right." She takes the flowers from him and breathes in the scent of one of the lilies. "Wait right there," she says, and puts the flowers on the dresser, then goes to her purse for a ten-dollar bill.

"*Thanks!*" he says. "You need anything else? Ice? I could go and get you some ice for your ice bucket."

"No thanks."

"You know how to work everything in the room?"

Probably not. The alarm clocks they put in hotel rooms by-passed her level of competence years ago. The television she never bothers with. But she tells him yes, she's all set. She'll figure out what she needs to know, or she'll get help later. She wants to lie down for a while now, and then she wants to take a walk with Esther. Since the time she was a little girl, sleep and nature have been fail-safe tonics. And besides, the dog will be left in the room tonight, and Candy wants to be sure Esther will be too worn-out to make trouble. This hotel is dog friendly and Candy wants to do her part to keep it that way. There is a room service menu for dogs: chicken and rice, or beef and gravy, or a hamburger. There are dog cookies in the shape of fire hydrants. You can order a tennis ball or a Kong toy, too. Candy brought Esther's usual kibble, but maybe she'll give her a treat tonight and get her a burger.

Her cellphone rings and she looks to see who's calling. Cooper. She contemplates not answering. But he'll know her plane has arrived, he always tracks her flights, and he'll keep calling until she does answer. She opens the phone and says, "Hi."

"You get there all right?" She can hardly hear him. He must be in the car and using his earpiece. It comes to her that she has no desire to know where he is or what he's doing, but she nonetheless asks, "Where are you?"

"Just running some errands," he says. "Are you okay?"

"I'm fine. The flight was perfect; I actually arrived early. A lot of people are here already. I saw—"

"I mean, 'cause I was thinking, you didn't plan on being there with all this *stuff* going on."

"I'm fine, Coop. I was just going to take a nap."

"Did you get something from me?"

"Oh! Yes! So sorry, of course; I got the most beautiful bouquet of flowers—they just arrived. Thank you."

"Yeah, I told 'em, you know, spare no expense. Should be a pretty over-the-top bouquet."

"It is."

"Like a million different types of flowers."

"Uh-huh, yes."

He waits, and so finally she says, "There are roses and lilies, and gerbera daisies and delphinium—"

"Yeah, blue, did they send blue delphinium? I know you like the blue ones. That's what I told them to send."

She sees herself in the mirror across the room, her shoulders drooping, her mouth thin and drawn. In the hotel with her are the people she went to high school with, the ones who knew her when. She straightens herself so that she is standing tall, untucks the hair that has fallen down her collar, and tosses her head. "You know what, Coop? I'm so sorry, but I am just beat."

"Well, I was just making sure the *flowers* I sent you had arrived. I wanted to make sure they were what I ordered. I paid enough for them."

"I'll bring them home and you can see them."

"I doubt you can get them through security." There is a kind of petulance in his voice.

"I'll get them through," she says. "The vase is the problem. But I'll wrap them in wet newspaper and plastic; I'll get them home. I'm going to lie down now, Coop. I'm *tired*. I'll call you tomorrow."

"We'll talk later tonight," he says.

She turns off her cellphone and puts it in her purse, takes off her suit and lies on the bed. She realizes she has never turned off her cellphone when she's been away from home. It's not *that* radical—he knows what hotel she's in. He can call the general number and ask to be connected to her room if he really needs her.

She picks up the hotel phone and asks for the front desk. "I wonder if you could hold my calls until further notice," she says, and the man says, "My pleasure, Ms. Armstrong," and as soon as he says it, she feels a thrilling zip of energy that all but eliminates her fatigue.

She lies back down anyway, and pats the space beside her for Esther to come up. But the bed is higher than the one at home, and so Candy has to reach down and help lift the dog. As she does, she notices a swelling on either side of Esther's abdomen and now she feels a deep stab of fear. Esther noses around, snorting and turning in tight circles, and finally lies down. Candy presses lightly on the dog's sides. Yes. A definite swelling, on both sides. Oh, please. It can't be. She presses harder, and Esther raises her head and licks Candy's hand.

She moves her face close to Esther's, looks into the dog's eyes. "Are you okay?" Esther licks Candy's nose and wags her stumpy tail. Candy pulls the dog closer to her and lies back down. Esther has been eating, drinking, sleeping, peeing, pooping. It's nothing. It can't be anything. It *isn't*.

She thinks she can probably take a good half-hour nap, and then she and Esther will take a walk (she'll watch the dog's gait, any change in her level of endurance) and then she'll get ready for the dinner and dance. She has a new dress for the occasion, one that she rather than Cooper selected.

She regards the mammoth bouquet on the dresser, the small white card stuck in it. She hasn't even bothered to look at the card; that's not right. Maybe, despite everything, he's trying. Maybe he wrote something romantic, some overture meant to try to get them onto a different path. She gets off the bed and goes over to the dresser to pull the card out of the little envelope. "Call when you get this. Coop."

She props the card against the vase, then throws it in the trash. She moves to the window and leans her head against it, considers again the information she was given by her doctor. She will seek a second opinion, even a third. But if she is dying, well, then she's going to live first. On her own terms. On the nightstand is her purse and in it is a chocolate bar and she gets it out. She breaks off a large square and carefully positions it in the exact middle of her tongue. Then she moves herself to the exact middle of the bed to let the candy slowly melt. While it does, she runs her hands over her abdomen, then up across her breasts and down her arms. She touches herself in a way that has nothing to do with eroticism and everything to do with simply acknowledging—thanking!—a body that has been ignored for a very long time, by Cooper and by herself, too. *Don't go,* she thinks.

At three-thirty, the bedside clock alarm goes off. Candy starts awake, then reaches over to shut the thing off. Who would set their alarm for three-thirty in the afternoon? Someone taking a nap, she supposes. Or someone like her, who distrusts the off switch and is wary of an alarm going off at five in the morning and so sets it for three-thirty in the afternoon. It makes Candy smile, thinking of someone else doing that, sitting on the side of the bed and fiddling with the alarm clock, arming themselves against what are supposed to be conveniences. She would like to meet someone like that; they could probably be friends, having lunch and complaining about the demise of hands-on reading and the way you can never get a live person on the line when you're trying to take care of some pressing business matter. On one particularly bad day when Candy had to call about a problem with her refrigerator, she got a recording offering endless choices for things she didn't want; and then she was rerouted to the beginning of the recording when she pressed 0. Same deal when she pressed *. And when she pressed #. Finally, Candy yelled into the phone, "I WANT A *PERSON,* I WANT A *PERSON,* THIS IS SO DE*HUMANIZING,* GIVE ME A *PERSON*!"

Later that afternoon, when she went out to deadhead the flowers in her garden, her neighbor Arthur was in his backyard. He saw her and waved, and Candy waved back. Then he came up to the fence and asked quietly, "Everything all right?" Candy flushed—he must have heard her screaming on the phone—and said brightly, "Yup!" It seems to her now that she might have shared with him her exasperation with recordings on the telephone and he would have understood. It seems like he would have nodded grimly and said, "It gets my goat, too, I'll tell you. The world's going to hell in a handbasket." And then she could have shared with him her idea for being a person whose job is to simply be a real person on the line. Not to do anything; just to be a real live voice, for the *relief* of it all. He would have laughed at that, Arthur, and his bright blue eyes would have disappeared into his face the way they did when he laughed. Such a nice man, Arthur. A kind man.

Esther is sitting before her, staring expectantly in her pop-eyed way. Candy pets her, and checks to see if the lumps are still there or if they have somehow disappeared. Still there. How has she not noticed this before? She tells the dog, "Okay. I know. I'm going to take you out. Just let me take myself out, first."

She uses the toilet, brushes her teeth, then goes to the window to look outside. Still sunny and warm, it appears, no one wearing a sweater or a jacket. She puts on a pair of white linen pants and a black linen blouse, a gold cuff bracelet, low-heeled sandals. She pushes the room key into her back pocket. Then she snaps Esther's leash on and goes out into the hall.

Standing at the elevator is a man whose face she thinks she recognizes. "Pete?" she says. "Pete Decker?"

"Aw, Jesus, *Candy Sullivan*? The last time I saw you, you were drunk at our graduation party."

She laughs. "Right back at you. How are you?" Oh, it's nice to see him. Pete Decker, all grown up. He looks fine—graying hair, a few wrinkles, a little looseness at the jawline, but he really looks fine.

"I'm great!" he says, and she can see that he is taking in her collateral damage in the same way she just quickly assessed his. He bends down to pat Esther. "How you doing there, Sparky?" He looks up at Candy. "What's his name?"

"Esther. She's a girl."

He laughs. "Great name. Great-looking dog. I like bulldogs, they always put you in a good mood." He leans closer to Candy to say, "*You* look fan*tas*tic!"

"Thanks. You do, too."

The elevator comes, and Pete holds the door for her and Esther, then steps in after them.

"You play golf?" Candy asks, as they lean on opposite walls of the elevator.

Pete looks down at his yellow knit shirt, with its little embroidered golfer teeing off at nipple level. "Well, yeah, I do; but I don't usually wear golf *clothes*. This was just . . . I spilled something on my clothes at the airport, whole cup of Coke, some kid knocked into me, so I had to quick buy a change of clothes. I was wearing jeans and a blue Zegna shirt. You know. These pants don't even fit me." He pulls with some pride at the waistband to show her the pants are too big, and Candy nods. They are also a bit short, she sees.

"I'm going to try to quick buy a suit somewhere," he says.

"Your suit got wet, too?"

He looks confused. "Oh. No! That, I . . . Would you believe it, I forgot to pack it!" He smacks his forehead. "Left it hanging in my closet!"

The elevator doors open, and Pete looks to the right and the left before he exits. "You seen anybody yet?" he asks. " 'Sides me, I mean. Course, *I'm* all you *need* to see!"

She smiles. Same old Pete. She tells him, "Just Pam, when I registered." But now she sees a couple standing outside, about fifty feet from the entrance. "Is that anybody?"

Pete squints. "I think that's . . . Oh my God, I *think* that's Lester Hessenpfeffer and Mary Alice Mayhew! Isn't it?"

Candy looks again. "I think you're right!"

"*There's* a match made in heaven!" He shakes his head.

Candy starts to say she always liked them both but felt inhibited in the old days from showing it, and why had they all been like that? But Pete's in a hurry and steps briskly down the hall, and Candy decides the people to talk to are Lester and Mary Alice, not Pete. She suspects if she asked Pete about why they marginalized people in that awful way back then, he'd say, "Well they were *nerds*." And then he'd look over at them and probably say, "Still are, come on."

But Lester and Mary Alice are engrossed in what appears to be a rather personal conversation, standing there with their heads bent close together, and she decides not to bother them. She'll tell them tonight, one way or another, that she regrets not having gotten to know them better in high school. She'll ask Lester for a dance. If she drinks enough, she may ask Mary Alice for one, too. It comes to her that she'd like to tell her the News, that Mary Alice would be the kind of person you'd want for your friend, if things got bad. Or even if they didn't. How can she feel this way, when she has not exchanged a word with Mary Alice in all these years? She never talked to her much when they were in school together, either. Still, she has this feeling about her.

Candy goes out the far door of the hotel and into the sunshine. She'll walk Esther for as long as there's time. Then she'll come back and get ready.

She takes a few steps, then suddenly stops and says, "*Essie!*" The dog looks up at her. She reaches down to pet her, avoiding touching her abdomen. "Good girl," she says. "You're a *good girl*! You ready?"

A snort.

"You *ready*?"

A few steps backward, and she barks.

"*Okay!*" Candy says. "Me, too. Me, too. Let's go."

FOURTEEN

A FEW MINUTES BEFORE THE DINNER IS SCHEDULED TO start, Pete Decker gets off the elevator and runs smack into his wife and that nincompoop, Fred Preston. Fred is wearing a suit you'd wear to a funeral: something muddy-colored and plain, with no style at all, and his tie is a nightmare. What is that, *cats* on there? Not that Pete should talk. Damn it. He was not able to find a suit, and so he's stuck wearing these stupid golf clothes. His shirt is untucked to disguise the fact that the pants are so loose at the waist. He, Pete Decker, Mr. GQ, looks like hell. That's right. He looks worse than Fred! But to put a new spin on an old axiom, even in tacky golf clothes, tomorrow morning he'll still be Pete Decker and Fred Preston will be the dickwad that he is, no matter what he wears. Nora has stopped in her tracks to stare at Pete, and he raises his hand in a little wave. "Hey," he says.

"Pete! What are you doing here? Why aren't you in the hospital?"

He shrugs. "Yeah, funniest thing. Right after you left, the doc came in and sprang me after all."

God, Nora looks good. She's wearing some blue-green dress with a short skirt that shows off her legs, and her shoulders are bare. She looks beautiful. She has on a necklace he didn't give her and hopes Fred didn't, either; he hopes she bought it for herself. It's blue-green, too, something made of glass or crystal or some such thing, and it has a very classy and contemporary look, like the jewelry Hillary Clinton wore when she was running for president. It's a youthful look. He remembers how Nora used to comment on how swell Her Hillaryness looked every time she spoke on the campaign trail, and he would think, *Yeah, well, maybe you should pay attention to the content and not the costume,* but the truth was that Nora did pay attention; she retained more about what the candidates said than he did. Another thing he'll do when he moves back in is give her the respect she deserves.

Fred reaches out his hand, and Pete reluctantly (though *graciously*!) shakes it. "Nice to see you, Pete," Fred says, and Pete says, "You, too," and aren't they both full of shit.

"Play a few rounds today?" Fred asks, smirking, and Pete looks down at himself and says, "Yeah, the airline lost my bag, what can you do." He feels himself blushing and tightens his buttocks as though that might stop it.

"Well, we'd better get going," Nora says, and there is—is there?—just the softest hint of regret in her eyes. Pete guesses that she wishes she were with him, that she has begun to feel exactly what he wanted her to, on account of all the memories being stirred up. He stares back at her, his high school sweetheart, the girl who wore his letter jacket, his wife, the mother of his children, his *friend,* and he feels two parallel lines in his throat begin to ache.

"Hey, Nora," he says. "Can I just . . . Can I talk to you in private for just a second?"

She hesitates, and Fred takes her arm and says, "We were just going in, Pete."

And God bless Nora, she pulls her arm away and says, "It's okay, Fred. You go ahead, and I'll be right there."

"I really don't know anyone, Nora," Fred says. "This is, after all, *your* high school reunion."

Right, Pete thinks. *Hers and mine. Not yours.* He wonders how Fred got a ticket, anyway. That damn Pam Pottsman. She probably just told him he could come for free, giggling the whole time.

Nora's right eye twitches, which it always does when she's getting annoyed. Not that Fred knows this. Or anything else. She says, "Well, could you just wait for me at the entrance to the ballroom? You might try speaking to someone. They're all friendly people." Her tone softens, then, and she says, "Just give me a second, okay? I'll be right there."

Oh, man, this is suddenly the happiest day of Pete's life. He won't take her from Fred right away. Let them have dinner, then he'll request that the DJ play "The Way You Look Tonight," which was the first song he and Nora screwed to, and then he'll walk right over and ask her to dance. She might get weepy, that would be good. But in any case, they'll dance a little and then he'll say, "Why don't you dump the excess baggage and come upstairs with me?" and maybe she will. He bets she will.

Nora comes over to him and he says softly, "How you doing, babe?"

She crosses her arms and sighs, and he sees that the scenario he just imagined is not going to happen. She's with another man. She's wearing a dress he's never seen before. A new scent.

He blows air out of his cheeks. "Okay, well, I don't have anything, you know, special. I just wanted to say that you look so beautiful. You really do."

"Well . . . Thank you. Thanks, Pete." She starts to walk away.

This can't be it! There's got to be something he can say that will get to her! He gently takes her arm and says, "Nora? I also wanted—" The cellphone in his pocket vibrates, making a buzzing sound, and he tries to ignore it, but she hears it, too.

"Better get that," she says, and there is something in her tone that makes him think she's pretty sure it's Sandy. He wants so much for her not to think that. He points to the phone and says, "Bet that's one of the kids."

Her eyebrows rise to the *Oh?* position.

He takes the phone out and looks to see who's calling. Damn it, it *is* Sandy. "I'll call them back," he says, but Nora knows. She smiles, turns away, and walks down the hall toward Fred, who's probably going to act like he's saving the damsel in distress. Asshole. He can't even play touch football. He doesn't *like* sports. Or cigars. Or *cars*! He "kiddingly" referred to Pete's Porsche as generic Viagra. And what does Fred drive? A *Nissan Cube,* an absolute joke of a car, and in the driver's seat he has some sort of wooden-beaded *orthopedic* device for his *back*.

Well, Nora is still his wife. They're not divorced yet, she is still his wife. He opens his still-buzzing cellphone and says, "What."

"Okay," Sandy says. "I have to do this while I'm feeling strong enough to do it, so please just listen. Okay. I want to say something. Which is: I don't think we should continue our relationship. It is too damaging to my esteem."

He pulls the phone away from his ear, looks at it, tries to think of what to say, and then just snaps it shut. It buzzes again, and when he answers, Sandy says, "Did you hear me?"

"Sandy," he says.

There is a long silence, and he hears her snuffling. "I'm sorry," she says. "I know this comes as a shock. I'm sorry to hurt you. But I just don't know if we can work this out."

Pete rolls his eyes. "I understand. We're done. Be happy. Goodbye."

"You *always* hide your *true* feelings," she says.

"Not this time," he says. "Take it easy."

He stands in the hall and watches his classmates come out of the elevator and head for the ballroom. He calls out to some of his football buddies, wonders who some of the other people are. There goes Pam Pottsman in her triple-X-size emerald green dress and her hair ratted up real high. She's wearing blue shoes. Women used to get their shoes and purses dyed so everything matched; now they seem to pride themselves on these outrageous color combinations. You have to pay attention to women; they're always shifting things around, always *changing* things. A guy can never trust that the chair that he has positioned perfectly for watching television will be left alone.

Dorothy Shauman gets off the elevator with her two girl-friends who always hung with her like she was the Queen of Sheba and they were her slaves. They're all still okay looking; the brunette, especially, what was her name, Jennifer, he thinks, something J. Anyway, he made out with her but good one night at a Homecoming bonfire. And the blonde, Linda, he had a session with her in the bathroom at a party he brought Nora to on their first date. He still feels kind of bad about that. The J woman and Linda say hi, but Dorothy hardly looks at him, what's her problem? He made out with her, too, one time, and it actually wasn't bad, she was most accommodating. Maybe she forgot. It's possible. He doubts it, but it's possible.

He recognizes Ben Small, who gets off the elevator alone, talking on his iPhone. That guy had been a really good actor. *Really* good. Pete watches him walk to see if he turned out queer. Hard to tell; Ben's got an easy, long-legged stride that could go either way. Same with the clothes: elegant, casual, expensive looking, but not sissy. He'll buy Ben a drink, see what's up. He might have become some Broadway star, who knows? The last time he saw Ben Small, it was the August before most of them left for college and Ben was mowing the lawn in front of his little white house. Pete had driven by with a handful of buddies and they'd all called out, "Hey, Small!" and Ben had waved and then stood still, watching them go. Everybody wanted to be in Pete's crowd in those days. Everybody did.

He looks at his watch and starts for the ballroom. Coming around a corner near the opposite end of the hall, Pete sees a woman in a blue dress pushing some old geezer in a wheelchair. The guy's all decked out in a suit Pete wishes he had on, nice blue tie, too. As they get closer, he sees it's Mary Alice Mayhew. God damn. She actually looks kind of nice! She recognizes Pete and smiles, waves. He waves back, then goes over to meet her and what he presumes is her father. He'll ask if he can sit with Mary Alice for dinner. She'll be a safe haven from where he can watch the crowd. Well, not the crowd. Nora. Nora Jane Hagman Decker, born September 9, 1952, at 7:07 A.M. via cesarean section. Favorite color: green. Favorite movie: *All About Eve*. Favorite food: sauces, the woman loves sauces, always asks for extra sauce on the side. It will be good for Pete to sit with Mary Alice Mayhew. If Nora sees him, she'll know he's *behaving* himself.

"Hey, what's up, Mary Alice," he says when he's beside her.

"Hi, Pete." She leans over and gives him a little kiss. She smells good, like just-cut grass. "How are you?"

"I'm fired up!" he says.

Mary Alice puts her hand on her father's shoulder. "This is my friend Einer Olson."

"Nice to meet you," Pete says, and thinks, *Hmm, not her father. Is he her* date?

He always did feel sorry for Mary Alice, but this takes the cake.

"Bet *you* were a senior superlative!" Einer says, looking him up and down. The dude's glasses must be three inches thick.

Pete smiles. "Pardon?"

"Senior superlative! Didn't you people have them? When I was in school, we had senior superlatives. They were the young men and women who truly excelled in one way or another. We had one guy, Cecil McIntyre, oh, that guy could throw a football, I'll tell you! Good friend of mine."

"Yeah, I played football," Pete says.

"No, he's been gone for years now," Einer says.

"No, I said, 'I played football,'" Pete says, loudly.

"That so? What position?"

"Quarterback."

Einer tilts his head back to scrutinize Pete more fully. "Well, the girls always like the quarterbacks, don't they?"

"Yes, sir, they do."

"I was a track man, myself."

"Nothing wrong with that."

"I could *play* football, just wasn't my strong suit."

"Einer, I'm starving," Mary Alice says.

"Move along, then! I'm not the one driving!"

Mary Alice pushes him slowly into the ballroom, and it seems to Pete that she's carefully scanning the crowd.

"Looking for someone?" Pete has to raise his voice to be heard over "Crimson and Clover," which the DJ is playing a little too loudly.

"Oh, no," Mary Alice says.

"She is, too," Einer shouts. "She told me on the way over that she really wants to talk to Bert Small."

"*Ben* Small?" Pete says. And then, pointing, "He's right over there. Let's go and sit with him; there's room at his table."

Now Mary Alice speaks quietly. "That's okay, Pete."

"Aw, come on!" Pete smiles the old killer smile. Let this be his good deed of the night: get Mary Alice Mayhew and Ben Small together. He doesn't remember ever seeing her with anybody in high school. In fact, now that he thinks of it, he recalls that kids were kind of shitty to Mary Alice. Oh, not Pete—he had bigger fish to fry. He picked on other jocks, especially those from other schools. Put a little spray paint a few places it shouldn't go, that kind of thing.

Pete takes over pushing the wheelchair for Mary Alice, and when they get to Ben's table and ask if they can sit there, he says absolutely, and seems happy. Pete sees in one instant that Ben Small is not gay. Sensitive, maybe, but not gay. He's not sure Mary Alice can see it, though. She's looking in another direction altogether. She's looking two tables over, where Candy Sullivan— Jesus, *gorgeous* in that white dress—is sitting with none other than Lester Hessenpfeffer. Mary Alice is probably worried about Candy moving in on Ben. All the girls used to worry about Candy Sullivan.

The dance floor is empty but for a couple Pete doesn't recognize—a couple of white-haired people dancing to "Proud Mary." The music isn't quite so loud now; Pete thinks maybe the couple asked them to turn it down.

"I had a lot of fun in high school," Einer says, and Pete moves closer to him. He'll make do having conversation with the old man during dinner. It's fine. The guy's kind of funny—interesting, too—and Pete has a clear view of Nora, who is engaged in intense conversation with another woman at their table—Gloria Gelman? Is that ancient-looking woman the formerly sexalicious Gloria Gelman?—while Fred sits there like some kind of stick-in-the-mud. That's because he *is* a stick-in-the-mud, a total loser, a namby-pamby, pissant girlyman, which, if Nora hasn't learned by now, she soon will. All Pete needs to do is take his time and play it cool. And oh, baby, he knows what cool is.

"I was a bit of a ladies' man until I met my wife," Einer says. "She was the editor of the school newspaper. Real bright girl."

"That right?" Pete says.

"Yup. So who do you think signed on to be a reporter?"

"Einer Olson?"

"Bingo," Einer says. And then, "Say, Pete, do you think you could get me a gin martini?"

"Einer," Mary Alice says. "I don't think you can drink with your medication."

Einer leans back in his chair and slaps his hands on his knees. "You're right. And guess who hasn't taken his medication the last couple of days?" He turns back to Pete. "How about it, son?"

"My pleasure," Pete says. And then, to Mary Alice, "What can I get you?"

"Well, a gin martini, I suppose."

"Ben?"

"I'm set," Ben says, and holds up what looks like a glass of Coke, complete with compensatory slice of lemon. He's probably an alkie. A lot of sensitive types end up alkies.

"Be right back," Pete says. He takes a path to the bar that will bring him close enough to see Nora better without her seeing him—she's sitting with her back to him. She's having red wine, and so is Fred. He hates that they're having the same thing. Fred looks over and sees him and his stupid smile disappears and his expression becomes tense and unhappy. *That's right, buddy.* Pete smiles, waves, and steps up to the bar to order the drinks, loosens his shoulders. Yup. He's starting to have a good time now. He looks back over at Fred, who has turned away from him and emphatically put his arm around Nora.

Pete leans against the bar and looks around the room. There's Kim Birch, she was a smart one, went to Wellesley. He sees Hodder Carter, weird name, great wrestler. He'll catch up with him later. He's talking to a woman Pete thinks is Angie McNair, who Hodder had a big crush on, and Angie would never go out with him. She told him if he'd just lose weight, he'd be a lot more popular and then she would go out with him. Well, who needs to lose weight now? Angie looks like *she's* the wrestler now, heavyweight division. Look at the neck on that woman!

Some guy Pete doesn't recognize is standing at Candy Sullivan's table, talking to her. Wait. Is that . . . ? It's Buddy Dunsmore! Damn! Poor Buddy, he really got shafted, having to marry Nance. Pete would bet money that they are long divorced by now. So Buddy's going to go after what every guy in school wanted: Miss Candy Sullivan, who looked every day like she walked right out of the pages of a magazine. *Beautiful* girl, and really very nice, too. Buddy never got her—hell, even *Pete* never got her, not even one kiss. She dated very few guys from their school, she mostly dated boys from the private school a couple of towns over, and by senior year was dating college guys exclusively. Nobody from their high school ever nailed her. She moved out East right after high school, she was going to become a nurse. She probably married a surgeon or something.

Candy was one of those happy types, always in a good mood. He'd enjoyed running into her earlier today and talking for the little bit that they did. There was something about Candy now, though. He couldn't put his finger on it, but she had a look in her eyes—or maybe behind her eyes—that reminded him of how his then five-year-old daughter looked one time when he'd yelled at her to put something back and he'd yelled way louder than he meant to. Katie had jumped, and she'd put the thing back very carefully, and then she'd looked over at him and her hands were clasped tightly together and she was smiling but she was scared as hell. Overcome with guilt, he'd held out his arms and said, "Aw, I'm sorry; come here, baby," and she had, but she'd kept that look on her face until he'd held her a long time. Candy had a look like that, only sadder.

The salads are being delivered. Pete pays for the drinks and starts to carry them carefully back to the table. A hugely over-weight man comes up and punches him lightly in the arm. "Hey, Decker, you asshole!"

"Hey!" Pete says. "How you doing?" The guy's not wearing his name tag. Pain in the ass. Pete's not wearing his name tag, either, he hates those things, but he doesn't *need* one.

"Remember me?" the guy says.

Pete smiles, says nothing.

"Aw, man, you don't remember me?"

"I'm sorry," Pete says.

"Benny Westman!"

"Oh, sure!" Pete says. *Who the hell is Benny Westman?*

"For fuck's sake, man! I can't believe you didn't recognize me. Although I look a little different now, huh?"

"I guess we all do." *Benny Westman. Benny Westman.* Oh yes, he remembers now. Tight end. Kind of a jerk. Always real mean to his girlfriends, or at least about them—revealed plenty of secrets in the locker room. Stuff a girl for sure wouldn't want known about herself. Stuff the other guys didn't want to hear, although of course they never admitted that, they just laughed and shook their heads.

"Few of us lettermen are getting together after dinner in the parking lot for a little recreational toot," Benny says. "Want to join us?"

"Yeah, sure, we'll see." Pete gestures with his chin to his table. "I'd better get back and deliver these drinks." *Lettermen.* He's got to remember to request "The Way You Look Tonight."

Benny looks briefly toward Pete's table, then turns back to him, his eyes wide. "Is that fucking Mary Alice *Mayhew?*"

"It is."

"You're sitting with *that* skank?"

"Yeah, I am. You know what? It's been forty years, Benny. You want to give her a break?"

Benny's face changes. "Oh, Jesus, sorry, man. Are you like . . . *with* her?"

"No, she's just a friend."

"You and Nora are still together, right?"

"She's here," he says, and then, "I'll see you later, Benny."

He returns to the table, passes out the drinks, clinks glasses with everyone. He watches Benny lumber back to his table and put his arm around a washed-out looking blonde. She's wearing a tacky black strapless dress, and she still has her purse hooked over her shoulder, a brown leather purse on which she has put her name tag. It's one designed for the spouses, and it says, "Hi! I'm with _____." He feels sorry for the spouses. Nobody wants the spouses there, unless they went to the same school. In fact, all of a sudden he feels sorry for *everybody*. Here they all are, all these people, all these years later just . . . what? Trying, he guesses. Just trying.

"Mary Alice!" he says.

"Yes!"

"Dibs on the first dance!"

She smiles. "How about the second? Einer beat you to the first."

"Well, the best man won," Pete says, and holds his glass up to toast Einer. Einer holds his own glass up, his hand trembling.

When Nora and Pete were still together, Pete had noticed Nora beginning to pay a lot of attention to old people. She would watch some bent-over octogenarian painstakingly making her way across the street. Or she'd stare at an old lady selecting a little can of beans from the supermarket shelf, or standing in line with a walker waiting for a prescription. "That'll be me in five minutes," Nora would say. And he would laugh. He didn't understand why she said that. Now, suddenly, he does. Einer, the high school star, holding a forbidden drink in his trembling hand.

Someone bumps into the back of Pete's chair, and he feels cold liquid spilling onto his shirt.

"Oh, *sorry!*" a woman says.

"It's okay," Pete tells her, dabbing at the mess with his napkin, and now he's got *orange salad dressing* on the shirt as well. What the hell. Nothing can make it look any worse.

"Are you . . ." The woman smiles. "Oh my God. Pete Decker!"

"Hey, Susie." Susie Sussman. *She* wore her name tag, like a sensible person. She was okay in high school, pep squad, cute little figure; he made it to third base with her, something like that. He knows her underpants were on his car floor, anyway. Hers or her sister Patsy's. They were twins. He got them both, but he never made out with them at the same time, which guys were always daring him to do. Patsy died the day after graduation in a motorcycle accident, Pete found that out at the five-year reunion, where Susie showed up looking like a million bucks. They'd had a nice little boozy kiss in the hall that year, couple of kisses, nothing else since. Susie looks a bit worn at the edges now. Well, she looks like hell, really. A good thirty pounds overweight, big circles under her eyes, one of those awful too-short spiky haircuts that women seem to think make them look younger but only make them look like Marines. He saw her at the last reunion, and she still had something, then. All gone now. Nada. Not that she seems to know it. Once in the Club, always in the Club, he supposes.

"How the hell *are* you, Pete?"

"Good," he says, nodding. "Yup."

"You look great!"

"Thanks. You, too." *What the hell.*

"Save me a slow dance, will you?"

"I will!"

She moves away without having acknowledged one other

person at the table. It was high school behavior she'd reverted to; the people at Pete's table had never made the cut then and apparently don't now, either. Pete feels ashamed, as though it's his fault Susie ignored them. He supposes that, in part, it is. He should have made introductions. Well, add it to the mea culpas. Add it to the long and ever-growing list. He drains his drink, looks over at Nora. It appears she hasn't touched her salad. Too busy talking, laughing. Look what a good time she's having, a Kleenex carnation pinned to her hair. See that? He knew she would enjoy herself like this, he *knows* her. What a smile she still has. He smiles back at her, though clearly she is not smiling at him.

FIFTEEN

"Now, there's someone I can get along with," Einer tells Mary Alice, as he watches Pete wend his way through the crowd toward the bar.

"He *is* a nice guy," Mary Alice says.

"Should have hung around with *him* when you were in high school!"

"Well." She smiles at Einer. "Yes, I suppose so."

Einer's having a great time. She hasn't seen him so enlivened since . . . since she doesn't know when. She herself is not exactly thrilled with the way things are going. She'd hoped—expected, really—that she'd be eating dinner with Lester, but there he is sitting next to none other than Candy Sullivan. Well, that's the end of that. Candy is wearing a simple white dress that sets off . . . everything. She remains a dazzlingly beautiful woman. Her hair is in a loose upsweep, and she wears a large pair of diamond studs that twinkle every time she moves. Her shoulders are bare, her arms, but she has a gossamer wrap draped loosely about them. Mary Alice sighs the tiniest of sighs. She can't justify getting angry: Candy doesn't know she has feelings for Lester; and what man could resist her? Moreover, Candy Sullivan never did a single nasty thing to her in high school and, on one momentous day, actually chose Mary Alice first to be on her field hockey team in gym class. There was a collective gasp when she did that, and at the time Mary Alice wondered if her being picked first wasn't as bad as being picked last—different stares, different whispers, but stares and whispers all the same.

No, and she doesn't blame Lester, who sits with his chair turned at an angle toward Candy, his legs outstretched, his arms crossed. Mary Alice puts a great deal of stock in body language, and would like to think that Lester's crossed arms indicate a certain unwillingness to let Candy in. But look at his face: open, friendly, and awfully attentive to whatever Candy is saying. At the moment, their conversation is exclusionary; everyone else at the table is talking to each other. Nance and Buddy Dunsmore. Sheila Grommer, class secretary. Linny Waterman, who, as captain of the cheerleading squad, wore a star on the sleeve of her sweater and could do multiple backflips and impossibly high jumps. Marshall Kind, whose father more than once got kicked out of his son's wrestling matches for arguing with the refs. Erik Betterman, a huge, burly guy who was rumored to be a fool over his ancient cat. Mary Alice remembers every single one of them. Still the popular table, except that Lester and Pete Decker ought to change places.

Einer rises a little ways out of his wheelchair to reach for the salt, and Mary Alice watches carefully. She won't help him unless she has to; she appreciates the fact that his own memories have erased many of his years, if only in his mind. After she "dances" with him, she suspects he'll have his choice of partners. The truth is, he looks adorable, his tightly knotted tie and gold cuff links, his stick-out ears and duck-fluff hair. She bets someone will end up in his lap.

Mary Alice sighs and contemplates her hands, clasped together in her lap. She and Lester had had such a lovely time together this afternoon. They had talked easily, their conversation running smooth and lively and seemingly unstoppable. They are aligned politically; they both like pancake breakfasts; he likes Beethoven over Mozart, just as she does. They both like line dancing, though Lester says he's better at watching it than doing it. And when it came to high school memories, well! Didn't they understand each other in that regard! The name-calling, the spitballs, the nasty notes shoved into locker doors, the "accidental" knocking of books from their arms, the churlish comments about them in slam books. Yet both of them had let go of all that, had in fact let go of it long before they graduated. "Did you even *care*?" Lester had asked, and Mary Alice had thought for a while before she'd answered. Finally, she'd nodded and said, "Yes. But I cared about other things more. The world was quite a bit bigger than the halls of Whitley High School."

"It sure was," Lester said.

He had told her about his wife, briefly, mostly by way of explaining why he'd devoted himself more to work than to pursuing a relationship. There'd been one time when they were standing in the middle of the field—which, as promised, had been full of red-winged blackbirds—and Lester's hand had rested on Mary Alice's shoulder when he showed her one of the birds sitting motionless on a wire and looking up at the sky. "It's like he's contemplating the cloud formations," Mary Alice said, and Lester laughed and said, "It's true! I have never seen a bird do that. Have you?" Mary Alice turned toward him and allowed as how she had not. Their faces were very close together then, and the moment was charged not so much with any kind of sexual energy as with *ease*. Lester asked if she'd ever been bird-watching in a more formal way, if she'd ever risen before dawn, slung binoculars around her neck, and headed out to join a group that moved together like one organism, whispering and pointing and then going out for a breakfast that felt more like lunch. No, she said, she had never done that. And he said, well she really ought to. That moment hung in the air, it felt like an invitation from Lester was forthcoming, inevitable; and then she made a mistake. She looked at her watch, which prompted him to look at his own and say that they'd better get going. *No, that's not what I meant!* she wanted to say. *I was looking because I wanted more time!*

But she'd figured she'd have an opportunity to bring up the subject again. He'd said, "See you at dinner?" and the late afternoon had been gilding the side of his face and making the tips of his eyelashes seem to glow; and besides looking handsome, he'd looked kind and capable and rich in the soul, and she'd said yes, she would see him at dinner. Yes, she'd said, and she'd wondered how she would look to him in her new dress.

She went home and got ready in a kind of grounded ecstasy, and applied a little makeup to the best of her ability. And she thought she looked quite nice. She looked in the full-length mirror at her front and back and sides; and she approved of herself in a way that was new to her. She sang "It Had to Be You" under her breath, and laughed at herself for her presumptuousness, then decided she wasn't being presumptuous at all, she was just being hopeful—realistic, even!—and responding to the encouragement she'd been given.

She called Einer before she left home, telling him she was on the way to pick him up, and he could release Rita to leave for her dinner date with the man she'd met in the grocery store. Rita had promised to come back in a couple of hours; she and Mary Alice had incorrectly assumed that Einer wouldn't want to stay for long at the reunion.

When Mary Alice arrived to pick up Einer, he was still in his bathrobe. He told her he was sorry, but he had to use the bathroom before he finished getting dressed. *Finished?* Mary Alice had thought. *You haven't even started!* But she stood in her heels and perfume, clutching the little evening bag she'd borrowed from her sister, and Einer shuffled to the bathroom at his turtle pace, the newspaper under his arm, and what could she do? The choice was to be furious and unhappy or to make herself useful. She'd put her purse on the nightstand and turned down Einer's bedcovers invitingly and plumped his pillows. She'd gone down to the kitchen to get a glass of water to put on his nightstand. Then she'd sat at the foot of his bed with her back straight, her knees together, breathing in and breathing out and feeling grateful that she never had to give her bowels a second thought. Einer farted explosively several times, and then called out "Sorry!"

"It's all right!" she called back.

"I'm having a little trouble getting going!"

"Take your time," she said.

"What?"

"It's *okay;* take your *time,*" she said, and looked out the window at the darkening sky. She would not give him a suppository. Absolutely not.

As it happened, Einer succeeded on his own ("Now you're talking!" she heard him mutter), and soon he came shuffling out of the bathroom. He dressed slowly and with great deliberation, and then he fussed with the knot in his tie, and then he combed and combed his sparse hair while he squinted into the mirror. Next he deliberated over which cologne to wear, citrus or spice? By then it was all she could do not to drag him out of his room by the scruff of his neck. "Women like citrus," she told him, and he looked at her doubtfully, but then shrugged and put on that scent.

At last, he was ready, and she helped him out and into the car, and they headed for the hotel. And then what? A freight train!

Once Mary Alice walked into the hotel, she calmed down and was most accommodating to Pete Decker, who asked if he might sit with them. She'd always found him lovely to look at, the photo of him had looked nice on her bedroom wall, but a crush? No. Despite what her sister thought, she had never had a crush on Pete Decker. No reason for him not to sit with them, though. He was still lovely to look at.

Mary Alice had told Einer on the way over that she wanted to talk to Ben Small because she did want to talk to Ben Small, but only because she was curious about whether or not he'd ever become an actor. But now look.

She turns and glances again at Lester, who is still engrossed in conversation with Candy. What are they *talking* about? Each so serious. She doubts he's even noticed that she is here.

Pete comes back to the table and delivers the drinks, and Mary Alice takes such a large first gulp of hers, it gives her the hiccups. She's embarrassed by this, but Ben Small puts his hand on her arm, nicely, and she leans back in her chair and smiles. Then she hiccups again and he laughs and so does she. What can you do? Love the one you're with. The main courses are placed before them by grim-faced waitstaff who are banging the platters down in a way that is not exactly gracious: *Here! Here! Here's your food!* They want to get this dinner over with, it's clear; and so does Mary Alice. Because although she has missed her opportunity to have dinner with Lester, there's still the rest of the night to come; the DJ is already setting up for the dance in the corner of the ballroom. In third grade, Mary Alice once asked the most popular boy in the school to dance. And what do you think he said? *Okay,* that's what he said.

There is the sound of a spoon against a water glass, and the loud chatter in the room gradually quiets. Pam Pottsman is over by the DJ, and she takes his microphone. "May I have your attention?" she says. "Now, I know you just got your dinners, and I want you to go ahead and enjoy them. But I have a surprise. I think most of you know that Walter Vogel has passed on; his class photo is over on the memorial table, you probably saw it. And gosh, we all remember Walter Vogel, don't we?" She leads the audience in a confused kind of applause.

Mary Alice has not yet looked at the memorial table, and she suspects she is not the only one who is putting off doing so. But she has no memory of Walter Vogel. Not one memory. *Walter Vogel*, she thinks. *Walter Vogel*. And then she remembers: a thin boy in ill-fitting clothes who had seemed pathologically shy—he'd never talk to or even look at anyone. He lived alone with his father; his mother was dead, and there were rumors that his father beat him with a board. He did poorly in school; Mary Alice remembers that he had a driver's license long before the rest of them, because he'd been left back a few times. Unike her or Lester, Walter wasn't picked on. He was simply ignored. Unseen, really.

Pam continues talking exuberantly into the microphone, though it's obvious she's not quite sure what she's doing—or should do. "Right! Okay! So, Walter Vogel, he . . . You know, he was quite the . . . And of course I think he also played on the basketball team! Walter unfortunately died of cancer two years ago, and—" She looks off to the side, where a young man stands in the shadows. "Pardon? . . . Oh, I'm so sorry, it was three years ago, but anyway, the good news is that his son, who was the one who got the invitation to the reunion and then called and told me about his dad's passing, *he* has come here tonight, and he would like to say a few words. It's just a wonderful *surprise* for *all* of us, and, well, here he is, Ron Vogel. Walter's son."

The young man steps into the light, and now Mary Alice remembers his father clearly; his son is his spitting image. Ron is wearing jeans and a plaid shirt, a sweatshirt jacket, heavy work boots. "Okay," he says. "Well, first off I just want to say thank you to everyone for letting me talk to you. Which I did not plan to do, to be honest. But I remembered you all were going to be here tonight, and I thought . . . Well, I just wanted to come over.

"My dad, he was not an easy guy. I guess that's what you'd say. He was a hard dude to live with, he wasn't so nice to us kids. He was real nice to my mom, he always was, he treated her like she was a princess or something.

"What I really wanted from my dad was a way to know him. I never did *know* him, he wouldn't hardly ever talk to me. Or anybody, for that matter. He never did. But I think you all must have known him. He used to talk about this group of guys he hung around with in high school. Glory days, you know, that is the one thing he would talk about is this group of guys he hung around with in high school. Pete Decker is the guy he talked about most, he just loved Pete Decker. Is Pete Decker here tonight?"

"Over here," Pete says. He's smiling, but his eyebrows are furrowed, and Mary Alice suspects he, too, is trying to remember who Walter Vogel was.

Ron says, "Hey, Pete! Good to meet you, man! Wow. Okay, so . . . I just want to . . . I just want to thank *all* of you, really, for being such an important part of my dad's life. It's good to know he *had* a time when he was . . . you know . . .

"Well, I'll let you get back to your party now, and thank you very much."

"Hold on!" Pete says. He gets up and heads over to where Ron is standing. He puts his arm around the younger man's shoulders and takes the microphone from him. "I did know your dad, we all did, and we all really liked him, too. And I'll tell you, back in those days, one of the things he talked about most was how he couldn't wait to get married and have a kid. We got a six-pack one night, and we went down by the river, did he ever tell you about that night?"

Ron shakes his head no.

"Well, *I'll* tell you about it. So . . . we got a six-pack, your dad talked some guy going into the liquor store into buying us a six-pack. I was too chicken to do it, so your dad did it. We drove over to the river and drank it, and your dad opened up about what he hoped would happen in his life. And you know, he didn't say one word about jobs or money or status or any of that stuff. What he really wanted was a son. He said he wanted to make sure his son got taught the things he'd never been given the opportunity to learn. He said he could hardly wait to see his boy grow up in front of him, his own son would be . . . would be just the best thing that ever happened to him. He could not wait for you to arrive. And I was . . . you know, I was still young and a little wild, and the last thing on my mind was marriage and family. But when I heard him talk about it that way, even I wanted it."

A few people laugh, and Pete holds up his hand. "No, really. The way he described it made me want it, too. So your dad knew exactly what he *wanted* to do. He had big plans. But as I'm sure you know, Ron, sometimes things in real life don't work out the way they do in our imaginations. And men aren't always so good at showing emotion, at showing appreciation for the things that mean the most to them. We *feel* those things, but we don't show them. Although I think your generation is a lot better at that. I guess our generation was told that real men don't do this and real men don't do that, but your generation, you know better. And that's good. It's important to tell the people closest to you how much you care, and not to take them for granted. Because otherwise you might lose them."

Mary Alice steals a look over at Nora, who is staring into her lap.

Pete takes his arm from around the younger man's shoulders and faces him. "I guess there's a lot we don't do in our lives, no matter who we are. I guess there's a lot of important things we mess up. But I want you to know that, even if your dad didn't share much of himself with you, he *wanted* to. I hope that counts for something. And I want to tell you, too, that I was proud to call Walter my friend." Pete offers his hand to the young man, who shakes it, and everyone applauds. Then he starts back to the table, refusing to meet anyone's eyes. Ron calls out a final "Thank you!" and leaves the room.

Immediately afterward, Mary Alice hears the questions start: "*Who* was he?" "*Our* class?" She hears someone else say, "Not on the basketball team. He wasn't on any team." And she hears, "Pete Decker and *Walter Vogel*? No way."

When Pete sits back down, Mary Alice puts her hand over his, and when he looks up, she nods.

By the time they are through with the entrees, both Einer and Pete have finished their second martinis, and Einer is slumped decidedly to the left, though he keeps telling Mary Alice that it's only because he's trying to hear Pete better. Mary Alice has mostly talked to Ben Small, who *did* try to be an actor in New York, but mostly ended up working as a waiter in a deli that got shut down for having rats in the kitchen, and that was the final straw: Ben left behind the city and his dreams of becoming an actor. She's enjoying talking to Ben, but she's having trouble hearing him, because the music is so loud. And then there's the exuberance displayed by Einer talking to Pete. Once she heard Einer say, "Right back *at* it!" and now he lifts himself partway out of his chair to yell, "Well, son, that's exactly what I'm saying! You decide what's worth fighting for, and what isn't! That's the critical decision you got to make! And once you make it, why, then you stand up and be a man!"

"Einer," Mary Alice says.

"*What?*"

Pete looks over at his wife, then at Mary Alice. "You know what? He's right." He says loudly to Einer, "You are absolutely right!" and begins to pound his fist lightly against his thigh.

"Tell you what, I'll help you," Einer says. "All right? I will help you. I'll be right by your side! I'll be the commander and you be the infantry, by God!"

"Einer?" Mary Alice says.

He turns to her, his face flushed. "Look here, Mary Alice. Have you heard this man's story? Do you have any idea what he's going through?"

"Are you *okay*?"

He stares at Mary Alice, and then leans back in his chair. "I have never been finer. I've got a mission. I and my friend Pete. Which we are going to run right after I have one more martini."

Mary Alice puts her hand on Einer's arm and leans in close to him. "Einer, please don't. You've had too much already. I know you're having fun, but I'm afraid of what might happen if you drink another martini. Please don't do that. I feel responsible for you."

"You're not responsible for me! Rita's responsible for me! That's why I pay her, is to be responsible for me!"

"Rita is out on a date tonight! I'm responsible for you until she comes home! And I don't know when that's going to be! She still hasn't called!"

Einer squints at her, and she knows he's thinking about whether or not to fight her on this one. But finally he says, "Oh, all right. All right! Let me get back to my friend now, you don't have to babysit me. I'm through drinking, all right?"

"I'm not!" Pete says. "I'm going for a refill. Mary Alice?"

"I'm fine, thank you."

"Ben?"

"Just another Coke, thanks."

Mary Alice leans back in her chair to let the server remove

her dinner plate. "Still working on this?" he'd asked, and Mary Alice had, as usual, despaired of hearing that particular turn of phrase. Whatever happened to "Still enjoying this?" or "Have you finished?" or "May I remove this?" "Still working on this" always reminds her of pigs at a trough. Oh, but why fuss about such things? She supposes she's getting old and cranky.

She watches Pete as he talks to this person and that on the way to the bar. He glad-hands all the men, charms all the women. The man holds his liquor well, she has to give him that. Except for an overemphasis on certain words, he seems fine. He just showed everyone at their table photos of his children, of his wife and himself. Mary Alice, aware now of what's going on, feels bad for Pete. It can't be easy, sitting there in tacky golf clothes, across the room from a man who is dressed in a well-made suit and overtly courting your wife. She has switched from sneaking looks at Lester and Candy to sneaking looks at this Fred person. He has kept his arm around Nora the whole night, except when he cut his meat. And now she sees Pete go over to the table and say something to Fred and Nora. Whatever he said makes Nora look down and Fred leap up. Nora grabs Fred's arm, and Fred flings her hand off angrily, then steps closer to Pete and punches him in the face. Someone screams and the room goes deathly quiet.

Pete carefully puts the drinks he's still holding down on the table. Before he can straighten up, Fred has punched him again, hard enough that Pete actually falls onto the floor. "Stop it!" Nora yells, she and several others, and now people are all standing, trying to see what's happening. And then Einer takes off in his wheelchair.

"Einer!" Mary Alice calls after him. "Come back here!"

It's useless; the man is hell-bent on rushing to the aid of his new friend. Mary Alice looks around for Lester. He's not a doctor, but he's a vet; if something happens, he'll be better than nothing. But Lester is not at his table any longer, nor is Candy

Sullivan. Mary Alice doesn't see either of them anywhere. *When did they leave?*

She looks back at Einer and sees him trying to stand, then giving up and instead trying to kick Fred. And then he suddenly slides out of his wheelchair.

Mary Alice tries to push her way over to him. "Hey! Hey!" the DJ says. "Let's everybody calm down, now. Just calm down."

People start talking; it gets louder and louder. Someone says, "What's going *on*?" and someone else yells, "Is there a doctor in the house?"

"I'm perfectly all right!" she hears Einer say, and then she finally reaches him. He's resting on his elbows, his hair sticking straight up, and Pete is lying flat beside him. And then Pete slowly gets up and wipes the blood from his upper lip. He bends down to lift Einer back into his chair, and then wheels him toward their table, saying, "It's okay, everybody, it's all over. No problem. No problem."

But when they get back to the table, Mary Alice sees that Einer is not all right. He's pale, and she sees him putting his finger to his wrist, checking his pulse. She grabs her purse. "I'm taking Einer to the hospital," she says, and Pete says, "I'm coming," and Einer says, "I'm not going anywhere until this thing gets settled! Now, let's re-strategize!"

Mary Alice leans into his face and says, "Einer? We're going to the hospital," and he says, "Fine. Suit yourself," and gingerly touches his cheek, where a bruise is already beginning to form.

In the parking lot, Pete says, "I'm awfully sorry, Mary Alice," and she shrugs. Then—who can account for why?—she starts laughing. And then Einer does. And then Pete does. "Well, that was a good time," Einer says.

They drive the short distance to the hospital, and the ER is empty, so Einer is brought into the examining room right away.

Pete and Mary Alice sit quietly in the waiting room. Mary Alice points to a new stain on Pete's shirt and says, "Is that blood?"

Pete puts his hand to his nose and then looks at his shirt. "Guess so."

"I'll bet Einer would lend you a shirt."

"I don't think it would fit," Pete says. And then, looking down at his chest again, he says, "Ah, what the hell. Badge of honor."

They sit quietly for another minute or two, and then Pete says, "Damn. We missed dessert."

Mary Alice smiles. "I know."

"It was red velvet cake with cream cheese icing, too."

"Yes."

Pete crosses his arms and bounces his knee, looks around the waiting room. Scratches the side of his neck. Then, his face brightening, he asks, "Would you like a candy bar? There's a vending machine down the hall. I saw it when we came in."

Mary Alice smiles. "Why, yes, I would. I would like a Snickers with almonds. Or if they don't have that, Oreos. Or if they don't have that, Skittles. And also I would like you to help me get Einer home."

"Done," Pete says, and heads off for the vending machine, and Mary Alice picks up *Vogue* magazine, which she has never in her life looked at. Never. But it's *good*, quite interesting, not the superficial waste of paper she always thought it was.

In a few minutes, here comes Pete back into the waiting room. He hands her a Snickers. Then Oreos. Then Skittles.

SIXTEEN

"BUT CAN YOU BELIEVE IT?" DOROTHY SAYS. "CAN YOU BE-lieve how he just made up that story about drinking beer with Walter? Who would ever think that in addition to every-thing else Pete Decker would turn out to be such a *mensch*! I wanted so much to tell him how wonderful it was, what he did. And now he's gone! Everyone's leaving, and I won't have had a chance to say one word to him!"

"Everyone is not leaving," Linda says. "And I'm sure Pete will be back. Why don't you just *relax*."

Well. Easy for Linda to say. She's on her fourth drink. Judy has had more than that. Dorothy has not had one bit of alcohol because she has to pay attention to what she's doing. If Pete does come back, he's likely to be upset. She'll need to have her wits about her. Oh, the nerve of that old man showing up and wreck-ing everything! Why in the world would Mary Alice Mayhew bring an *old man* to the reunion? Aren't they all old enough? Do they really need to be reminded of the wizened old creatures they'll become in fewer years than any of them wants to admit? An old man in a wheelchair, no less! Say, that's a sexy thing to see! That'll put you in a great mood! Maybe they should have decorated with anti-embolism stockings, with colostomy bags!

She checks the entrance and then looks around the room yet again, to see if Pete and stupid Mary Alice have slipped back in without her noticing them. No. Well, the DJ is supposed to play for another hour. She supposes there is still time.

If Pete does come back tonight, Dorothy hopes Nora will be gone. Her date keeps yawning (without covering his mouth), and Nora has stopped chatting with everyone and is just sitting at the table stirring her drink with a swizzle stick, staring down into it as though it's a crystal ball. Dorothy wishes it were a crystal ball, and Nora would be seeing some gypsy wearing big hoop earrings and saying, *You will soon be leaving the room.* Dorothy needs time to get Pete to focus only on her; she doesn't need his eyeballs shifting around all over the place, trying to keep track of what Nora is doing. Can't he see that they're over? Dorothy can see it! Everyone can! Where is his pride? Spend a little time with Dorothy and he'll get his pride back, no problem!

Candy Sullivan has disappeared. And with Lester Hessenpfeffer! "Who'd a thunk it?" Judy said, when Dorothy remarked on their absence.

"Well, he is good-looking," Linda said. "And he's a vet. He probably makes a pile of dough."

Judy's nose wrinkled. "I know, but he's still . . ."

Linda shrugged and looked back toward where Candy and Lester had been sitting. "I don't know," she said, kind of sadly. And then, "I'm going to fix my face. You guys want to come?"

Judy did, but Dorothy stayed put, even though she could have used a little pee. It was important not to miss Pete if he came back. She needed to be the first one up to him so he wouldn't encounter any *other* distractions. She hoped the old man got admitted to the hospital and Mary Alice went home. Though even if she came back, she'd be no problem.

Dorothy had done a beautiful job of ignoring Pete when she first saw him, but he saw her, all right. *Saw* her. He couldn't help but see how nice she looked. No one could help but see that. Oh, that makeup person should win an Academy Award. At first, she was being all listless and kind of snotty, but then Dorothy confided in her about how this was her night to try to recapture an old flame, and boom! the girl went into high gear. She was a very young blond woman with three-inch-long black roots, wearing no makeup at all, which certainly gave Dorothy pause, you can just imagine. But it turned out she knew her stuff. Boy, did she. And she made Dorothy look like a million bucks, both Judy and Linda agreed.

"You look twenty years younger!" Judy had said, which was not true, of course. Maybe five years younger, though, especially if she remembered to keep her head held high.

And then hadn't Judy and Linda done just what she'd thought they'd do, and gotten made up themselves. But they hadn't looked as good as Dorothy. The makeup girl had to rush because she had other appointments coming: there was a formal that night at their old high school. Oh, the poignancy! Dorothy had wanted to take those young girls aside and give them a little talking-to. "Girls, don't do what I did. Listen to me. I was you once, going to dances at this very same school, full of hope and happiness, and then my life went straight to hell. Just watch out, girls. Just be careful. *Think* about things before you do them, will you promise me that?" She'd seen it just like in a movie, the girls all quiet and dewy-eyed, staring up at her, so grateful to her for taking the time. Though that probably wouldn't have happened. Probably what would have happened if they'd listened to her at all was that they'd have told her to fuck herself. Or sat there texting each other the whole time she was talking, saying things like *Gag me w spn. Cn u belv ths fat cow?*

But anyway, because of those bratty girls, Judy and Linda hadn't gotten the full treatment, which included partial false lashes, and that was a pity, because what a difference *they* made. When Dorothy had gone up to her room to get ready, she'd hardly taken her eyes off herself, and she wasn't being vain, no she wasn't, she was just admiring craftsmanship, or art, or something. She'd decided not to wash the makeup off that night; she wanted to have the same face at the breakfast. She'd asked the makeup girl if there was something like hair spray for the face and the girl had said, "Oh, don't worry, unless you use a ton of cold cream, this stuff isn't going anywhere. It could even last a couple of days. I mean, don't *rub* it real hard or anything." Then Dorothy had gotten a little nervous, thinking of Pete and how he might inadvertently do that, he might even give her whisker burn. But he'd seemed clean-shaven, and anyway, he wouldn't be spending that much time on her face, Dorothy isn't that crazy about kissing, if the truth be told. She's never admitted it to anyone, but she could do without it. All that parrying and thrusting and saliva. Just get to it, is Dorothy's policy. She likes her nipples to be kissed first, that's what she likes, she'll show him. And then a straight shot to the nether regions. And she'll give *back,* of course. You don't get to be this old and not know a thing or two about a thing or two. As far as she's concerned, they can skip the old in-and-out. She never did care for that so much, either, and besides, now it kind of hurts. From what she can recall. If her *long-term memory* serves her well.

The DJ puts on Wilson Pickett's "In the Midnight Hour," and Dorothy's hips start undulating in her chair in spite of herself, moving back and forth in the time-honored rhythm. Oh, was she a sexy young thing the last time she danced to that! She feels a tapping on her shoulder and turns to sees Ben Small.

"Dorothy Shauman," he says.

"Ben Small." She smiles in what she hopes won't appear to be an artificial way, even though it is.

"May I have this dance?"

She starts to refuse, but what the heck. Ben wasn't so bad. She'll dance a bit, and still be able to watch for the whole reason she even came to this reunion.

She and Ben walk out to the dance floor and when Wilson sings, "and do *allll the things I told you,*" she and Ben sing along. He's not so bad. You'd never know he'd had such acne. He asks her something, and she stops dancing and steps up closer so she can hear him. She thinks he's asked her if she's married, and she looks at him more carefully. She decides she'll go out to dinner or a show with him, if he lives anywhere nearby. No sex, no. Not interested.

But what he asks is if Judy is married.

"Why don't you ask her yourself, if you're so interested?" Dorothy says, and walks off the dance floor.

She gets her purse and goes out into the hallway, blinking back tears. She stands there for a minute, trying to calm down, and then calls her daughter. "Nothing is working out!" she tells Hilly. "Pete isn't even here and no one is interested in me at all!"

"Oh, come on, Ma," her daughter says.

"No, it's terrible, Hilly! I shouldn't have come. This was such a waste of time and money!"

"Have you had a drink?" Hilly asks, and Dorothy says, "No! I have to stay sober!"

"Why?"

Dorothy stares out the large plate-glass window of the hotel into the darkness. "I don't know."

"I think you're just nervous," Hilly says. "Just get a drink and sit down and relax. You don't have to control everything, you know. You can't, anyway! Just sit down and have a drink and see what happens. And try to *enjoy* what happens, even if it's not ex-actly what you planned. If you would just stop trying to *control* everything, I think you would find that your life is much easier."

"I guess."

"It's true, Ma. I had to learn that myself. You know what I did the other day? I told Mark he could pick out the cake totally without me. 'Surprise me,' I told him. And I was a nervous wreck because the cake is such a symbol, you know. Such a centerpiece! But he picked out the loveliest cake I ever saw. It's very simple and understated, botanic-inspired accents in the frosting, and groups of nasturtiums here and there. And you know what flavor it is? Orange! I would never have picked that, but I tasted it, and it's the most delicate, delicious thing! Now I'm thinking about letting him pick the bridesmaids' gifts. You see? Sometimes you just have to step back and get out of your own way, and things start coming to you."

"*Orange* cake?" Dorothy says.

"It's delicious," Hilly says. "And Ma? See? My cake is *not your decision*. Your job will be to eat it and enjoy it. Or not."

"Okay," Dorothy says.

"I'm just trying to help you."

"You did help, Hilly. Thank you. I'll call you tomorrow."

Dorothy snaps her phone shut and heads back to the ball-room. She walks quickly over to the bar. Hilly is right. Enough is enough. What if Pete doesn't come until the breakfast tomorrow? She tells the bartender she wants vodka, straight up and *cold*. When he hands her the glass and tells her that will be seven dollars, her perfectly colored and arched eyebrows go up.

"*Seven dollars?*"

"Yes, ma'am."

She holds up the glass to eye level. "Tell you what," she says. "You put some vodka in this glass, and I might *give* you seven dollars."

He hesitates, then adds a tiny bit more vodka to the glass. And she gives him seven dollars exactly. Some people tip no matter what. Not Dorothy. She tips according to how well she was *served*. Which is what tips are *for*. Which everyone seems to *forget*.

Back at her table, she takes out the mirror from her purse and inspects her face to see if tearing up smeared her eye makeup. No, thank God. She sees Linda on the other side of the room, blabbing away, apparently having a bang-up time. She crosses her legs, swings the top one in time to the music, drinks her vodka. She forces herself to keep a little smile on her face though she does not feel like smiling. She watches Ben Small and Judy dancing. For an artsy-fartsy type he certainly has no sense of style on the dance floor. Judy throws back her head and laughs, and Dorothy throws back her drink and then, teeth clenched, goes up to the bar for another.

After Dorothy sits back down at her table, Wendy Striker comes over and sits heavily beside her. "Remember me?" she says breathlessly, leaning in way too close to Dorothy. The woman is bombed out of her mind. Dorothy leans back a bit and offers a tight smile.

"*Do* you remember me?" Wendy asks.

"Well, of course I do," Dorothy says. "Wendy Striker. We were in Future Homemakers of America together. You and I teamed up for beef Stroganoff." Dorothy remembers that because Wendy had been such a slob. She'd gotten sour cream all over both of them and Dorothy's mom had gotten mad because she'd had to take Dorothy's skirt to the dry cleaner's.

"And *chorus*," Wendy says.

"And chorus, yes," Dorothy says, though she does not remember this.

"When you signed my yearbook, alls you wrote was 'Good luck to a nice kid.' I really wanted you to say more. Like, at *least*,

'Thanks for covering for me on our class trip.' I covered for you that time we went to Washington, D.C., and you snuck out with Pete Decker, remember? You could have said something about that."

"Sorry," Dorothy says. "I must have been in a hurry."

"Isz okay. I forgive you." Wendy thrusts her chest dramatically forward and then back, a kind of stretch, Dorothy supposes. A vulgar one. "Are you having a good time?" Wendy asks.

Dorothy shrugs.

Wendy peers into her face. "Is that . . . Are you wearing *false eyelashes*?"

Dorothy moves her chair back. *"No."*

"You are, too."

"So what?"

"So nothing. Jeez. Just asking. Don't have a cow." She laughs at herself, laughs and laughs, then abruptly stops. "So listen. *Are* you having a good time? Is it what you expected? This is your first reunion, right?" She gently burps. "Ecshuze me."

"Who told you it was my first one?"

"I *know,* because I've been to them *all*. But also Pam Pottsman. She told me. She tells everybody evvvvverything. What a fucking blabbermouth. But *is* it what you expected?"

"Not yet."

"Whattdya mean?" Wendy leans closer, savagely hikes up a bra strap. "What'd you think would happen? Huh? Did you think something would happen? Because oh. *Oh! I* did. That's what I thought, is that something would *finally* happen because this is the *last* one. Oh, my God, we're almost *dead,* all of us!" She sniffs, looks wistfully around the room, and some sort of whimpering sound escapes her. "Oh, we all got so old, we all look like *old* people." She turns back to Dorothy. "But *anyway.* I was getting ready in my room tonight? And I was just so *happy* thinking of all the things that could *happen* and you know what?

You know *what*? Not one damn thing has happened! I'm divorced," she adds, seemingly apropos of nothing.

"Hmm," Dorothy says. Where the hell are Judy and Linda?

"I'm divorced, so, I mean, anything *could* happen." She throws her arms up in the air. "I'm a free woman. YOO-HOO, BOYS! OVER HERE! I AM FREE!"

"I have to go," Dorothy says.

"Wait, wait, wait a minute," Wendy says, grabbing her arm. "I want to ask you something. Okay? I just really want to ask you something."

Dorothy raises an eyebrow.

Nothing.

"What did you want to ask me?"

Wendy lists to the left. "Huh?"

"I have to go," Dorothy says, and walks quickly away from the table.

"*Waaaaiiit!*" Wendy cries.

Dorothy keeps walking.

"*Doooorothy! Waaaaait!*"

Dorothy turns around and starts back to the table. *Hush!* she'll tell her. *Get hold of yourself, why don't you!* But then she sees that Wendy has found Dorothy's unfinished drink, and her attention is now taken up with something else. Look at her. Barefoot, her legs spread widely apart. Oh, it's awful the way some people behave!

She wanders over to the table where Nance and Buddy Dunsmore are sitting and plops herself down. "Hi," she says, miserably.

Buddy takes a quick look at her name tag and says, "Dorothy Shauman. Well. Hello."

Nance says nothing. She just holds her mouth in that well-well-well way. *Well, well, well; look what the cat dragged in.*

Dorothy regards the two of them. Nance and Buddy. Still going strong, she guesses.

"So how are you guys?" she says.

"We're just *fine*," Nance says. "Surprised?"

"Nance," Buddy says.

Nance turns to her husband. "What? Don't you remember what she did?"

Buddy smiles at Dorothy, then tells his wife, "It was a long time ago, hon."

Nance scratches at the top of her arm, says nothing.

Dorothy sighs. "Okay, you know what? I'm sorry. I am! Here it is, a formal apology: I'm *sorry. Really.* And I'll bet it has bothered me all these years a lot more than it has bothered you. Look at you! You're still together and you're happy!" She looks back and forth at their faces. "Aren't you?"

Buddy shrugs. "Yup."

"And your family is just perfect."

"We're not *perfect*," Nance says. She practically spits it out.

"Well, close enough," Dorothy says. "I heard about you guys. Pam Pottsman told me."

"Well. Pam *Pottsman*," Nance says, and now her voice seems to have softened a bit. Then she says, "Did you know Pam hit on the DJ?"

Dorothy turns around to see if she missed something attractive about the DJ. Absolutely not. He's a short little guy, exceedingly thin, with a beard he should never have tried to grow. It looks like a beard that some kid tried to color on his face with a crayon.

"She's three times his size!" Dorothy says.

Nance laughs. "I know. But I heard they're getting together after the dance is over. I'll bet they *hook up*."

"*What?*" Dorothy says.

"Some guys like large women," Buddy says. "For some guys, that's their thing."

"Well, good for them," Dorothy says bitterly. She stares into her lap.

"Dorothy?" Nance says. "How come you did that thing?"

"Aw, come on, Nance," Buddy says.

"No!" she says. "I want to know."

"Well, then I'm getting out of here for a while," Buddy says. "I'm going out to the parking lot and talk to the boys." When Nance starts to say something, he says, "What did I tell you? Don't worry, I won't. I told you I won't and I won't."

Dorothy watches him walk away. Then she asks Nance, "What won't he do?"

"Drugs," Nance says. "They're doing drugs out in the parking lot. The Lettermen's Club."

Dorothy's hand flies to her chest. The idea of doing drugs appalls her, but the thought of all the lettermen together, that kind of attracts her. Maybe she could go out there on some pretext or another. Just to see if anyone's there she might have forgotten about, now that that damn Pete still hasn't come back. She should have had a second choice in mind all along.

"What kind of drugs?" she asks.

Nance shrugs. "Pot for sure. Probably cocaine, too."

"Oh, my God," Dorothy says.

"Hey, Dorothy?" Nance says. "Can I give you some advice? *Don't tell.*"

Dorothy looks at her. "I *know.*"

"But why *did* you tell on us?" Nance asks.

"I thought it was wrong," Dorothy says. "I thought it was immoral. I guess I was kind of scared by it. I thought the others should know, in case they wanted to leave."

"Uh-huh. Know what I think?"

Dorothy sighs. "What?"

"I think you were jealous of us."

"You're right." She nods. "I still am. Now more than ever."

Nance waves to someone across the room and tells Dorothy, "I'm going over to talk to Betty Williams."

"Okay."

Nance grabs her purse. "You can come, too."

"That's all right."

"Oh, come *on*," Nance says, and Dorothy rises gratefully.

Following Nance across the room, she sees some people she remembers, and many she doesn't recognize at all. A group of women is standing around some guy demonstrating what looks like a yoga pose. Downward dog or whatever—Dorothy wonders if he teaches yoga. Judy and Linda are at the bar, talking to John Beckmeier, who was captain of the debate team. They would never have talked to him in high school, but they seem to be enjoying him now. They seem not to want to be with Dorothy, and she doesn't blame them; all she's talked about since they got here is Pete.

On the dance floor, two women are jitterbugging together in their bare feet, shrieking with laughter. A couple seated at a table in the shadows are kissing. She tries to see who it is and runs smack into a chair. Nance grabs her to keep her from falling, then links arms with her as they continue to walk. "Come on, you old tattletale," she says.

Dorothy can't look at her. She stares at the floor and holds back some strong feeling that could be laughter or could be tears, either one. Or both. It comes to her that all of the people in this room are dear to her. As if they all just survived a plane crash together or something. All the drunks and the show-offs and the nice kids and the mean ones. All the people she used to know and all the ones she never knew at all. And herself, too. She includes herself and her stingy little soul. And oh, what a feeling.

SEVENTEEN

Betty Williams is deeply engrossed in conversation with Pam Pottsman. But when she sees Nance and Dorothy coming over, she waves at them and points to the empty chairs at her table.

"Listen to Pam's great idea," Betty says, when they have seated themselves. "It's a really great idea. Tell them, Pammy."

Pam's face is flushed, her hair has fallen flat, her mascara is smeared, and the top of her bra is showing and it is not meant to be; no, that kind of Valkyric bra is not for display. But there is such excitement in her eyes that she looks lovely, Dorothy thinks. A happy person just looks good, no matter what. And a depressed person? Well, that's the opposite. You get some gorgeous woman who's all sad, and she doesn't look good. You don't want to be around her. It comes to Dorothy now that that's what "Pretty is as pretty does" means. She was always terrible at interpreting aphorisms. When she was in ninth grade, her English teacher, Mr. Hannigan, said, " 'Fish and visitors smell in three days.' Meaning? Dorothy?" She'd started when he called on her; she hadn't had her hand up, she'd been doodling daisies in the margins of her paper and hadn't been paying attention. "Pardon?" she'd said. And Mr. Hannigan had drawn himself up the way he always did if he noticed someone wasn't hanging on his every word and repeated coolly, " 'Fish and visitors smell in three days.' What does this mean?"

Dorothy had scooted her butt around a little in her chair and smiled at him. She'd had no *idea* what it meant. She remembers thinking, *Why do people* speak *that way? Why don't they just say what they* mean? *Why must their words wear little* costumes? But she wasn't going to say that, she wasn't going to delve into some completely unrelated subject like Wendy Peters, who one day raised her hand in history class and asked the teacher, "What is truth?" Imagine! But anyway, everyone had been staring at Dorothy that day, all the kids turned around and leering in that piranha-like way kids did when someone got in trouble. Dorothy had run the sentence through her head again: *Fish and visitors smell in three days.* Well, of course they did! And so she'd said, "Well, I think it's self-explanatory," which she thought sounded kind of smart. But Mr. Hannigan had sighed and called on Donna Whitby, that little National Honor Society, prissy nerd weirdo, and Donna had said, "It means 'Don't overstay your welcome,' " and then she had looked over at Dorothy and smirked. And Dorothy had looked down at her desk and thought, *So what. At least I have friends. And a figure.*

"Okay, so here's what I thought," Pam says. "I thought we would get a whole bunch of people to sit around the table and really open up. I'll ask certain questions, and they'll answer *really honestly* what their lives have really been like since we last saw each other."

Nance and Dorothy look askance at each other and Dorothy

gets a little thrill, thinking that she and Nance are now actually friends. Nance says, "Well, Pam, that's kind of a tall order, isn't it?"

"Yeah," Dorothy says. "Nobody's going to do that."

"Oh?" Pam says. "Well, I already asked four people, and they said yes and they're going to get more people. They're all coming back here. A whole bunch of them. And Betty and I were just coming up with the questions, and we've got some good ones."

"Nobody's going to sit in a *circle* and answer *questions*," Dorothy says, again.

"Well, your friends are," Pam says. "Linda and Judy."

"They are?"

"Yes."

"Who else?" Dorothy asks.

"Tom Gunderson, he's just getting another drink and then he's coming. President of the student council, in case you forgot. Lettered in four sports, in case you forgot. Really good-looking, still, in case you hadn't noticed. And *available*."

"I don't care about that," Dorothy says, but Betty has her number. Dorothy pulls her chair closer to the table. She's in. "So what are the questions?" she asks. She wants a jump on them so she's not caught off guard.

Pam holds the napkin close to her breast. "That's for me to know and you to find out. But if I were you, I'd get another drink."

"I've had enough," Dorothy says.

"No you haven't. Trust me, go and get a drink."

Dorothy asks Pam to save her place, and goes over to the bar. Annie Denato is ahead of her, ordering red wine. Annie Denato, class slut, but my goodness, hasn't she cleaned up! Dorothy heard two things about Annie: one, that she went to both medical school and law school; two, that she lives in New York City, on Park Avenue, thank you very much! Her streaked hair is in an elegant chignon, she's wearing a pale blue shantung suit, and it fits her so perfectly Dorothy thinks it must have been tailor-made. Annie turns around and Dorothy sees that she is wearing diamond studs at least half a carat apiece and Dorothy doesn't think they could possibly be cubic zirconium, although later she will find out. "Dorothy?" Annie says, and Dorothy nods. "Hi, Annie."

"It's Anne now," she says, and then hugs Dorothy like they were old friends. And Dorothy hugs her back, God knows she's not going to hold a grudge or whatever after all this time! Though it's hard to escape memories of how Annie used to be. Hard not to think of her beneath the bleachers on the football field, humping away, everyone knew she did that.

"Know what I heard about you?" Dorothy says. "That you went to law school and medical school."

"True," Annie says.

"Why both?"

"Well, medicine is a symphony, and law is hip-hop. And I discovered I like hip-hop better than classical. Do you know what I mean?"

"Sure," Dorothy says, nodding, though she has no idea what Annie means. Who would?

"I use a lot of what I learned in medical school in my law practice," Annie says. "In my life, actually. But on a day-to-day basis, I prefer to practice law. How about you? What are you up to these days?"

"Oh, well," Dorothy says. "This and that. Not much. Nothing, actually."

"I'm going over to Pam Pottsman's Table o' Truth," Annie asks. "Are you coming?"

"I am," Dorothy says, and Annie waits for her while she gets another glass of wine. Finally, she's starting to have a good time! She doesn't even care if Pete ever comes back!

Well, yes she does, but not as much.

When Dorothy gets back, she sees that a sizable crowd has gathered. Three tables have been pushed together to make for a kind of round table, and many chairs are pushed up to it. Several people stand behind the chairs, too. *There must be twenty-five people here!* Dorothy thinks, and counts. *Well, twenty, but still.*

She claims her chair and looks around at the people. Tom Gunderson is across from her. Ron Rubin, the preacher's son, is on one side of her, and Marjorie Dunn is on the other. Tommy Metito is here, and he's still in terrific shape—he's taken off his suit jacket and tie, unbuttoned his shirt a few buttons down, and rolled up his sleeves. Yup, he's still in pretty good shape, even if his chest hairs are all white and wiry and stick-outish. He's wearing a gold necklace that Dorothy thinks is tacky—way too Tom Jones, but hey. Why not? Let the man be what the man wants to be! Here comes that soulful expansiveness she felt before.

Linda and Judy arrive, and sit in the last two chairs left at the table. Buddy is standing behind Nance, and now more people, drawn by the setup and the noise, curious about what's going on, have made their way over. "What's going on?" someone asks, and when they're told, some laugh loudly and others stand still, their expressions a mix of eagerness and apprehension.

Pam dings a spoon against the side of her wineglass and speaks loudly. "Everyone? Everyone?" A few people stop talking, but most people keep right on. Then Tom Gunderson stands up and claps his hands once, and everyone quiets down. Good old Tom. Dorothy remembers how he used to lean so earnestly on the lectern when he spoke at student assemblies. He began one speech by saying, "What does 'pep rally' really mean?"

"Thank you, Tom," Pam says. "Okay, everybody. Here's the deal. Betty and I were talking and it seems like we're all curious about certain things that don't exactly come up in general conversation. So we thought we'd just make it a kind of game. I'll ask questions and anyone who wants to can answer. But if no one volunteers, I'll pick someone. And if that person won't answer the question, they have to buy a round for everyone."

"Oh, fuck that, I'm out of here," a man says, and strides off angrily. It's someone Dorothy doesn't recognize, and then she hears someone say, "Well, Donnie Funderman, he'd never talk to anyone about anything. He never did. He was just always pissed off about everything. He got suspended about five thousand times, once for putting a cherry bomb down the toilet. He hated our school. He hated everybody *in* our school."

"Well, why'd he even come?" Judy asks, and no one answers.

Then, "Terrorist plot?" someone says, and everyone laughs, if ruefully.

"Well, the hell with Donnie Funderman," Pam says. "Let's start." She looks down at her list. "Okay. The first question is, What scared you about coming here tonight?"

"How I'd look to everybody!" Nance says immediately, and a number of people nod their heads, agreeing with her.

"Who'd not be here because they died," Ron Rubin says. "I guess everybody thinks about that, but it was on my mind particularly because *I* almost died not long ago. I wasn't going to tell anybody because it's not exactly . . . I mean, I thought I might get lucky tonight and I didn't want anybody thinking I'd keel over on them. In fact, just in case I do get lucky, I want everyone, especially Sally Harding, to know I'm *fine* now." He looks over at Sally and winks, and she smiles and winks back. "Six months ago," Ron says, "I had a stroke."

Steve Hoffman puts his hand on Ron's shoulder. "Whoa," he says. Then it gets very quiet.

"Aw, come on, didn't anybody *else* have a stroke?" Ron asks, and no one raises his or her hand.

"Heart attack?" he asks, almost gaily, and two hands go up, two men. "Okay, then!" Ron says. "Well, so, like I said, I had a stroke. I was cleaning the leaves out of my gutters, up on a ladder, you know, and I got this really weird feeling. I came down the ladder, and the whole way down I was feeling more and more numb on one side. By the time I reached the ground, I was listing way over and my mouth was drooping and I thought, damn it, something's really wrong. And then I realized what was happening. I sat on the ground and called my ex-wife, who's a nurse. When she answered and I told her what was going on, she said, 'Call 911, you idiot!' and I said, 'No, I'd rather ride over with you.' We're still real good friends, and she only lives a couple of blocks away. I figured, if I'm going to die, I don't want to be with strangers. So she said she'd come, and I leaned against the house to wait. I looked up at the sky, and it was a real pretty blue with a kind of zigzag cloud I'd never seen before, and it occurred to me that every day of my life, there had been a different kind of sky overhead, and I was sorry I hadn't paid more attention. Then I saw the pack of cigarettes in my pocket and I thought, *Well, either I'm going to die or I'm going to quit smoking. Either way, I'm having these last two cigarettes.* So I smoked 'em, and then my wife came and we went to the hospital. On the way, I told her everything wrong in our marriage had been my fault. And she started crying and said cut it out or we'd get in an accident and both of us would die. 'I mean it,' I said, and she said, no, it was her fault, too, and she was sorry and she would always love me even if I was a ghost. But of course I didn't die. And after I got out of the hospital we got a little more estranged again. Still friends, but . . . you know. And here I am. Here I am with you guys again. And goddamn, I'm glad to be here! Sally, I'm really glad you're here, too."

"Well, *I've* had a hip replaced," she says, and everyone laughs.

But Dorothy has been deeply moved by Ron's story, and she gets out of her chair and goes over to him and puts her hands on either side of his face and gives him a little kiss. He puts his hands over hers when she does this, and she is surprised and gratified by their warmth. "Ron Rubin," she says. And he says, "Dorothy Shauman," and smiles. "You're all right," he says, and she says thank you and goes back to her chair.

"Don't let's do health anymore," someone says. Dorothy agrees. She visited the memorial table, she saw those photos of classmates who are no longer with them. Vietnam. Disease. Accidents. There was a bouquet of flowers there, a black ribbon around the vase. Dorothy looked carefully at each photo, into the eyes of the unsuspecting young person. She looked at their collars and their ears and their shiny hair. *It's good we don't know our own futures,* she thought. *It's merciful.* A couple of other people came up to the table when Dorothy was there, and she moved away before they could say anything. There was nothing to say.

So yes, they should move on from this morose topic. Imagine if, when they were kids, they'd gone on and on over health concerns, their measles and mumps, their skinned knees and broken wrists and cavities. *Yeah, I was really worried about a staph infection with that skinned knee!* Or *Broken wrist, man alive, what a problem. I have to write with my left hand! I can't take a bath! Can't play volleyball! What will* happen *to me?* No. They did not complain when they were kids, with rare exception. They just went on with their temporary ailments, waiting to get right again. They got their casts signed and made it fun!

It's different now; Dorothy and her peers are on the other side of the incline. When something happens, they do not assume they'll get right again. They fear getting worse. And they wait for the next thing, and finally for the inevitable tap on the shoulder, that icy singling out.

When they were in their forties, Dorothy and Judy and Linda had made a vow never to talk about health problems the way their mothers did. "Well, I just don't know *what* to do about my *gall*bladder," Judy had said that day, joking around. And now look. Just a week ago, she said that very same thing to Dorothy, and it wasn't funny at all. Dorothy thought, *Are you sure it's your gallbladder? Are you sure it's not your pancreas?* And then she started thinking about how she could not go on without Judy and Linda in her life, but at some point in the not-so-distant future, she'd have to. Or they'd have to go on without her. Unless they all died in a car wreck together, that actually might not be so bad. Bam! *Done.*

"Okay," Pam says. "Here comes the next question. Does anyone have any dirt on any of the teachers?"

"I screwed Miss Woodman in the art supply closet," Sam Noerper says, and a few people, including Dorothy, gasp.

Tommy Metito says, "I got her, too. Same place. A tube of oil paint came undone beneath her and she got cerulean blue all over her ass."

"Are you *kidding*?" Pam says.

Marjorie Dunn says, "I had sex with her, too."

"You so did not!" Linda says, and Marjorie laughs and says, "You're right. I didn't. But I did have sex with Mr. Garvis, that real young math teacher who came for the latter half of our senior year, but it was after graduation."

"But this is awful!" Dorothy says. "I had no idea!"

"Oh, come on," Buddy says. "Teachers used to flirt all the time. Remember how Mademoiselle Florin used to sit on the top of her desk and cross her legs and her skirt used to ride up real high?"

"*Noooo,*" Dorothy says.

"Well, she did it in our class," Buddy says. "Remember, guys?"

A few members of the Lettermen's Club look at each other and nod, grinning.

"Okay, *moving on*," Pam says. "Here's the next question. Did your life turn out to be anything like you thought it would be?"

Silence.

"Anybody?" Pam asks.

Jenny Freeman, who was always so quiet, always the great observer, speaks up now. "Not mine. All I ever wanted was to get married and have children. I thought it was a noble goal. But then the women's movement came along, and I felt compelled to work outside the house. It sounded great, you know, live up to your potential, everybody pitch in, it's going to be Equal City. Which, actually, it was not, and *is* not, but at the time I bought into it. When my second was two months old, I put her in day care and I got my real estate license and I got a job. I walked around in this horrible mustard-colored blazer, selling houses. Paid a fortune to get my face put on a bus stop bench. I sold a million houses, I swear, I made a lot of money. And I so regret doing it, because I don't feel like I ever got to know my daughter, not like I did my son. I had a red phone, it was a separate business line, and every time it rang, I'd stop whatever I was doing and talk to some client. I was afraid not to answer that goddamn phone, I might miss out! And the irony is, I did miss out. I've never been able to achieve the kind of relationship with my daughter that I have with my son."

"Oh well," Pam says. "That's girls, isn't it? Boys are just easier."

"No," Jenny says. "It's that I wasn't available to her. I can remember her trying to talk to me when she was growing up and I was always putting her off. The truth is, I was an awful mother."

"Oh, for God's sake," Judy says. "You set a good example for your daughter by having a successful career!"

"No, I didn't," Jenny says. "I was a fucking anxious wreck. I was always tired, always feeling so much pressure. I quit cooking, which I really used to enjoy, especially baking, I used to love to bake. But after I started working, I used to have a *fit* if I got a notice to make something for a bake sale. Have you seen what bake sales have become, by the way? Nobody makes anything. It's all supermarket crap! Remember when everything used to be homemade? Remember the pies and the banana breads and the cookies, all tied up in ribbons? Remember the *cakewalks*?"

"Yeah," Judy says. "And remember when women used to medicate themselves in order to get through a day because they were so damn bored? You're being too hard on yourself."

"My daughter has been institutionalized three times for drugs. She's had four abortions. I can't . . . We don't really talk. She lives with a man I can't stand; I don't think he treats her right. I go to visit her and I want to be nonjudgmental and loving and try to repair our relationship but her apartment just reeks of cigarettes and dirty dishes and garbage overflowing from this big can they keep in the kitchen, and the cats are eating from it and . . ." She starts to cry and then laugh, saying, "Oh, I can't believe I said all this. I'm so embarrassed."

"Don't be," Karen Komall says, little Karen, who never measured more than four feet eleven and was regarded as a kind of pet for the student body. Everybody liked Karen, she was such a sweet girl. She ended up marrying her high school sweetheart, Tim Swift, who is one of the guys on the dead table. Vietnam. "I had a lot of problems with my son," she said. "A lot. It's hard to raise a son without a father. But he's okay now. It took a long time, but he's really got his life on track, now. If there's anything I've learned about life, it's that things always change. Which, for me, means that there's always hope. I'll give you my email—I'll be glad to talk to you about this anytime."

Jenny nods. "Thank you. I'm so . . . Thank you. Okay. Let's change the subject!"

Annie—Anne—Denato says, "Well, I have a question. What

did everyone hope to find, coming here tonight? And I'll answer first. I wanted a chance to show how much I've changed. I wanted you all to know how much you misjudged me."

"We did misjudge you," Nance says. "I for one am sorry. I knew you were smart, but you were . . ."

"I know," Anne says. "I had *reasons* for being that way. If you guys had had *any idea* of what went on in my house . . . My father did a number on me, okay? But I'm past it. I'm past all that stuff, I'm really happy now, I'm successful, and I wanted you all to *know* it. And yet, being here makes me feel like that girl in high school all over again.

"You know, when I told one of my colleagues I was coming to my fortieth high school reunion, he said, *'Don't go.'* We're good friends; he knows what life was like for me in high school. But anyway, he said so many people who go to reunions think that doing so can somehow change what happened to them. That the person you've become might erase the person you were then. But of course that doesn't happen. In some respects, this reunion has shown me that it's not that you can't go home again; it's that you can never leave." She swallows what's left of her drink and then offers a big smile. "Well, but here we all are, talking to each other in a way that's not bullshit. I say that counts for a lot. What about the rest of you? What did you want to find here?"

"Dorothy came for only one reason," Judy says, and Dorothy's eyes grow round and she says, *"Judy!"*

"I didn't say who," Judy says, but then Pam says, "Well, who is it?" and Judy says, "Pete Decker," and there it is, right out in the open for everyone to know.

"He's married, isn't he?" Ron asks, and Tom Gunderson says, "Getting divorced."

"Fair game then," Ron says, and winks at Dorothy.

"I'm going to the bathroom," Dorothy says, and Judy says, "Oh, Dorothy, sit down!"

"I have to pee!"

Pam picks up her purse. "Maybe we should all go, so none of us misses anything."

"If we all go, the momentum will be lost," Linda says.

"She's right," Judy says. And then, "Sit down, Dorothy."

"I'm not sitting down," Dorothy says, and Linda says, "Sit *down*!" so she does. Then she says, "Okay, I have a question. Who do you think is going to hook up tonight, besides Lester Hessenpfeffer and Candy Sullivan?"

"Lester and *Candy*?" Anne asks.

Dorothy nods gravely. "Somebody saw them on the elevator going up. They've been gone for a long time."

Susie Black says, "I don't think I'm going to hook up with anyone, but I did get kissed in the hallway. And you know who it was? It was Bill Anderson."

Bill Anderson! Dorothy thinks. He stayed for such a little while, she doesn't think he even finished his dinner. He was a wreck, nothing like his former self, Dorothy couldn't imagine what had happened to make him that way and wasn't inclined to ask. He was sort of scary, sitting alone at a table by the bar, staring off into space. Dorothy avoided him because he looked so sad and odd. It seemed like most people did. Susie had gained quite a bit of weight, but she still had a little left of what used to make her so cute. Still with the big blue eyes, the high cheekbones.

"It was the most extraordinary thing," she says. "The sweetest thing. We walked past each other in the hall—I was coming back from the bathroom and he was leaving, and we nodded at each other. Then he called my name, and I turned around, and he asked if I had a minute. Sure, I said. So he came up and stood real close and looked me right in the eyes for a long time. Then he told me he'd had a crush on me in high school, that he had loved me for years and he'd kept my picture in his helmet when he went to Vietnam. He said he'd wanted to ask me to the prom senior year, but he was too scared. And you know, I sat alone on prom night. Well, not alone, I sat watching television with my parents, which was worse than sitting alone. I said, 'Oh, Bill, I would have gone with you,' and he said, 'You would?' and I said 'Yeah, I thought you were really cute!' and he said, 'You did?' and I said '*Yeah,* in fact I had a crush on *you.*' Which I did, I liked how shy and mysterious Bill was, I liked that. And he was really cute, that black hair, those green eyes. Real tall, and he had a little dimple in his left cheek. He said, 'You had a crush on me?' and I said yeah, and he said, 'Huh. I wish you'd told me.' And I said, 'Me, too.' And then he put his finger under my chin just like in the movies and gave me the most gentle kiss. And I thought about how we were both pretty good-looking in high school and now we're both kind of wrecked, and here we were, sharing a smooch in the hallway under bad fluorescent lighting, and I thought we were more beautiful than we had ever been. You know?"

"Why don't you call him?" Betty says.

"I thought of that. I asked for his number and he said he'd rather not give it to me. He said he had a lot of problems; he wasn't really able to be with a woman. Wasn't able to be with anyone, really."

She shrugs, and Dorothy can see that she's close to tears. "It's too late. It really is. He was such a sweet guy, too. I knew him, and he was just so *sweet*." She shakes her head. "Man oh man. There's just a million ways a life can go. Isn't there?"

EIGHTEEN

Lester and Candy are lying on their backs on her hotel bed. The lights in the room are out, but the drapes are open, revealing the bright moon and the many stars. Esther the bulldog lies between them at shoulder level, her head on her paws, her forehead wrinkled and worried looking. Lester and Candy are fully clothed, on top of the covers, and Candy is holding Lester's handkerchief pressed against her nose. After a moment, she says, "Okay, I think I'm done crying now. Sorry."

Lester looks over at her. "Oh, no; don't apologize. I'm honored! Truly. My wife used to say that to cry in front of someone was to offer them a compliment."

"She did?"

"Yes."

"What else did she used to say?"

He looks out at the night sky. "Well, she called stars silent commentators. Ancient, silent commentators."

"Huh. That's nice. What else?"

Lester's chest hurts now, but he says in as easy a tone as he can muster, "Oh, she said a lot of things." He thinks about how, after the reconciliation that came after their first major argument, he told Kathleen he feared he'd lost her forever. And she said, "You know that song 'Till the End of Time'? Please review the lyrics, and then report back to me." But what he tells Candy is, "She used to say this all the time: 'If you can't beat 'em, beat 'em harder.'"

Candy laughs, and it makes Lester's spirits rise. Then she props herself up on one elbow and says, "I'm sorry. I've taken you away from the party."

"You didn't take me away. I wanted to come with you. For one thing, duty called. A dog with love handles is a dog that needs attention!"

"Oh, I was so scared she had a tumor. What a relief that she's only fat! I love fat!"

Lester rubs the top of Esther's head briskly. She licks him and snorts happily into his hand. Her tail is wagging so fast it's nearly a blur. "Don't you listen to her; you're gorgeous," Lester tells the dog. "Liz Taylor should have such beauty marks!" And then, to Candy, "You're gorgeous, too, by the way."

He sees her pull back slightly into herself, the automatic response of many pretty women who have been complimented too many times for reasons more suspect than sincere. "Oh, well, money helps," she tells him. "I'm on a first-name basis with more than a few plastic surgeons. I think I alone support many branches of the cosmetics industry."

"I didn't mean how you look, I meant how you *are*."

This seems to surprise her, and she starts crying again.

"Uh-oh," he says.

She waves her hand and blubbers, "It's just . . . Well! I guess a lot of things are hitting me all at once."

He could say the same. They had talked about so many things! From a random and seemingly weightless remark at a dinner table to . . . this! He'd sat next to Candy Sullivan only to . . . well, to sit next to *Candy Sullivan*. To say a brief hello. And, if the truth be told, to have the opportunity to look at her close up—God, she was something. Then he'd intended to take a place at the nearly empty table where Ben Small was sitting. He was going to face the door so he could see when Mary Alice arrived, then wave her over to sit beside him—he had expected that, after their lovely afternoon, they might have dinner together. For starters.

But then he formed what felt like an immediate bond with the Homecoming Queen. "Candy Sullivan?" he said, and she turned around and looked up at him. He extended his hand and reminded her of his name—he'd discovered that not all of the people there saw well enough anymore to read the name tags.

"Oh, *Lester*!" she said. "I know you. I remember you very well!"

She removed her purse from the empty seat beside her and he sat down and said, "So. The last time I saw you was the day before you left to go to Boston for college, BU wasn't it?"

"It was! What a memory!"

"Well," he said. "What a goil. Everybody knew everything about you. That day, you were in line ahead of me at the Dairy Queen. Wearing . . . well, Candy, I think you would have to call them short shorts. And a white blouse, knotted at your waist. You were barefoot, and you had a daisy stuck between a couple of your toes. You were talking about how you were going to marry a neurosurgeon and have five children."

Her forehead wrinkled. "Did we talk that day?"

"Nah. I just overheard. You were surrounded by your usual friends and admirers. A guy couldn't wedge his way in with a . . . with a wedger."

Her eyes shifted briefly away from him. "Yes, well." She touched her right earring, her left. "And you were off to college, too. The University of Minnesota, right?"

Lester laid his hand over his heart. "I'm touched you remember."

She tilted her head and studied him. "I remember a lot about you, Lester Hessenpfeffer. I remember how smart you were, and how kind. How you were going to be a vet. How a lot of people were really awful to you. And how I never stood up for you when I could have."

He shrugged. "It didn't matter, really. I turned out fine. I'm happy! I'm a vet! So *did* you marry a neurosurgeon and have five children?"

"Not exactly," she said; and then her chin began to tremble, and she started telling him things that would have made him leaving her table rude, if not impossible. From the corner of his eye, he had seen Mary Alice come in, and he'd thought to give her some sort of sign—a finger held up in the air? A quick lift of his chin that would let her know he'd be right over? But then he'd noticed Pete Decker with her and thought, *Huh! Well, that's that.* Oh, he'd intended to validate his assumptions, not for nothing had he been trained in the scientific method. But as his talk with Candy grew more intimate, the idea of him pursuing a relationship with Mary Alice (sitting with *Pete Decker,* why was she sitting with *Pete Decker?*) became less and less urgent.

Dinner was delivered, and Candy sat staring at her plate. Then she began to cry into her filet mignon, tears suddenly spilling over and apparently taking her by surprise. "Oh!" she said, and quickly dabbed at her eyes with her napkin, her head down—embarrassed, he thought. "Gosh!" she said. The tears kept coming, and finally he gently took her arm and led her into the hall, where her crying turned into all-out sobbing. "Oh, for heaven's sake," she said. "I'm all right. Really. I'm so sorry. I'll just go up to my room. I'm fine."

"Well. No, you're not." He was frustrated by a sudden desire to do something for her without having any idea what that might be. He imagined himself picking her up, swooping her into his arms, her white dress and her sparkly purse and the dinner napkin she still held clutched in her hand, and . . . what? Asking her if she'd like to take a truck ride with him to visit Elwood Masten's eleven golden retriever puppies, seven and a half weeks old and each one better looking than the next? Abandon their reunion dinner in favor of brown sugar meat loaf and carrot mashed potatoes and heavily buttered green beans and gooseberry pie at the Clean Plate Club? Which fortunately or unfortunately (depending on whether he was wearing his medical professional hat or his starving man hat) was right across the street from his clinic? Samson the mastiff had availed himself of half a sandwich made from that meat loaf when Lester had carelessly left his take-out lunch on top of the reception desk and Jeanine had turned her back, and that is probably why Samson never cowered in the waiting room anymore. No, Lester decided. He would give Candy her privacy.

He did punch the elevator button for her, though, and when the doors opened, the people who stepped off stared with blatant, nearly openmouthed curiosity. Lester stepped between them and Candy and thus ended up on the elevator with her. When they reached her floor, he walked her to her door. She hesitated, then said, "I wonder . . . would you come in and have a look at my dog? I'm sorry to take advantage of you this way. But I just noticed this awful swelling on both her sides, and I'm so worried that she—"

"I'd be happy to have a look," he said, and when she slid the key into the door, he couldn't help it; his heart sped up. And it wasn't *that* (although who could be a straight man with a functioning brain and not have the briefest of scenarios occur to him when a beautiful woman like Candy unlocks her hotel room to him?). But it wasn't that he wanted to have sex with Candy Sullivan. It was that he felt retroactively invited to sit at the Table.

He supposes some things never go away. Jeanine's mother lives in an old-age home where there's a Popular Table. "It's just like junior high, I swear," Jeanine had told him. "The royalty still saving seats for each other."

"Is your mother a member of the royalty?" Lester had asked.

"No," Jeanine had said, "and it drives her crazy. She says she doesn't care, but when I go to have a meal with her, all she does is watch them. Oh well, one of them will probably die soon, and then maybe she can move up the ladder."

After Lester examined Esther, he and Candy kept a respectful distance from each other, but then Candy slipped off her heels and stretched out on the bed and said, "Oh, boy, this feels good. Do you want lie down, Lester?" And he did. By that time, each knew that "lying down" was simply acknowledgment of presumed aches and pains and a reduced capacity for alcohol. If Candy weren't so sad, the situation might have been funny.

They talked about how Candy had been living a life more and more distant from what she had wanted it to be; how lately she had been having difficulty making simple decisions, and this made her feel she no longer knew herself at all. (Do *I like strawberries?* she'd asked herself at the supermarket recently and was literally unable to answer.) She said a weighty despair had insinuated itself into her life and now it was just the norm—every morning, she opened her eyes and searched the bedroom ceiling for long minutes at a time, looking for what was wrong. "What I finally decided," she said, "is that *everything* is." She talked, in halting tones, about how she feared her husband in ways too complicated to be fully acknowledged, and how she was ashamed of that fear, and didn't feel she had anyone she could talk to about it.

"Does he hit you?" Lester asked, a question that seemed balanced between obscene and necessary.

She hesitated, then said, "No. Not . . . like that. But if he did, it wouldn't surprise me. Or even make me mad. I would just feel like it *belonged,* somehow." The elevator dinged out in the hallway and she tensed, then looked quickly at the door as though waiting for a knock. Then she looked back at Lester and sighed. "You know, this diagnosis has been a kind of gift. It's making me look at things and *see* them."

She told him she had begun to think about what death really meant and what life really meant—nothing like death to make you think about life! She said a friend's baby had died at only eight months old from an overwhelming bacterial infection, and that she found consolation in remembering what that mother had put on her baby's gravestone: "A brief life, but oh so joyful." Candy said she intended to move toward joy, if only for the last several months of her life.

Lester talked about himself, too. It seemed that a certain type of intimate exchange could elicit more and more soulful admissions, especially if you'd had a few drinks and were experiencing the kind of jaunty surrealism a high school reunion can bring. Lester told Candy that he loved his little neighbor girl like a daughter, and that she had used his house for her last sleepover party because her mother had said never again. He said he had served seven little tomboys spaghetti and meatballs at the picnic table in his backyard, and then made ice cream sundaes, which he believed he was not alone in thinking were absolutely fantastic. He told her he'd recently offered Miranda another such party and she had refused him because of the unacceptable amount of time he'd spent hanging around the girls last time, thus preventing them from talking. Which she hadn't wanted to tell him, but since he'd asked about doing it again . . . When Lester said he'd do better next time, Miranda said all right, how about two Saturdays from now, which by the way was the day he had promised to let her sit in on the day's surgeries, and he had readily agreed. Tacos, he was going to give those girls this time, and a repeat of the sundaes. Then he was going to turn over the living room to them, and retire to his bedroom to read.

He described to Candy the impact his wife's and unborn child's deaths had had on him, not only right after they happened, but also the ripple effect of the ever-transforming but never quite resolving grief. "I guess I believe I owe it to her to keep on feeling the grief," he said.

"Hmm," Candy said. "I wonder. I wonder if you asked her if she wanted you to feel such pain, what she would say."

"She would want me to remember her," Lester said. "I know that."

"Yes, but in pain? How about another way? How about honoring the love you shared by loving someone again?"

"Well, funny you should say that," he said, and told Candy about how he was very attracted to Mary Alice Mayhew, of all people.

"What do you mean, 'of all people'?" Candy said, and Lester said nothing; he was embarrassed he'd put it that way. Talk about the pot calling the kettle black.

"She just didn't *try*," Candy said. "She was too smart to."

Lester nodded. "You're right. And you know, I had lunch with her today, and I noticed . . . She smells like *outside*."

"Well, that *alone*!" Candy said, smiling.

"But she's down there with Pete Decker. So I don't know. I guess I kind of blew it."

"Oh, come on," Candy said. And something about the way she looked at him made him believe he still had a chance after all.

They have just agreed to head back downstairs when they hear the tinny sound of salsa music, and Candy sighs. "My husband calling," she says. "I'll bet you a million dollars. I should never have turned the phone back on."

She pulls the cellphone out of her purse, looks at the caller ID, then puts it back in her purse without answering it. "Yup," she says. "That's who it is. Cooper Anthony Armstrong. My husband."

"Does this mean I have to pay you a million dollars?" Lester asks. "Do you take Visa?"

Candy shakes her head sadly. "See? This is how he is. I ask him to come with me and he says no. But now the whole time I'm here, he'll keep calling. This is how he always is, these mixed signals, and it's so confusing. I wonder why he doesn't ever just say *yes* to *any*thing I propose. Why doesn't he ever say, 'Sure, I'll go.' Just like that. It's as though he just likes to say no to me. Or *needs* to or something. Maybe it's something he learned.

"You know, at my father-in-law's wake, my mother-in-law was sitting in a corner by herself. She was sitting up so straight, her purse balanced on top of her knees, clutching a hankie. I went to sit by her and asked her how she was doing. She said, 'He never played cards with me.' I didn't know what she meant, of course, and I said something like, 'Oh?' And then she told me that she used to wait for her husband to come home every night, that was the highlight of her day. Half an hour before he was due, she changed into a dress and heels, put on lipstick and perfume, and combed her hair. Then she set the table—candles every night—and served him a nice dinner. Almost every night when they had finished eating, she would try to get him to spend some time with her. Just a card game, perhaps gin rummy, she would suggest. And he never did. She said when the kids were home, she could understand it; he was tired—well, so was she. But even after the kids left, all the years they were together without children, she would still make him dinner every night and she would still ask him for a little card game and he never did play with her. But here's the thing: he didn't say, 'I don't want to play cards.' Or 'I don't like to play cards.' He would say, 'Later,' and then never do it. *Why?*"

Lester has a few ideas about why, but he keeps them to himself. The question seems mostly rhetorical. Besides that, Candy's figuring things out for herself. And the process is new, still delicate. If he criticizes her husband, he suspects she'll find a way to defend him. Let silence be his only comment. He's known men like Candy's husband seems to be, and the kindest thing he can say about them is that he will never understand them, the way they deny themselves happiness and contentment because of a kind of stinginess and general obstinacy toward their wives, if not a weird sort of hatred. He thinks that such men feel there is a pattern of behavior that must be adhered to during courtship; after that, the onus is on the woman—and the woman alone—to please.

"I wish I had the courage to leave him," Candy says. "But then I'd be alone. It would be hard to deal with all that's going on if I were alone."

"I don't know," Lester says. "I think there's alone-alone; and then there's feeling alone when you're with someone, which is worse."

"You're right," she says. "You're absolutely right. Alone-alone is . . . clean. Isn't it?"

"I think it is."

"To be alone without longing, that's the thing."

"That is the thing."

"I have never in my life been alone. I have always had a man."

"Yes?"

"Yes. Since I was eleven years old. My God. Since I was *eleven*. That's when my boyfriend Billy Simpson would come over every day after school. Every day, and you know I would spend a good half hour getting ready for him. Instead of being outside and riding my bike or something, I would sit in front of my dresser mirror trying out different ribbons for my hair."

"Didn't your mom say anything?" Lester asks.

"Oh, sure. She told all her friends how wonderful it was that I had such a dedicated boyfriend so young. She was quite proud." She is quiet for a moment, and then she says gently, "Bless her heart. It was such a different time."

It is quiet for a while, and then Candy clears her throat and says, "Lester? In your professional opinion, do you think I'm going to die soon?"

He looks at her. "I'm a veterinarian."

"I know. But do you?"

"Well, I think . . . You know what? I think people get hung up on statistics. The reality is that, when it comes to the individual, it's zero or one hundred percent. And I'm struck, too, by the way that people assume a medical diagnosis is what's going to take them out of Dodge. I could go out for a walk tonight and get hit by a bus."

"Oh, I hope you don't," Candy says. "Then I'll never get my million dollars."

There is the sound of a door slamming, and then they hear a woman giggling on the other side of the wall. She giggles louder, whoops, and then there is the sound of the headboard banging against the wall in an unmistakable rhythm.

Candy's eyes grow wide and she whispers, "Do you think that's one of ours?"

"Someone from the reunion?"

She nods.

"God, I hope so," Lester says. "I hope it's Dorothy Shauman and John Niehauser." Lester hates to impugn the character of John this way, he was pretty a nice guy who had the misfortune to have been seen eating boogers in fourth grade and it followed him right up to the last year of high school, but Lester always liked him. He was a math genius, which put another nail in his high school coffin, and, as if that weren't enough, he liked to bring the newspaper to read at lunchtime while he drank coffee from a plaid thermos. He was almost as big a nerd as Lester. But to pair Dorothy with someone so that they can put faces to the sounds of moaning and groaning is irresistible. He and Candy start laughing, just a little at first, and then long and loudly.

"Oh, *God*!" Candy finally says, her hand lying limp across her belly. "Whew!" She sits up and blows her nose and says, "All right. Let me fix my mascara and then we should go back down there. I've kept you here so long. I'm sorry."

"Hey, Candy. Would you do me a favor?"

"Stop apologizing?"

"Bingo."

"I know. One of the many habits I need to break."

"I'm *glad* we talked. I really am. I hope you know that."

"I'm glad, too. And now you've got to get down there and ask that sweet-smelling woman to dance."

Lester sits up, his face full of worry. "I am an awful dancer. Awful." He stares at his shoes, as though it's their fault.

Candy puts her hand on Lester's shoulder. "Here's what I know about Mary Alice Mayhew. She won't mind one bit."

"Yeah. I guess you're right."

"Ask her for a slow one."

"Slow's the ticket," Lester says, and Candy nods in a serious way like he's talking about all kinds of things, which he supposes he is.

When they get back to the dance, they see a large number of people sitting around a few tables that have been pushed together. "What's going on over there?" Candy asks, and Lester says, "Don't know. Let's go see." He scans the group quickly to see if Mary Alice is there. No. Nor does he see her anywhere else. Also missing: Pete Decker. *So.*

When Candy and Lester reach the table, there is a sudden silence. And then Pam Pottsman says, "Allllll right. Where have *you* two been?"

Lester drags two chairs over, and he and Candy squeeze in around the table. "We've been getting to know one another," he says, and the group says together, "*Ohhhhhhhh.*"

"And what are you guys doing?" Lester asks.

"We're telling the truth," Pam says. "Isn't that something?"

"About what?" Candy asks, and Buddy says, "Everything. We just finished horror stories about health a little while ago."

"Ah," Candy says, and it's all Lester can do not to reach over and take her hand. Then she says, "Here's something true. I just made a friend. Which I need. And always did need."

"Are you kidding?" Judy says. "*Everyone* was your friend in high school! And you had a date practically every night of the week!"

Candy nods, smiling. "Yeah, but you know what? The thing about *everybody* being your friend is that it can mean *no* one is.

"As for dating . . . Yes, I did date a lot. A *lot*. I took a kind of pride in it, too. I had a calendar hanging on my wall next to my desk, and I used to keep a tally at the bottom of the page, of how many dates per month I had. And I had a ritual I kind of enjoyed each time I got ready for a date. I'd wash and roll up my hair, and then dry it with one of those dryers you could put perfume in, remember those? I'd stand in front of the mirror putting my makeup on so carefully, trying this new thing or that. I'd debate for a long time about what outfit to wear. It was like a job, dating. It was what I did. I would go on all these dates, and when I came home, there would be my mother in her bathrobe, sitting at the kitchen table and smoking, waiting for me to tell her how everything went. I think she missed her own days of furious dating, and she would hang on every word I told her. But of course you don't talk to your mother like you would a girlfriend. You don't share certain things, you don't ask certain questions that you want to ask. I really needed girlfriends, and none of you ever really let me in."

"Why didn't you *ask* us?" Nance says.

"I couldn't," Candy says. "It was too embarrassing to admit how lonely I was. But I'll admit it now. I have lived a pretty lonely life, and I am ready for women friends!"

Linda puts her arm around Candy and says, "I'll be your friend."

"Can I . . . ? I want to say one more thing about health," Marjorie says, then adds quickly, "It's not a bad thing." She re-settles herself in her chair and says, "I saw this picture in the paper the other day. It was bicyclists in a race, and the weather was awful, rain just pouring down. The riders looked so bedraggled and miserable, nothing like those cool Tour de France posters you see, where the bikers are in such impossibly good shape, and the day is perfect, and they're taking a turn with such grace and precision. I mean, they look like ballet dancers on wheels. The riders in the photo I saw were nothing like that. They were not in good shape, they had their heads down, and a lot of them were frowning, it seemed like they were gritting their teeth, just working so hard to get through the thing they'd signed up for, never thinking it would be like *this*. And I thought, that's what I am now. I'm a rider in the rain—out of shape, operating under less than optimal conditions, just trying to finish the race and not give up early. But I *like* myself better now. I like all of us better now. I think I had to get this old to understand some things I really needed to know. I needed to suffer some humiliation and to pick up a few battle scars. It's made me less shallow, and far more appreciative of *everything*. I've finally gained some perspective that lets me laugh about things that used to make me want to tear my hair out. Getting older is hard, you lose an awful lot. But I don't know, I think it's worth the trade. And, Candy? I'll be your friend, too. I always wanted to be your friend. Want to go shopping for rain gear?"

Lester's cellphone rings. He looks to see who it is, then answers quickly. It's Jeanine. More to the point, it's Samson.

NINETEEN

MARY ALICE STANDS WITH PETE AT THE ENTRANCE TO the ballroom. She doesn't see Lester anywhere, nor does she see Candy Sullivan. Well, there's *that* reunion story. For a moment, something seems to deflate inside her, but then she reminds herself of how pleasant an afternoon she and Lester had spent. There's always the breakfast, which he'd said he would definitely attend. "I'd never turn down breakfast," he said. "Even the *name* is right. And then if you add bacon, well . . ." He looked at her with some concern then, asking if she was a vegetarian, and she told him only in her ideal vision of self, which she never lived up to; and that she had recently seen a recipe that featured bacon crumbled on top of ice cream and thought it was brilliant.

She sees Pete scanning the crowd—looking for his wife, she supposes. She touches his arm and points in as unobtrusive a way as possible to where Nora is dancing with Fred. Mary Alice doesn't know Fred at all, and she doesn't really know Pete that much better, but the time she spent with him this evening has made her think his wife really should give him another chance. Mary Alice sees him as an essentially kindhearted man a little derailed by his good looks and charm. But he has a generosity about him, a kind of *willingness* that, in Mary Alice's book, anyway, makes up for a lot.

She and Pete had put Einer to bed. "Drape my socks over my chair!" Einer ordered Pete. "I only wore them half a day!" Pete complied, aligning the socks with great care on the top of Einer's easy chair, the one he keeps stationed by the window. Pete also hung up Einer's suit jacket, pants, and shirt, and complimented him on his choice of fabrics. Before he left Einer's bedroom (Einer himself propped up on his pillows, as yet refusing to give in to the fatigue that was making both his mouth and his eyelids droop), Pete sat at the old man's bedside and shook his hand, thanking him for his friendship and counsel.

"That's all right," Einer said. "You ever make your way out here again, you know where to find me."

"I might take you up on that," Pete said.

When Pete stood to leave, Einer said, "Say, how about a little touch before you go? I've got some good scotch downstairs. Rita knows where it is, she likes a touch herself, every now and again. She thinks I don't know, but you have to get up early in the morning to fool this old bird."

Pete told Einer they'd have some on his next visit, and then he and Mary Alice made their way downstairs, where they waited at the kitchen table for Rita to come home. She arrived about fifteen minutes later. "Sorry," she said, "but boy, do I have a good excuse! Want to know what it is?"

"Tell me later," Mary Alice said, though there didn't seem to be too much mystery as to what had delayed her return.

On the drive back to the hotel, Pete told Mary Alice about his father, who was a philanderer of some note. "He didn't even try to hide it," Pete said. "His pockets were a treasure trove of evidence—he'd have matches from hotel bars, numbers written on scraps of paper; once, even, a tube of lipstick. My brother and I used to go

through his pockets to spare my mom—and to see if we could figure out if he'd seen the same woman twice. We also stole whatever
change was in there and spent it on candy." When his father was
home, which wasn't all that often, he had a heavy hand with his
children, especially with Pete, because Pete had the balls to give him
a little crap back. Pete admitted that he had cheated on his own wife
and then left her but now realized his idiocy. "I know this sounds
like bullshit," he said, "but I don't know who that *was,* the guy
who did that. I feel like all of a sudden I'm starting to come to, to
realize some things I should have known a long time ago." It was
quiet in the car, and then Pete said, "You probably don't believe me
when I say that, huh?" and Mary Alice said, "In fact, I do."

He said he had schemed to get Nora to come to the reunion,
where he could see her alone and begin the process of getting her
back. "I thought if I could just get some time with her," Pete said.
"Whenever I come over to the house, she's itching the whole time
for me to leave, I can tell. I wanted a chance to talk to her away
from there. She doesn't really want a divorce; she's just hurt. And
I don't blame her! I fucked up! But I figured if she came to this reunion, if she thought about how we used to be . . .

"And then that *clod* had to come with her. Mr. Personality.
Let me tell you, that guy doesn't stand a chance in hell with
Nora. He may be fine for now, something for her to do, a guy to
take her places, you know; but believe me, I know my wife, and
Fred Preston is not going to last much longer. He is on the way
out. She's bored silly."

Well, not by the look of things. Fred and Nora are dancing to
a slow song, and the look on Nora's face is anything but bored.
Deeply content comes to mind.

Mary Alice can almost feel Pete's heart sink. She smiles at
him, trying to think of something that will make him feel better,
if only in the smallest way. But look at him, standing there with
his hands in his pockets, his shoulders slumped, unable to turn

away from the thing that is causing him such pain. What words that she could offer would provide any solace? She feels so bad for him in his golf clothes, his shirt stained with blood and salad dressing, and now as well as with the lurid orange of a Cheeto he dropped on himself as they sat waiting for Einer in the ER.

"Pete?" she says softly.

He looks over at her, his face full of weariness. "Know what my kids would say about this situation?" he says, gesturing with his chin toward his wife and Fred.

"What?"

" 'Game over,' that's what they'd say."

"Your kids wouldn't say that," she says, though of course she doesn't know Pete's children at all. "They'd say, 'Game on!' "

Mary Alice looks over at the couple again. Fred's still got Nora held up against him tightly, and now they both have their eyes closed.

"I was going to ask the DJ to play 'The Way You Look To-night,' " Pete says, sadly. "That was our song."

Mary Alice puts her purse down at an empty table and reaches for Pete's hand. "Come on. Let's do that."

He hesitates for just a moment, then takes her hand and follows her to the DJ, who agrees to play that song right after this one finishes. Then Pete follows Mary Alice out onto the dance floor. "Okay, here's the plan," she says. "We dance with each other for a few seconds, and then we cut in on them. When the song ends, you keep hold of Nora for 'The Way You Look Tonight.' "

"What if she won't do it?"

"What have you got to lose?"

And so they position themselves next to Fred and Nora, dance a few steps, and then Mary Alice gives Pete the slightest of nods. He moves over and taps Fred on the shoulder. Fred opens his eyes, and when he sees it's Pete, opens them wider. He steps away from Nora, his hands in the air, as though he's being held up.

Pete holds his own hands up. "No worries, Fred; I'm just cutting in. Gentleman's prerogative."

Fred looks at Nora, who raises one shoulder: I *don't care*. But Mary Alice can see the concern in her face when she looks at her husband: his disheveled state, his obvious need.

Mary Alice taps Fred on the shoulder. "May I have the honor?" she asks, and Fred looks once again at Nora, then reluctantly takes Mary Alice into his arms.

"So you're Fred?" Mary Alice asks.

"Yes, that's right," he says. And automatically, mindlessly, he asks, "And you're . . ."

"I'm Jayne Mansfield," Mary Alice says.

"Uh-huh," he says, his eyes glued to Pete. The song ends, and, fortunately, the next one starts right away. Pete keeps hold of Nora, and she doesn't seem to mind. "*Someday*," the Lettermen sing, "*when I'm awfully low, when the world is cold . . .*"

Fred dances stiffly, badly. Mary Alice tries to make conversation, but everything she says falls flat. Finally, "I live in a tree," she says.

"Is that right," Fred says, but then he looks at her. "Did you . . . What did you say?"

"I said, 'I live in a tree.' The very top branches. Lovely view."

He continues to stare at her, but before he can think of how to respond, the song ends. Mary Alice looks over at Pete and can tell instantly that their ploy did not exactly work. Nora is walking quickly back to Fred, shaking her head, and Pete is standing still, empty eyed.

"Last dance!'" the DJ says and starts playing another slow song, an instrumental that Mary Alice doesn't recognize. And now here come Dorothy Shauman and Pam Pottsman, from opposite sides of the room, headed straight for Pete Decker. Dorothy sees what Pam is doing and actually runs over and elbows her out of the way. "Wanna dance?" she asks breathlessly, and Pete takes her in his arms like an automaton, then looks over the top of her head at Nora and Fred, holding hands and walking back to their table.

Pam stands beside Mary Alice, trying to catch her breath. She watches Pete and Dorothy dance, mindlessly anchoring a piece of hair that has fallen again from where it was pinned up. "Nuts," she says. Then, brightening, "Oh well, there's always breakfast."

Ben Small comes up to Mary Alice and shrugs. "How about it, toots?" She smiles and takes his hand. They dance right next to Pete and Dorothy. Neither she nor Ben talks, and Mary Alice is pretty sure it's so that they can better listen to Dorothy putting the moves on Pete. They hear her say, "I have wanted to dance with you all *night,* but I haven't had the *chance.* You look great, Pete! Which I'm sure you know. You look just great! Even in . . . those clothes."

Pete makes some sort of grunting sound.

"What are you driving now, Pete?"

"What?"

"What are you *driving* now?"

"Oh. A Nissan *Cube,*" he says, bitterly.

"Oh, I love those cars!" Dorothy says, and Pete says, "I was *kidding.* Jesus! I've got a Porsche. And a 'fifty-seven 'Vette."

"Oh, a vintage 'Vette!" Dorothy says. "Yes, that does sound more like you." She pulls him closer. "You know, I have to tell you, ever since I got the invitation to the reunion, I've been think-ing about that time we had together, do you remember that *time* we had together? I do. I remember that time."

At last, Pete looks at her, and his face is full of misery. "Yeah, I remember," he says. "I think I got to second base." Now he smiles the smallest smile. "You were a cute girl."

"Well," she says, "we're a lot older now, aren't we? I mean, more mature and all. More *experienced.* But we're still kind of cute, aren't we?"

"Dorothy," Pete says. "Dorothy, Dorothy, Dorothy Shau-man. Would you like me to bang your britches off? Is that it?"

And Dorothy giggles and says, "Yes, please."

Mary Alice squeezes her eyes shut and rests her head against Ben's shoulder. *Ah, Pete,* she's thinking.

The song ends and there is the sound of applause, and then the faint sounds of . . . *cheering?* Yes. In the corner of the ballroom, Judy and Linda are doing a cheer.

"I gotta see this," Pete says. "I always loved the cheerleaders." Mary Alice and Ben, Dorothy and Pete, they all move to where people have gathered around the two women.

Dorothy stands watching Pete smile at them, and then suddenly she's doing the cheer, too, her heels off, her dress held up to miniskirt level. Judy and Linda were cheerleaders, and Dorothy was always trying out, but she never made it. The truth is, she made a fool of herself every time she auditioned; she was no athlete, but she just kept trying. Now, she makes the moves as best she can, and along with her old friends chants the words to the Tony the Tiger cheer:

WE'VE *got the boys on* (clap!)
OUR *team*
They're grrrrreat! (clap clap!)
WE'VE *got the spirit that*
A great TEAM *needs, it's*
Grrrrreat! (clap clap!)

At the end of the cheer, the women leap into the air for a stag jump, but Dorothy slips and falls. Her friends rush over to her, and she says, "I'm fine, I'm fine," and looks anxiously into the crowd for Pete, who is no longer there. Mary Alice didn't see him go, but he is definitely not there.

Dorothy scrambles to her feet, yanks her dress down, and puts her heels back on. "Pete?" she calls. *"PETE?"*

A woman's voice calls back, "He's *gone,* Dorothy," with a

distinct note of satisfaction. Mary Alice turns to see who it was: Nora. And Dorothy bursts into tears.

Mary Alice turns to Ben and he shrugs, then says, "Pretty good Sturm und Drang, huh?"

She smiles, shakes her head.

"You headed out?" Ben asks.

"I think so." She walks over to the table to retrieve her purse, and Ben goes with her.

"A bunch of us are going to the lobby bar for a nightcap," he says. "You want to come?"

"No, thanks," she says. "I'll be back for the breakfast, though."

"I'll see you then," Ben says and adds, "Did I tell you this? You look lovely, Mary Alice." She looks down at her dress, her shoes, this outfit she assembled with such care, and thanks him.

Mary Alice makes her way to the bathroom. She'll pee, then head on home. She thinks she has some leftover pizza in the refrigerator; she'll eat that. She's hungry, she realizes.

When she walks into the ladies' room, Mary Alice is met with a great cloud of smoke. Sitting on the floor, leaning against the wall, are Dorothy, Judy, and Linda. Dorothy is weeping into her hands while her friends puff on cigarettes and attempt to console her.

"Mary Alice!" both Judy and Linda say when they see her. She suspects she's a welcome diversion.

"Hey," she says, and she considers for a moment backing out of the room and using a bathroom elsewhere, or even waiting until she gets home.

But, "Sit down!" Judy says with an outsize, drunken generosity, mixed, Mary Alice suspects, with a kind of curiosity. Well, she's curious about them, too. Who are they now? For that matter, who were they then?

And so—why not? Mary Alice always did want to hang out in the bathroom with the popular girls, and even if these three weren't *Candy Sullivan* popular, they'd held their own. She sits on the floor next to Judy.

"Cigarette?" Linda says, taking her pack out of her purse, and Mary Alice starts to decline—she's never smoked—but then she accepts a Marlboro, and Judy lights it for her.

She coughs immediately, and they all laugh, except for Dorothy, who continues to hold her face in her hands.

Judy rolls her eyes. "Hey, Dorothy," she says. "Look who's here! Mary Alice Mayhew!"

Nothing.

"Hi there, Dorothy," Mary Alice says. "How are you?"

And then, oh, terrible, she and Linda and Judy start laughing. Now they hear Dorothy's muffled voice saying, "It's *not funny*!"

"Well, it *kind* of is," Linda says, in a tentative voice. "It's a *little* funny. If you could see that it's funny, then you wouldn't feel so bad." To Mary Alice, she says, "Take a smaller puff. And then hold it in your lungs just for a second. You have to get used to it. It burns a lot, at first."

Mary Alice tries again, successfully this time, although, good grief, she has no idea why people would want to go through this kind of thing. Still, "Can you teach me to French-inhale?" she asks, and Judy and Linda say together, "Absolutely!"

Dorothy takes her hands off her face, revealing scattered pink patches. "Fine. Don't pay any attention to me."

There is a lengthy silence, and then Linda says, "Well, yes, we are paying attention to you, Dorothy. We're giving you space. We're being respectful."

"Yeah," Judy says.

"If you're ready to talk, we're ready to listen," Mary Alice says.

"Oh, sure, Mary Alice *Mayhew*," Dorothy says. "My lifelong confidante." Then, "Oh, I'm *sorry*." She gives Mary Alice a quick once-over. "Huh! You look *nice*."

"Thank you." Mary Alice notices a false eyelash hanging perpendicular to Dorothy's eye, but now is probably not the time to tell her.

Dorothy reaches over and takes a cigarette from Linda's pack. "I gave these up years ago," she says. Judy lights the thing, and Dorothy takes in a deep drag and exhales slowly. "I might take it up again, though. Nothing else to do. Because I give up. I do. I just give up. I guess I'll never spend time with a man again. That's all over for me. I am D-U-N done."

"Hey, remember how we used to meet every day after math class and smoke in the bathroom just like this?" Judy says. "Remember that one time I told you guys I had a dream about a gigantic slide rule that Mr. Schultz was making me walk up and down? And then Miss Falk came in and busted us for smoking but she didn't turn us in to the principal because she was always trying to be our friend?"

"Well, of course I remember," Dorothy says. "I'm not senile. Yet." She honks her nose into some toilet tissue she has wadded in her hand.

"*Dorothy*," Linda says. "*Stop* it, now. You'll have another chance at breakfast. You'll see him then. And his wife won't be there. I saw her when everyone was leaving and she said she definitely wasn't coming tomorrow."

"Big deal," Dorothy says. "It won't matter. I made a fool of myself tonight. He was going to make *love* to me, he asked if I would like it if he made *love* to me and I said *yes* and then I had to try to do a *cheer*. A *cheer*! What was I *thinking*? Well, I know what I was thinking. I was thinking he'd think I was cute, like the old days, but all I did was pull up my dress too high and I'll bet he saw I was wearing Spanx and you know I have that one varicosity behind my knee, and *then* I had to go and fall *down*. God! It won't help if Nora's not at the breakfast. *Nothing* will help. He doesn't care about me. He never did! And I know why. It's because I'm a terrible person. I *am*! Even if I don't *want* to be, I just *am*!

"You know what I discovered tonight? Everyone is so much nicer than I thought. And it makes me so mad! Because I never knew that, I was always so poised to defend myself. And now it's too late. I was so mean and awful all the time, and now it is too late, the cows have come home to roost. I'll die a bitter old woman, alone. I'll be found weeks after the fact!"

"Yeah," Linda says. "And probably your stinky old corpse will be in a very unflattering position, too. They'll photograph you like that. They'll have to, for the police files."

"Wait," Judy says. "The *cows* have come home to roost?"

"You know what I mean," Dorothy says. She sniffs, wipes at her eyes. She's laughing a little, in spite of herself.

"Gosh," Linda says. "When you were fifteen and crying in the bathroom over some guy, did you ever think you'd be sixty years old and crying in the bathroom over some guy?"

"I'm not sixty yet!" Dorothy says.

"Oh, just say you are," Linda says. "I say I'm sixty-five because I love to hear people say how young I look."

"I do that, too!" Judy says.

"I know. I told you to."

"Oh yeah."

"My daughter hates me," Dorothy says.

"Oh, for Christ's sake," Judy says. "Will you *stop*? No woman's daughter likes her. But factoring that in, I'd say your daughter loves you very much."

"I'll bet my grandchildren will hate me, too. I'm not fun. I'm nervous and too critical. I have a bad way about me. If Hilly has kids, she'll never let me babysit."

Linda says, "I saw this show on TV? A dog that was missing for nine years reappeared! He was real cute. One of those shaggy guys. He just showed up, nine years later!"

"*And?*" Dorothy says.

"It just goes to show you," Linda says. "It's never too late. Except for dead people. Oh, wasn't it sad to see Patsy Sussman on the dead table? To die in a motorcycle accident right after graduation! All that studying for finals, and for what? She must have worked so hard, she always had a hard time keeping her grade point average up."

There is a long silence, and then Judy says, "Didn't she sort of have buck teeth?"

"What does that have to do with anything?" Dorothy snaps.

Judy shrugs. Then, quietly, she says, "I don't know."

"It's too late for the dead people *and* me," Dorothy says.

"Oh, that's an awful thing to say," Judy says.

"Why?" Dorothy says. "It's true. You know what I have in my life? Nothing."

"Dorothy?" Mary Alice says.

"What."

"Why would you insult your friends this way?"

"*What?*"

"I'm wondering why you would say you have nothing in your life, when your friends of so many years are sitting right beside you. I think it's insulting to them. Not that it's any of my business, really."

"Oh, it's your business," Judy says quickly. And to Dorothy, Judy says, "She's right. In a way, you're telling us we're losers."

"I am not!"

"Listen, Dorothy," Linda says. "We love you. All through high school, and all these years later, we *love* you."

"Though it wouldn't hurt for you to get some therapy," Judy says, and Linda says, "Judy!"

"What?" Judy says. "Let's just be honest here. You and I have talked about how she could use therapy. In a *loving way,* Dorothy! We want you to be happy, that's all."

"Oh, who's happy," Dorothy says.

A moment, and then Mary Alice raises her hand.

Dorothy looks at her. "Really?"

Mary Alice nods solemnly.

"Huh," Dorothy says.

Another woman comes into the bathroom, no one from the reunion. She wrinkles her nose, waves at the air, and says, "You are *not* supposed to *smoke* in here."

Mary Alice blows out a stream of smoke toward her and says, "Really?"

"Disgusting!" the woman says and exits the little room.

"We'll get you your black leather jacket and motorcycle boots in the morning," Linda says, and Mary Alice says, "Thank you. Please make sure there are zippers *everywhere*." And then, looking at her watch, "It already *is* morning."

"Let's go to sleep, now," Judy says, as though they are at a slumber party.

The women struggle to get up off the floor, and Mary Alice, who is first to stand, offers a hand to Dorothy.

"Thanks," Dorothy says. And then, "Mary Alice? Mary Alice Mayhew. Is it too late to say I'm sorry for the way I treated you in high school?"

"I never think it's too late for anything," Mary Alice says. "I have an appointment to try skydiving next week."

Dorothy straightens the shoulders of her dress, brushes off the back. She smiles, and Mary Alice sees in it the pretty, open-faced girl she used to be. "See you tomorrow," Dorothy says. "Want us to save you a seat at our table?"

"Sure. Thanks."

On the drive home, Mary Alice sings along with the radio. She hopes she'll be with Lester tomorrow, but if not, she's got friends who will keep a seat for her, no matter how late she gets there.

TWENTY

"WELL, HOW MUCH IS *THIS* GOING TO COST ME?" ALAN Heck asks Lester. His hands are on his hips and he's glowering at his dog, a small black collie mix named Lady with a white blaze down her nose. She'd be a good-looking dog if she were well cared for. As it is, her ribs protrude, her coat is dull and full of burrs, and Lester can tell from the smell that her right ear is probably infected.

"I'm not sure yet," Lester says. "I'll have to see how deep the cut is."

Alan shakes his head. "Fell right down the basement steps. How stupid is that?"

Lester doubts the dog did any such thing. One of his clients, Anna Pearson, lives next door to Alan Heck, and she told Lester he constantly abuses the dog.

"Aw, hell, put the damn thing to sleep," Alan says. "I suppose you're going to charge me for that, too."

Lester is tempted to punch the guy. He was up all night with Samson, and he is in no mood to deal with Alan Heck. He always dreads seeing Alan, but this time is worse than usual. "I'll tell you what," he says. "You want to put her down? Why not just let us find her another home? If you do that, I'll treat her for free."

"Really?" Alan says. And then he makes some phony effort to show concern. "Hate to do it, of course," he says, furrowing his brow, shoving his hands in his pockets, and hunching his shoulders. "My wife loved the thing. But I just can't . . . I just can't keep it if it's going to keep costing me like this. There's always something, shots I'm supposed to get it and whatnot. And my business isn't what it used to be."

"I understand," Lester says. "A man's got to do what a man's got to do." He gives Alan a form to sign, releasing his rights to the dog.

Alan signs it without reading it, then hikes his pants up. "Okay! Well, so, that's that." He reaches down to pat the dog, and she lowers her head, her eyes rolled up in fear. "You be good," he tells her, and Lester nearly laughs out loud.

"See you around town, Doc."

"Right." After Alan leaves, Lester stands gently stroking the top of Lady's head and listening to Alan trying to joke with Jeanine, who ignores him, then tells him pointedly that she's *busy*.

"Whoa," Alan says. "That time of the month?"

Lester is gently lifting the dog off the table to bring her into the back when Jeanine bursts into the examining room. "If you ever let that man bring another animal in here, I'm going to have you put away."

"If I ever let that man bring another animal in here, I'll put myself away."

"Why did he even keep her after Rose died?" Jeanine asks, and when she looks at Lady, her eyes fill. "Oh, look at her. You can see every rib."

"Let's get her settled. I'm going to fix her up and then I'm going to find her a home that deserves her."

"He gave her up?" Jeanine says.

"Yeah."

"The bastard. I'll take her."

"You have four dogs, already."

"You only have one," she says hopefully, and Lester says, "Jeanine."

It is Lester's policy, his desire, his need, to have only one dog at a time. He likes it that way. Jeanine knows this, but she regularly argues that dogs like it better when there is more than one.

Together, they clean Lady up, put drops in her ears, temporarily dress an abrasion that runs long across her side, give her a dose of antibiotics, and then put her in a roomy cage with a soft blanket. "She'll probably need a few stitches," Lester says. "I can do it under local. You can help me. I doubt she'll put up much resistance. But let's feed her—and us—first." They give the dog food and water, and she immediately empties both dishes. Jeanine refills the water dish, and then she and Lester go into the staff break room for a bagel. Jeanine reaches out to touch Lester's arm. "You okay?"

"Yeah."

After they eat, Jeanine helps him put in the sutures Lady needs—the vet tech they most recently hired has called in sick. "She calls in sick way too often," Jeanine says. "You're going to have to fire her and find someone else."

Lester secures the dressing onto the dog's side. "I know. You do it."

"We'll have to find someone else, first," Jeanine says, and again Lester says, "I know. You do it."

As Lester predicted, the dog resists not at all. Nor does she attempt to go after her dressing, so they don't have to put a cone around her neck. Instead, they simply put her back in the cage, and she lies down and curls in a little ball in the far back corner. Lester stands watching her. At this point in his career, he's become pretty good at shielding his heart, but this dog is getting to him. He remembers Alan's wife bringing her in as a puppy, how full of hope Rose had seemed, probably at the prospect of having something that would love her back.

"You must be exhausted," Jeanine tells Lester.

"You must be, too."

"I'm okay," she says. "I'll tell you, though—I can't believe Samson made it. That dog thinks he's a cat—nine lives."

Samson had been recovering well from his infection when he suffered another, unrelated problem: gastric volvulus, a sudden twisting of his stomach, rare and usually fatal. Luckily, Jeanine recognized what it was and called Lester immediately, and the dog went back into surgery. Now he is sleeping soundly, his "parents" beside him in lounge-type lawn chairs. They will not leave him until he comes home. Betty brought a picnic basket and a pile of library books, and Stan brought his transistor radio.

"All right, I'm going to bed," Lester tells Jeanine. "Call me if you need anything."

"You aren't going back to the reunion? Don't you have a breakfast?"

"Too much going on here," he says.

"I just called John Benning," Jeanine says. "He said he'd cover for you all day today. He's on the way. And he said he's glad to do it—you bailed him out lots of times."

"True," Lester says. "And he still owes me fifteen dollars from our last poker game."

"So, how *was* the reunion?" Jeanine says. "Did you have fun?"

"I did."

"Did you . . . meet anyone?"

"Sort of."

Jeanine is all business now. "Okay, you get back there. You go to that breakfast."

"Yeah, I don't know." He looks at his watch. "It'll be over pretty soon."

"Oh, no you don't," Jeanine says. "I know you. If you don't go back, you'll never see whoever you met again. That always happens whenever you meet anyone you're interested in. You just talk yourself right out of it. You let the whole thing drop!"

"Well, I don't know if there's a whole thing *to* drop, really. I met someone I kind of like, but I don't know if—"

"And that's exactly why you're going back."

"Jeanine, I'm too tired to drive. Really." Pete Decker, she was with.

"I'll call you a cab."

"I don't need a cab."

"Go and change. And *shave.*"

Lester goes into the back room once more to check on Lady. The dressing is fine, and the dog is lying still in her cage. She'll be here all day, with the exception of the times she'll be let out to pee. Lester pokes his fingers through the cage and gently scratches behind Lady's ear, and the dog looks up at him.

Ah, what the hell. It's a nice day, not too hot, not too cold. "Want to go for a car ride?" he asks, and one ear moves. Lester opens the cage door and strokes the dog's back. "Want to come with me?" Her tail wags. He lifts her out of the cage and carries her into the waiting room. Jeanine is at the door, on her way out. "Where are you going?" she says.

"You told me to shave."

Jeanine points to the dog, and Lester says, "She's coming."

"In a cab? Town Taxi is on the way."

"Jeanine, not for nothing did I go through training. I can go three days without sleep if I need to. Cancel the cab. I'm going to sleep for half an hour. Then I'm going to drink some more coffee. Then I'm going to the breakfast. Then I'm coming home to sleep for the rest of the day."

"All right, good," Jeanine says, and reaches out to pet Lady. "I *could* have five dogs," she says wistfully, and Lester says, "Too late. We've bonded."

In fact, Lester sleeps for over an hour, and when he wakes up he sees that he has just enough time to get to the breakfast before it ends at noon. He leaves Lady sleeping on his bed while he quickly gets ready, then carries her downstairs to pee. He lays her on Mason's blanket in the front seat of the truck and lets Mason ride in the back, strapped into the harness he hates but will tolerate for the feel of the open air.

When Lester pulls into the parking lot, he narrowly misses hitting another car on its way out. Maybe he'd better drink a lot more coffee at the breakfast; he's more tired than he thought.

In the conference room where the breakfast is being held, Lester sees no sign of Mary Alice. She could be in the bathroom, he supposes, but he can't help feeling disappointed. What if he missed her altogether? He could call her, he knows now where she lives, but what he wanted to do at this breakfast was assure himself of a mutual attraction before he . . . Well, before he did anything.

He moves to the buffet table, which looks like it has been set upon by a pack of wolves. Bits of scrambled eggs are spilled onto the ripped paper tablecloth, none of the remaining pancakes are whole, and the syrup container sits in a sticky pool, with what must be a very happy fly directly in the middle of it. There's still a fair amount of bacon, and Lester lays a few strips on a plate, along with two slices of curled-up, overbuttered wheat toast. He has to tip the coffee urn to get out the last of what's there, and thinks the brand might most aptly be called Mississippi Mud.

"Not much good left here," he hears a voice say, and turns around to see Mike Massey, one of the star jocks in the old days, and someone who in the old days would never have deigned to speak to Lester.

"Nah, I got here too late, I guess," Lester says, and then notices Mike's outfit: a golf shirt with stains, a cheap pair of khaki pants. It is very close to what Pete Decker wore last night and in fact is still wearing—there he is, sitting at a table with Candy Sullivan. Mary Alice is still nowhere in sight.

Mike notices Lester looking over at Pete and says, "Can you believe what Decker's wearing? There's five or six of us got together in a little show of solidarity. Went out to Kmart this morning and got ourselves some shitty-looking golf outfits." He shrugs. "Turned it into a goof, you know, so he wouldn't feel so bad." Mike shakes his head. "Poor guy's a wreck."

Lester nods. "Yeah, it's too bad." Pete doesn't look like a wreck now, however, sitting there with Candy, smiling. Has he moved on from Mary Alice, then? Is that why she's not here?

Lester gives the buffet table one more glance and sees a cheese Danish in decent shape in a metal bin at the end of the table. He points to it, saying to Mike, "I think I'll grab that pastry. Unless you want it."

Mike pats his stomach. "Nah. I got diabetes. Doc kept telling me to watch my weight, and I thought, *Yeah, yeah, mañana,* you know? And then damned if I didn't get it, just like he said I would. I can't have *any* fun anymore. My doctor is a sadist, man. He likes to tell me all the things I'm going to get. He was ecstatic when I had to go on high blood pressure pills. Hey, you're a doc, aren't you? What do those pharmaceutical companies do, cut you in or what?"

"I'm a veterinarian," Lester says.

"So's Don Summers. But he didn't come. Pulled out at the last minute—death in the family."

"That's too bad. Yeah, I was kind of looking forward to talking to him. That's one of the reasons I came."

A shaft of light suddenly broadens and fills the room with light, and Lester sees Candy shade her eyes against it, then stand and put on sunglasses. She's apparently leaving.

"Nice talking to you," Lester tells Mike.

"Well, hold on—*do* you get cut in with the pharmaceutical people? I've always wondered. I mean, for animal pills and shit?"

Lester looks at Mike and sighs. "No. Okay?"

Mike steps back, offended. "Yeah, okay. *Sorry.*"

Lester heads over to Candy and reaches her just as she's about to walk out the door. "Hey," he says. "Taking off?"

"Oh, Lester! There you are!"

"I got here late. Had an emergency. I've got two dogs with me."

"Where are they?"

"In my truck. I can't leave them for long. I think I'll take off now, too."

"Mary Alice just left a few minutes ago," Candy said. "We had a nice talk. I can see why you like her, Lester. I'm crazy about her. I asked her to come and visit me in Boston."

"Uh-huh, good for you." He keeps his face carefully neutral. He doesn't ask any questions about Mary Alice. He doesn't know, suddenly, if he *wants* to ask anything about her. On the drive over, with Lady curled up beside him and occasionally wagging her tail, apropos of nothing (though it *was* possible, he guessed, that she sensed she was now free from Alan Heck), Lester was thinking about what he'd say to Mary Alice when he saw her. Invite her to get together for dinner? Take in a show, a concert in the city? Oh, it was wearying, really, to even contemplate. He honestly didn't have time for a relationship, nor did he have the *need* for one, Jeanine's thoughts to the contrary notwithstanding. Good old Jeanine. He wants to give her another raise, but she won't let him. She says he has to wait at least six months because he just gave her a raise. She said, "Pretty soon, I'm going to be making more than you!" And he said, "You should!" Why not? His expenses are minuscule compared to hers. He doesn't need much money. He doesn't *want* much money. He was lucky to find a wife who felt that same way.

When he and his wife had just started dating, they'd been talking one day about money because Kathleen's brother's wife had just left him, saying he was never going to amount to anything, i.e., not provide her with the material things to which she felt entitled. And Lester asked Kathleen how much a man would need to have so that a woman like her would feel secure. They were sitting in a booth at Sunday's, eating chicken-fried steak with milk gravy and mashed potatoes and collard greens, which they did on the first of the month, every month, and which he continues to do. Kathleen had just untucked her napkin from around her neck when he asked her this, saying she couldn't eat one more bite, not one more, *nothing,* unless maybe he'd like to share some lemon meringue pie. But when he asked her that question about income, she settled back in the booth and looked over at him, her arms crossed, her expression grave. And he silently cursed himself, thinking he'd blown it now, he'd asked too soon, and besides, the look on her face made him think she was going to quote an amount that ultimately would be beyond him. She was a direct and unfailingly honest person. She took in a breath and pooched out her lips. "Hmmm. How much would you need to have. Well, let's see." She searched the ceiling, as though using it for her calculations. Then she said, "Don't you have a bunch of lilacs on the hill behind your house?"

"I do," he said. "I have many lilacs. Acres. A small state, if not a veritable *nation* of lilacs."

"Well, that's enough," she said. "That and this here chicken-fried steak once a month."

He swallowed, then put his hands around his coffee cup and gripped hard. "This is too soon, I know, but would you—"

"Yes," she said. "A *small* wedding. Amid the nation of lilacs."

Ah, who could come close to her? That's what Jeanine didn't understand. Besides, he was *busy*. He was perfectly content. He was a fifty-nine-year-old man who had grown at least a little set in his ways, and he didn't mind, he *liked* it. Why set himself up for a life of compromise—and make no mistake about it, a relationship was all about compromise—when what he really wanted now was something he'd solemnly declared to his mother as a seven-year-old: "I want to do whatever I want whenever I want to, forever." To which she'd responded, "Oh my. Good luck, honey."

Still, that pretty much *was* his life, now: he did whatever he wanted, whenever he wanted. His work was his passion: there wasn't a day he wasn't eager to get to the clinic. His free time was spent in ways he wanted to spend it, whether it was mountain climbing in Peru or bass fishing in Montana or sitting on the front porch with a glass of raspberry lemonade and doing nothing but watching the liftoff and descent of butterflies on his front yard bushes. The relationship he'd had with his wife was one that poets dream about, and he did not ever expect to have such a partnership, such a love, again. How much is one supposed to ask from life, anyway? He knows his own luck. He knows he's had more than his share.

When they reach his truck, Candy pets the dogs, especially Lady, especially after Lester tells Candy about the dog's circumstances. "But she's going to live with you now, right?" she says, and Lester says, "Yup. In *style*."

Candy stands with her arms crossed, smiling at Lady. Then she sighs and says, "Well, I've got to go and get my own dog and then get a cab for the airport."

"Want a lift?" Lester asks. "I'd be glad to take you. Of course, you'd get dog hair all over your suit. Nice suit, by the way."

"I like dog hair," Candy says. "I'm tired of this suit. And I'd love a ride with you."

Lester walks the dogs while he waits for Candy to come back. After she does, he drives slowly, because he is enjoying her company.

When they arrive at the airport, Lester gets out of the truck to open Candy's door. He pulls a card from his wallet and gives it to her. "Let me know how you're doing, would you?"

She nods, and tears come to her eyes, but she is smiling. Her phone rings, and she ignores it. "I want to thank you," she says.

"And I you."

She wheels her suitcase toward the terminal as he watches. Several other men watch, too. Candy Sullivan. He sighs.

He goes to the back of the truck and unhooks Mason from his harness so that he can move the dog into the front seat with Lady. After Mason hops in, he sees Lady and freezes. "It's going to be a little different around here," Lester tells the dog. "You might think at first that you won't like it, but you will."

TWENTY-ONE

"WELL, I *TOLD* YOU NOT TO GO," SARAH JANE, MARY Alice's sister, says. "Didn't I? I told you. All it did is make you sad. I absolutely *knew* that would happen!" She shakes her head. "Why would you possibly want to go back to be among people who were nothing but cruel to you? What good could possibly come of it?"

"I'm not sad!" Mary Alice tells her sister. "And a lot of good came from it! I don't know what you think you just heard, but what I *said* is that I had a really good time! Don't forget your purse when you go," she says, pointing to the little evening bag lying on the kitchen table.

"I *see* it. What, is this a hint? You want me to go now? Fine, I'll go."

"I don't want you to go, Sarah Jane, but as it happens, I have an appointment to get to."

"For what?"

"Just . . . a routine check. A Pap smear."

Sarah Jane narrows her eyes at her sister.

"It's true! I have an appointment in twenty minutes. Do you want to see the appointment card?" *Oh, please don't say yes.*

Sarah Jane puts the evening bag inside her larger purse. "Well, call me later if you want. I hope you feel better."

"I'm fine!" Mary Alice watches her sister pull out of the driveway, scraping against the bushes as she always does, then attempting to straighten the car and scraping against them even more. She can see her sister's mouth moving, swearing, no doubt. And of course it is the bushes' fault, which translates to Mary Alice's fault.

She cleans up the lunch dishes and then goes up to her bedroom to lie down. It is Wednesday afternoon, chilly and gray, and she took off from work, a personal day. She never lies down in the middle of the day and so she admits at least to herself that perhaps her sister is a little bit right.

She puts her arms around David the pillow, closes her eyes, and reviews again the events of the reunion. She had enjoyed being around so many people, being so talkative for so long. She likes living alone, but the reunion sparked something inside her, brought forward a need she has long denied. Maybe she'll ask Marion to take English classes and she'll take Polish classes. Maybe that way they'll be able to advance their relationship to a more satisfying level of intimacy. Maybe she's ready for that. One needs, on occasion, to unpack one's heart, to share observations riskier than those about the weather.

She wishes things hadn't taken a nosedive with Lester. He saw her pulling out of the parking lot; he nearly crashed into her! He could have waved her over; they could have made some plans to get together. But he chose not to acknowledge her and instead drove on, intent, she supposed, on getting more time with Candy Sullivan. Clever of him to arrive just as everyone was leaving— that way, they could leave together. She wonders if they did leave together. Maybe she'll call Candy later and ask; she and Candy had established a bit of a friendship that Mary Alice looks forward to deepening.

He drove a nice truck, Lester; it suited him. And had a glad-eyed dog in the back to boot. Mary Alice knows she shouldn't, but she envisions herself riding in that truck beside Lester, on the way to . . . oh, anywhere. A ball game, the Cincinnati Reds against the St. Louis Cardinals. A picnic in the fall, the leaves drifting down onto the plaid blanket, cocoa and marshmallows in a thermos. A driving trip to Texas, to see the tumbleweed. She knows she shouldn't do this, dip into such outlandish wishful thinking, but she does it anyway. She falls asleep holding David close up against her.

She is awakened by the phone ringing, and answers it like a teenage girl, hope in her throat. But it is not Lester. It is Marion, asking in his halting way if she would like to take a walk this evening. She turns onto her back and contemplates the ceiling. She thinks maybe she'll find a church that has Evensong. A surprise about her is that she has a lovely voice: let someone hear it.

"Marion?" she says. "I was thinking. Would you like to go into the city with me tonight? Would you like to drive to Cincinnati and have dinner there?"

A moment, and then he laughs and "Ho! What would you think!"

She'll wear her reunion dress. It wouldn't be out of line. It might as well get used again, and even again.

She climbs out of bed and goes to look out the window.

"I'm not *sad*," she says, but look at how she presses her hand flat against the glass.

TWENTY-TWO

Einer looks out the window at the fine morning, remembering again the events of the reunion one week ago. To think that he might not have gone! Why, it took years off him, filled up his tank but good. When Rita comes up with his breakfast, he'll tell her to take the night off. He's going to invite Desiree over for dinner. He'll order out Italian, and *he'll* wait on *her*. She'll come, he knows she will, she gets a kick out of him. She's told him that: *You old buzzard, you're a gas, do you know that?*

What a day! Not a cloud in the sky, the humidity lifted, the birds singing. He knows he's developed a reputation for being a cantankerous old man, but today his heart is light, and if he could, he would stand on the rooftop and shout out glad tidings. "Blessings on the world!" he would say. "Blessings to us all!"

No bodily aches and pains today, either, it's a miracle! He breathes in deeply, and then, as he draws his head back in through the window, he bangs it hard.

He cries out and puts his hand to the back of his head. He can feel the goose egg starting to form already; it's going to be the size of Toledo. Well, isn't that the way? Isn't that life? Right when you're on top of the world, something happens to take you down a notch. And vice versa, thank God.

He shuffles over the few steps to his chair and sits down. He presses again on the sore spot at the back of his head. He'll endure the pain a bit longer—enjoy it, even, in the odd way people do, before he calls down to Rita to bring him some ice.

He stares at his pill bottles. He supposes he should get busy on doling them out. He picks up the first bottle and suddenly feels a crushing sensation on the right side of his head, nowhere near the bump he just got. *Now* what? It feels like a terrible, terrible headache, and it keeps getting worse. "Wait," he whispers. "Wait a minute." He lets go of the pill bottle, pushes it away from himself, as though it were the cause of his pain. The pressure increases even more, and he opens his mouth to breathe. He leans back in the chair and regards the ceiling, notices for the first time a cobweb at one corner. He opens his mouth to call Rita, but cannot speak.

Desiree, he thinks. Then, in his mind's eye, he sees the yellow centers of the daisies he was just looking at, the ones that grow in his garden. His wife planted them there, she loved daisies, and he remembers her face now with a clarity he has not enjoyed for years.

His vision starts to fade, and then he is bombarded with memories: a dogfight in World War II, the ironed scent of his mother's apron, a bakery screen door, the flash of tadpoles in a stream, sleeping on the porch in summer, a painting he once dared to straighten on a museum wall, the fedora he wore for so many years. Now the pain seems to lessen, but he remains powerless to move, to speak. He blinks, struggles to stay alert, aware. *My name is Einer Olson. I live on . . .* What street does he live on? He must remember!

He counts in his mind to five; then, less ably, to ten. He tries to recall one by one the people he saw at the reunion: *Think! Stay alive!* But it is unequivocally upon him, death; he knows it now, and suddenly he is not afraid. He relaxes; his hands loosen their grip on the arms of the chair, his face goes peaceful, and time seems to achieve a kind of elasticity that makes him feel he sees the future: someone over for Sunday dinner at his ex-wife's house and shaking the hand of her new husband. A woman moving the last of her things into her new house, a place full of light and flowers. A couple seated on a blanket in a park. A woman bending over her granddaughter and guiding her along, helping her learn to walk. And now, look: here are his tomatoes, they have ripened to perfection and they are sliced and laid out on a green platter and ready to be eaten, every one.

There is one more thing, he's got to do just one last thing, so important. He struggles to get up, then slumps to the side of the chair. Rita finds him there like that.

TWENTY-THREE

At eight-thirty on a Friday morning in February, Candy Sullivan awakens in her condo and sees quarter-size flakes of snow drifting down. She moves to the window to look down at the Charles River, as she does every morning, to take comfort from its graceful progression forward. Today she has another checkup and she supposes it's natural for her to be nervous, yet there is a calmness at her center that makes her believe she will once again test negative.

"It happens, this kind of cure," Dr. Johnston told her. "It's rare, but it happens." And she knows it does; she knows she's not the only one. Still.

She'll shower and go to see her doctor, and then she'll meet with a group of women who have been diagnosed with ovarian cancer. She does this every Friday, goes to a small room the hospital has provided and that she, with permission, had repainted. Rather than a bile-yellow color, it is now a soothing blue; and there is an oil painting on the wall of a field of lavender in late afternoon sun—Candy decided it would be better here than in her bedroom. She sits in a circle of women holding Styrofoam cups of coffee, their purses on their laps, their coats over the backs of their chairs, everything that belongs to them kept close to them, because familiarity is comfort.

Usually, at first, the women are full of fear, or they display a false bravado. Sometimes they cry together; more often, they laugh. Candy's favorite story is one that a woman named Carolyn told: "So about an hour after I get home from being diagnosed, my best friend calls and says, 'Well, I am constipated as hell. I probably have cancer of the poop shoot, so I guess this is goodbye.' We used to joke around like that all the time. I take in a big breath and I look at the clock—I have no idea why, but I look at the clock, it says four forty-three—and I say, 'Ginny? I just found out I have ovarian cancer.' My mouth feels like I'm a puppet and someone else is making me talk, and I laugh. She says, 'That's not funny,' and I say, 'You're telling me?' She gets real quiet and then she says, 'For real?' and I say yes. And she bursts out crying and says all jerky, 'Boy. I guess that beats the hell out of c-c-constipation.'"

When a new person comes, Candy tells the story of how it was this disease that brought her to herself, that let her find the kind of peace and happiness she'd craved and despaired of ever finding. She says that the diagnosis let her recalculate the meaning of time and of relationships. Mostly, though, she listens. She understands the relief in being heard, the cure there is in that, at least.

After the group, she'll go to work at her part-time job at Winston Flowers; and then she'll join Don for dinner. She met Don Seaver a couple of months ago in the waiting room of Dr. Johnston's office. He's the exuberant Man Who Will Not Die, although he would be the first to admit he's getting closer, now. But, as he says, so is everyone else.

They enjoy each other, she and Don. She's so glad to be with someone so deeply appreciative of everything, such a cornball. He makes her laugh. He makes her cry, in the good way. They watch old movies together under his grandmother's quilt, they have long, searching conversations about everything from politics to the various meanings of the color red in art. They go to the Children's Museum to watch children; they go to flea markets and buy; they go to the Huntington Theatre to see plays or to the ballet or to the symphony and then to Rosie's bakery for dessert. Don's partner, Michael, died of AIDS many years ago, but Don loves him still, and so sometimes they go to Michael's grave and Candy sits a fair distance away on a bench while Don kneels at the headstone, his hand pressed against it.

Candy pulls her gloves on and steps out into the hall of her building. It's overly warm out there, as it always is, and she likes this. She likes almost everything, lately. The last time she talked to Mary Alice Mayhew, who has become a close friend, she remarked on her own optimism, and said it felt kind of silly admitting to it, almost embarrassing.

"It's not silly," Mary Alice said. "It feels great, doesn't it?"

And Candy said, "Yes. Yes, it does. It feels like I was wearing a big belt that was way too tight, and it has finally loosened. Loosened and fallen off! And I've looked down and said, 'Oh. I had a *belt* on.'" She laughed and said, "If *that* makes any sense."

And Mary Alice said, "Of course it does."

Candy asked how Lester was, and Mary Alice said, "Well, I moved in with him last week."

"Oh, my God," Candy said, and Mary Alice said, "I know."

"Oh, my God!" Candy said, and Mary Alice said, "I *know.*"

"Will you come and visit soon?" Mary Alice asked, and Candy said, "Turn back the covers on the guest bed. I'll be there before you know it."

"Come for Valentine's Day," Mary Alice said. "And bring Don." Candy hesitated for just the briefest moment before she said okay.

It's cold outside, and a bit icy. Candy turns her collar up and walks slowly down the sidewalk. In every window she passes, there is so much to see.

Pete Decker hurries in the shower. He's late for dinner at his ex-wife's house. The whole family will be there, and it's been a while since he saw his children. He chooses a blue sweater to bring out his eyes, a nice pair of gray woolen slacks, loafers. He wouldn't be caught dead in galoshes. He applies some cologne Nora was always crazy about and races out the door.

When he arrives, he looks through the window and sees them all gathered at the dining room table: Nora, his sons and daughter, and Fred with his new wedding ring flashing like a semaphore. His chest starts to hurt in that familiar way and he reminds himself to do what his therapist, Suzanne Collins, always tells him to do: take a breath, then look to see if there isn't another side. And so he looks at the table and sees the place that's been left for him. She's right, there is always another way to look at things. She's good, Suzanne. Beautiful, too, a smoky brunette with legs from here to oh-my there. He told her that once, how beautiful she was, and she said, "Thank you. That's not what we're here for."

"Would you like it to be?" he asked, and she said nothing, only looked at him. He hates it when she doesn't say anything and just looks at him like that, and meanwhile the meter's running. She does that when he should know the answer, but couldn't she just *say* that?

Though he thinks this therapy finally might be working. Which it should be; he could have bought a small country for what he's paying her.

He rings the doorbell, rocks back and forth on his feet. And when Nora answers the door, he embraces her quickly, warmly, and then lets go.

"Who loves you?" Dorothy asks her granddaughter.

The toddler points to the exact center of Dorothy's chest.

"That's right!" Dorothy says. She lifts Jill from her crib and carries her down to the kitchen. "Grandma made you a sandwich," she says. "And after you eat it, guess who's coming over to play in the snow with us?"

"Ehwer!" the girl says, and Dorothy says quickly, "No, not Edward. Edward is all gone. Allll gone! Remember, Grandma said, BYE BYE, Edward! Remember? BYE BYE! Edward is *all gone*!"

The child leans around Dorothy to look at the sandwich cut into fours on her Elmo plate.

"It's *Ronnie* who's coming over," Dorothy says. "Remember Ronnie?"

A baleful glance.

"Well, you'll remember when you see him," Dorothy says. And then, more to herself than to her grandchild, she shrugs and says, almost happily, "Or not."

What a wise daughter Hilly is. She was absolutely right about getting out of your own way. As soon as Dorothy decided not to be in charge of getting a man into her life, didn't they start showing up like crazy! And at her age! She dated a man from her French conversation class. She dated one she met in the popcorn line at the movies and another one whom she met when she was having her car serviced, and he was, too. "Come here often?" he'd said, that was his pickup line. Oh, she'd liked that one, he was very witty and he had old-fashioned manners and knew things like how to help a woman out of her coat and back into it. But they sort of petered out after a couple of months. Nothing seems to last for very long, but who cares? It's not really a man she's looking for. Turns out it never was. When Jill was born, Dorothy was the first one to hold her. Well, the first one after Hilly. Her daughter looked up at her and said, "Here, Mom, you want to hold her?" *That's* what she had been looking for, but she hadn't known it until that moment. She looked into that baby's eyes and made sure they had an understanding, and then she handed Jill to her grinning—and weeping—father.

"Diddle diddle dumpling!" Dorothy says to Jill, and her granddaughter slams down her sippy cup, says, "My son *John*!"

"Peas porridge hot!" Dorothy says, and Jill says, "My son *John*!"

Dorothy laughs and tucks one of Jill's golden curls behind her ear. She thinks of the afternoon hours before them. They'll read books. They'll rock baby dolls. They'll play grocery store. Also, Dorothy will offer Jill the new puzzle she bought for her the other day, she'll spread it out on the floor and remember *not to put it together herself*. Hilly has pointedly reminded Dorothy of this more than once. "Mom," she has said. "You have to let Jill do it. Let her make mistakes; let her get frustrated; that's how she'll learn." So Dorothy will do that. When she puts the puzzle pieces out, she'll remember to sit back and just watch, trusting that things will, in their own time and in their own way, come quite satisfactorily together.

ACKNOWLEDGMENTS

Many thanks to Erin Weiss at the Hartford Animal Clinic in Hartford, Wisconsin, who shared stories about animals and the practice of veterinary medicine with me, some of which were then fictionalized for use in this novel. Any mistakes are my own. Erin is a veterinarian par excellence, the one you really want when your pal is in trouble or just needs those pesky shots. If only she'd take my advice and serve as my doctor, too.

The usual gratitude is due to my longtime and beloved editor, Kate Medina, and to my agent, Suzanne Gluck, who is smart, upbeat, and really *fun*. Thanks also to the team at Random House, who take care of everything from cover design to copyediting to publicity to making sure I get a window seat on the airplane or a copy of the new Random House title I really need *right now*. I want to single out Avideh Bashirrad, Susan Brown, Gina Centrello, Sanyu Dillon, Barbara Fillon, Ashley Gratz-Collier, Kathleen McAuliffe, Beth Pearson, and Lindsey Schwoeri. And at

WME Entertainment: Claudia Ballard, Sarah Ceglarski, and Caroline Donofrio—I love you guys.

I spent a lot of time looking at high school yearbooks when I was writing this novel, and I want to offer a shout-out to Ed McGraw and Bill Cocos, who in their own ways kept trying to tell me that my high school wasn't so bad. They were right.

the last time i saw you

ELIZABETH BERG

A READER'S GUIDE

Elizabeth Berg on the Writing of
The Last Time I Saw You

I write novels for different reasons. Sometimes it's my attempt to understand a certain issue or point of view. Sometimes it's to pay tribute to someone or some thing. Sometimes it's to explore relationships. Sometimes it's all of the above, all at the same time. *The Last Time I Saw You* came about in a kind of different way.

I was in my study one day, peacefully minding my own business, when Dorothy Shauman Ledbetter Shauman came into my brain and began talking in her loud voice. And let me tell you, I knew from what she was saying and the way she said it that if she were a real person, she would never be a friend of mine. She was loudmouthed, judgmental, and politically incorrect. She seemed awfully superficial. And yet I was oddly fascinated by her. The image I had was of her in her bathroom in a black half-slip and bra, fussing over herself for a fortieth high school reunion that was still a week away. I thought, *Hmmmmm. High school reunion, huh? I wonder why she's going.*

This led me to think about why anyone would go to a high school reunion, particularly a fortieth. But then it came to me that Dorothy's high school reunion was the last one her class would ever have, and therefore it was laden with a particular poignancy. In addition to that, for Dorothy, the reunion was her last chance to try to snag a man she'd been smitten by since they were in high school together.

So I began writing the first chapter of the book, in the voice of Dorothy. And after I finished that first chapter, I had an idea of who else would be coming to the reunion, and so I started writing chapters featuring those characters' points of views. It ended up that there were five characters in all, two men and three women, all going to their high school reunion, three of them for the first time, all of them for very different reasons. The pages—and the time—just flew by. These people knew themselves and they told me all I needed to know to write about them. Their personalities created the story more surely than any plot device might have: *The Last Time I Saw You* is a story first and foremost about people. When my agent first read the novel, she said, "These characters own the book!" And so they do.

The people who populate the novel are only part of the reason I wrote it, though. I also wanted to look at the nature of nostalgia. I wanted to show how sobering a realization it can be to understand that one is entering old age; and I also wanted to show the value of aging. I wanted to ponder the question of whether or not people can and do change. I wanted to suggest that, sometimes, meeting with people you knew at another time in your life can give you the wisdom and courage to make necessary changes in the life you are living now.

I recalled the one and only high school reunion I'd gone to, where I saw that people were very much different from the selves they used to be, and yet they were also very much the same. When I saw my class's heartthrob, he looked a lot different, but only for a while. Soon I saw the boy he used to be through the scrim of the man he had become. This happened for all of us, I think. I came to the reunion as a fairly attractive woman who had achieved a certain level of success, but was seen by others (and myself) as a girl wearing a flip and black cat-eye glasses, a painfully shy girl whose blouse was perpetually half untucked from her A-line shirt, and whose kneesocks were always sliding down into her loafers.

I think this is what happens at high school reunions: all the work you've done to create a new persona disappears and you're busted, revealed once again as the kid you once were and still are. That's what reunions do, is remind you that although we grow up (some of us more than others) we nonetheless remain all the other ages we've been.

This is not to say we don't evolve, however. It's not to say we don't become better—or worse—people than we used to be. It's not to say that we can't continue to learn new things about each other, and ourselves, and make changes. And it is certainly not to say that we can't come to a fuller appreciation of people we once didn't have much time for or, conversely, see through some of the pretense and posturing of people we once worshipped but no longer admire in any way.

After I got home from my reunion, I realized I'd come away with certain understandings and realizations that have stayed with me ever since. What I hoped for my characters in *The Last Time I Saw You* was that they, too, would have this happen, only in far more dramatic ways. I wanted them to experience something at their reunion that would make them feel their lives had irrevocably changed. And guess what? That did happen. If you've read the book, you'll know exactly what I mean. If you haven't, I invite you to dive in right now.

Questions and Topics for Discussion

1. Many people say they're going to a reunion for one reason, when it's really for another. Why do you think most people attend reunions?

2. Berg portrays an interesting and diverse group of high school classmates in her novel. Did you have a favorite character before the reunion? After?

3. Much of what we learn about Berg's characters comes from stories told by others. Which one seems best known by his or her classmates? Which classmate are people most wrong about?

4. Which characters were actually the happiest in high school? Does this match or contradict the perceptions of others?

5. In your opinion, is nostalgia generally a good or a bad thing? Other than reunions, what are some examples of things that happen in our lives that lead us to think, sometimes obsessively, about the past?

6. Dorothy Shauman is obsessed with seducing her high school crush, Pete Decker, at the reunion. She finds the perfect outfit, confers with her friends on strategy, and even sends herself flowers at the reunion hotel. But things don't go as planned come reunion night. Why do you think Dorothy strikes out with Pete?

7. In high school, people often go to great lengths to disguise their "real selves." Which of the characters did this in high school, and which of them are still doing it as the novel opens? What do you think it is that allows us to be, and to accept, our most authentic selves?

8. Pete and Candy were the king and queen of high school. But no matter what the others think of them, their lives post–high school have not always gone according to plan. Discuss Pete and Candy and how differently they seem to have handled their popularity—both during and after high school.

9. Mary Alice may not have been popular in high school, but it didn't seem to bother her. So why are the people in her life (her older sister and her elderly neighbor, Einer) so worried about her going to her reunion?

10. Why was Lester initially so hesitant to go to his reunion? Why do you think he changed his mind? Was it just the pressure from Jeanine, or something more?

11. Many of the characters in the novel assume, going into the reunion, that their classmates will be exactly as they remembered them. Of course, that's not the case. Which of Berg's characters has changed the least since high school? The most? Do you think people really can change?

12. Toward the end of the reunion, Pam Pottsman organizes an activity in which classmates gather around and tell the truth about a variety of issues. Were you surprised by the people who participated and the stories they shared? Why or why not? What would you share if you played this game with your high school classmates?

13. When you look back on your own high school days, what do you remember about yourself and your fellow classmates? Equipped with the knowledge and experience you have now, if you could do high school over again, what would you do differently?

14. Have you been to any of your high school reunions? If you haven't, talk about why you decided not to go. If you have, what was your experience like? Discuss.

Turn the page for a preview from
Elizabeth Berg's next novel,

ONCE UPON A TIME, THERE WAS YOU

PROLOGUE

When John Marsh was a young boy, he used to watch his mother getting ready to go out for the evening. He stood beside her dressing table and listened to the *mbuh* sounds she made tamping down her lipstick, and he took note of the three-quarter angle with which she then regarded herself in the mirror, as though she were flirting with herself. He watched how rouge made her cheeks blossom into unnatural color, and how the little comb she used to apply mascara made her blond lashes go black and spiky. She always finished by taking her hair down from pincurls and brushing it into a controlled mass of waves, which she then perfumed with a spicy scent that reminded him of carnations and oranges, both. Finally, "How do I look?" she would ask him, and he never knew what to say. For though he had stood beside her, watching her every move as she transformed herself, he was never sure that the made-up woman before him was still his mother, and this made for a mixed feeling of fear and confusion. Yet he always smiled and said softly, "Pretty."

Before he turned six, she was gone—off living in another state with a man who did not care for children. The rare times he saw her, she came and stayed in a nearby Howard Johnson, and she would buy him dinner there, and while he ate she'd sit smoking and sneaking looks at her watch.

Many years later, on the eve of his wedding day, thirty-six-year-old John sat in a bar talking to his best friend, Stuart White (Stuart himself happily married for twelve years), about how he was suddenly consumed by doubt. John sat morosely on the stool, chatting now and then with one of the women there, many of them beautiful, and understood that it wasn't that; it wasn't that he wanted anyone else. When the blonde on the bar stool next to him offered him a cigarette, John took it.

"What are you doing?" Stuart asked. "You don't smoke. And Irene *hates* cigarette smoke!"

"Yeah, I know," John said. "I think she has an allergy or something." He put a match to the end of the cigarette.

"Whoa," Stuart said. "Are your *hands* shaking?"

"No. What? No! My hands aren't shaking!"

"They are too, man. Look at them."

John looked at his hands, and his friend was right: there was a fine tremor. He ground out the cigarette, shoved his face into his hands, and moaned.

Stuart said, "Okay, okay, buddy, you just need to calm down. Try this. Think about when you asked Irene to marry you. Why did you ask her?"

And John said, "She didn't wear makeup?"

When Irene Marsh was a young girl, she used to have a play space in the basement where she lined up her many baby dolls. One by one, she fed them, burped them, and rocked them to sleep. It brought her a rare peace, to care for her babies. It took her away from what went on between her parents, the yelling and the hateful silences, which were worse than the yelling. She sang lullabyes into plastic ears and rocked inert little bodies;

she prayed each night on her knees to get old enough to live with someone else, in love.

Which was why it was a little surprising that on her wedding day, she sat weeping in the bride's room, fifteen minutes before the ceremony was to begin. The room was ornately decorated: a multitiered chandelier, embossed ivory wallpaper, two elegant club chairs upholstered with tangerine silk, a polished wooden table between them holding a bouquet of white freesia, a small gold lamp with a cream silk shade, a Waterford crystal bowl full of Jordan almonds—for good luck, Irene knew. There was a gold-trimmed white dressing table with a coordinating bench and oval mirror for the bride to apply makeup, and a claw-footed, full-length mirrror for the final inspection. Floral brocade drapes with brass rosette tiebacks framed diamond-paned windows. In the adjoining powder room was a vase of creamy white roses, pristine linen hand towels, and a basket of might-needs decorated by a length of wide satin ribbon. Irene had called Sandra in to show her this when they first arrived, and Sandra had said, "How pretty!" Irene had stood mutely, her hands clasped tightly before her. For what she had felt was a sense of outrage at the excess.

Irene was sitting on the bench before the dresser with her back to the mirror. She had just put on her wedding gown, a dress that was purposefully plain and might in fact work for everyday, were it not floor length and made from ivory Qiana. Her hair was loose about her shoulders, as yet unstyled into the upsweep she'd planned; her satin heels lay in a little jumble on the floor beside her, her veil across her lap. The bridal bouquet sat unpacked in its box in a corner of the room.

"But I thought you were *sure*," Irene's best friend, Sandra Cox (herself happily married for nine years), said. She was standing before Irene, holding her friend's trembling hands in her own. "You said you were absolutely sure!"

"I know, but I want to go home. Will you take me?"

"Well . . ." Sandra didn't know what to do. She spoke in a near whisper, saying, "Irene. You're thirty-six years old. If you want children—"

"I know how old I am! But you shouldn't get married just to have children. I can't get *married* just to have children!" She drew in a ragged breath, snatched a tissue off the dressing table, and blew her nose.

Sandra spoke slowly, carefully, saying, "I don't know; getting married to have children isn't such a bad idea. And besides, you *love* John. Don't you?"

Irene turned away from the mirror and stared into her lap, picked at one thumbnail with the other.

"Irene?"

She looked up. "I can't go through with this. Please, Sandra. It's wrong. Go and get the car, okay? We have to hurry. If you don't want to, I understand. I'll take the bus. There's a bus that goes by here."

Sandra cracked open the door to see if anyone was out in the hall yet: no one. Then she knelt on the floor before Irene and looked directly into her eyes. "Listen to me. If you do this, you can't take it back. Do you understand that? It's not just a little tiff and then you apologize and get married next week instead. If you do this, it's the end of you and John. Do you understand that?"

Irene nodded. "I do. So to speak." She tried to smile.

Sandra stood. She crossed her arms and sighed. "What about all those people out there? There must be two hundred people! Do you want me to make an announcement or something?"

"Oh! Yes. Yes." Irene stood and draped the veil over one of the club chairs. "Apologize for me, okay? Say I'm sorry. I *am* sorry. And be sure to say that I'll send all the gifts back, right away. Tomorrow. I know this is hard, Sandra. I'll make it up to you, I promise."

But then Irene's father poked his head in the door and said gruffly, "Let's go," and Irene put her veil on, stepped into her shoes, and linked her arm through his.

"Irene?" Sandra said, and Irene said, "No."

ONE

When eighteen-year-old Sadie Marsh comes from California to visit her father in Minnesota, she sleeps in a bedroom decorated for her much younger self: a ruffled canopy bed, a white dresser with fairies painted on it, wallpaper with pink and white stripes, a bedside lamp with a wishing-well base. Neither John nor his daughter has ever made a move to change one thing about that room; Sadie still sleeps under a pile of stuffed animals, the ones she left behind.

It's a warm day in August, and John is sitting on the front porch, feeding peanuts to the squirrel that has ventured up the steps and over to him. He's waiting for his daughter to burst out the door and announce that this is really it; she has everything now, she's ready to go to the airport. She's been here for the usual length of time—one week. She's not even gone but already he is feeling a wide band around his middle start to tighten. When he drops her at the airport, neither of them will express any regret at her leavetaking: it is an unspoken agreement that they keep every parting casual, that they do not make a bad situation worse with what they both would describe as fussing and carrying on, a phrase that John's Atlanta-born mother was fond of using, and one that she in fact employed every time *they* parted. "No fussin' and cahn' on, now," she would say, her white gloved hand beneath his chin, her eyes crinkled at the sides the way they did when she smiled. "I'm gon' see you real soon, just you wait; you won't hardly know I've been gone."

He did wait. And wait.

Sadie has Irene's looks: sandy hair, hazel eyes that lean toward green, a fair complexion that burns at the mention of sun. She's tall, with a delicate bone structure, wrists so tiny she can almost never find a watch to fit her. But her nature is more like her father's: she's an outdoor type, confident in athletics, a person who is more irritated than inspired by poetry, an even-keeled young woman who rarely takes things personally. She has a loud laugh, an infectious one; even when Sadie was a toddler, Irene would say, "You can't hear her laugh and not join right in, even if you're mad at her. *Especially* if you're mad at her."

John hears Sadie coming down the stairs, and tosses the rest of the peanuts into a corner of the porch. The squirrel stands there on its hind legs, its tail flicking, then opts for running off the porch rather than heading for the feast. "Hey!" John says. He moves to the top step to watch the squirrel run to the elm tree on the boulevard, then rapidly ascend. From the highest limb, it stares down at John. "Get your *peanuts*," John says, pointing, but the squirrel only stares.

"All set, Dad," Sadie says. She has her overstuffed backpack in one hand, her suitcase in the other, and he can tell from the tone of her voice that she, too, is having a hard time keeping upbeat. Never mind a deep and abiding love; he and his daughter really *like* each other. One week four times a year is not enough for either of them, but it is the best solution for now. In winter and summer, Sadie comes to St. Paul; in spring and fall, John goes out to San Francisco, where he stays in a hotel and visits with both Irene and Sadie, but that never quite works out—if he sees Sadie alone, she seems to feel bad for her mother; if they all get together, it's excruciating. The truth is, John doesn't like Irene at all anymore, and he doesn't think she cares much for him, either. They've grown apart in large ways and small. Irene identifies herself as a liberal conservative now, which John can't fathom. She's overly concerned about order and cleanliness in her flat—it's impossible to relax there. She prefers cats to dogs, which is almost worse than being a conservative. She's taken to wearing makeup and recently dyed her hair to cover the gray. Sadie says it's the influence of her latest man friend, a guy named Don Strauss who believes aging people should "fight the good fight."

"Please," John said, when Sadie told him this. And Sadie shrugged and said, "He's not so bad. He makes really good vegetable lasagna. He puts goat cheese in there."

"Well, that counts for something," John said, but privately he was thinking, *Right, I'll bet he's another vegetarian. Another Unitarian vegetarian who holds up peace signs at street corners every Saturday afternoon and aspires to live in a Mongolian yurt.* He waited for Sadie to say more about Don, but she didn't, and he didn't ask. Another unspoken agreement. He didn't ask about the men in Sadie's mother's life; Irene didn't ask about the women in his. Not that there were many to ask about. The last time he had a relationship was five years ago, and that blew up when he wouldn't agree to lock his black lab mix, emphasis on mix, out of his room on the nights she slept over. The woman complained that the dog snored and farted; John said that she did, too, and that was that. Festus died last year, and John thinks he's almost ready to get another dog. An Irish wolfhound, he's thinking, mostly because Sadie said she knows of a rescue group that recently took one in. "They're awfully big," John told her, and she said, "Exactly."

On the way to the airport, John looks over to see Sadie fooling around with her iPod. "Don't you dare put those plugs in your ears and disappear for the last fifteen mintues of our visit," he says. "Please."

She rolls her eyes. "I'm not. I'm just getting it ready for the plane."

"I don't see why you young people can't step away from electronics for ten seconds of your life." *Young people!* Well, that's it: he's officially old now.

"Dad. I hardly used anything at your house the whole time I was there. I texted, like, twice."

John doesn't believe her. He saw the light under her door when he went past at night, and he heard the tap-tap-tapping. But he doesn't challenge her; at least she was courteous enough not to be constantly online in front of him.

Sadie puts the iPod in her backpack and zips it shut. "I'm going to get you one of these," she says. "I'll load it up with good music; you can see what I listen to."

"Sweetheart?"

"No, you'd like a lot of the songs! You really would."

"No rap," he says.

"Some rap," she answers.

He stops for a red light and looks over at her. "You're a pretty girl, you know that?"

She laughs.

A great sadness overtakes him but he makes his voice light to say, "So! What's in store for the rest of the summer?"

"Well. A challenge. A bunch of us are going rock climbing. *If* Mom will let me. So far she says no way."

"What are you going to climb?"

"Just Mount Tam, and only the lowest slab. Some people wanted to go to Monmouth Mountain, myself included, but that's a six-hour drive."

"Since when do you know anything about rock climbing?"

She shrugs. "That's Mom's point. I *don't* know anything about it. But I want to learn. I'll be with people who do know a lot about it. My friend Ron has been climbing with his family since he was six. He says it's great. He says the only way to know yourself is to challenge yourself—in a hard way, so that you're really scared. He says what you do in times like that is what you *are*."

John nods. "I suppose there's some truth to that."

"You think?"

"Yeah."

"Have you ever done that? Taken on a challenge that really, really scared you?"

Marrying your mother. Didn't work out so well. "Not really," he says.

"Maybe you should try rock climbing."

"No thanks. So are you going to need ropes and pickaxes and oxygen masks and all that stuff?"

"Dad."

"Well, what do I know?"

"All I need is climbing shoes. Ron gave me a pair of his sister's—they're almost brand-new, and they fit just fine."

"I'll get you your own pair."

"Let's see if I like it first," Sadie says, and John feels a rush of pride in his daughter for being so practical and unselfish, for not taking him up on every offer he makes to buy her things. There's no doubt she understands that guilt is a pretty good wallet-cracker after a divorce, even many years after a divorce, and she chooses not to capitalize on that. She was a child who would never dump a bowl full of Halloween candy left untended on someone's porch into her bag, or even take more than one piece. He used to worry sometimes that she was too good, and he took an odd sort of comfort in the times she did act up.

"What you could do," Sadie says, "is talk to Mom and convince her to let me try climbing."

"Okay. I'll tell her it's fine with me. I'll tell her it's important that you take on physical as well as mental challenges. I think I can bring her around."

"Thanks. And what's your next challenge?"

"There's an old building on Wabasha I'm trying to buy. I'm just starting negotiations. My God, the ceilings on that place are—"

"I mean a personal challenge."

"Renovation is personal to me. Since I was your age. Since before that."

"I know. I know all about your matchbox cities when you were a little boy, and how you tried to buy your first building when you were sixteen, and how you won first prize in the science fair for your city of the future."

"That was an incredible city."

"I'm sure it was. But I meant more along the lines of when are you going to date again? That kind of challenge."

"I'm fifty-six years old, Sadie."

"And?"

"I think I'm all done with that."

"You so are not!"

"I'm not really interested."

"Well, you should be. It's not good to be alone. To be honest, I worry about you a little bit, Dad. You don't even comb your hair half the time. You don't eat well. I don't think you're uninterested; I think you don't know how to go about meeting single women. Why don't you go online? That's what Mom does. Just put up a profile, and see what—"

"Absolutely not. I am not dating someone I meet *online*." He will never admit that one night he looked around on Match .com. Sat before his computer in his shorts and T-shirt, drinking a beer, looking for something that wasn't there. Not even close. Something occurs to him. "Are you meeting people online?

Are you going *mountain climbing* with someone you met on-line?"

"*No,* Dad. I'm going with kids from school, if I go. I'm just saying you should get *out* more. There's more to life than work."

"As I've been told. And told."

"Well, there is."

He signals for the exit to the airport. "I'll tell you what. If you climb a mountain, I'll ask a woman out."

"Yeah, how will you meet her, though?"

"I have my ways."

"Name them."

"You'll see."

"You have one week," Sadie says. "That's when the climb is."

"Deal." He pulls over to the curb to let her out and puts the car into park. He puts his hand to the side of daughter's face and sighs. Kisses her forehead. "All right. Get out of my car."

"I thought you'd never ask." She leans over to embrace him. "Don't *call* me all the time," she says into his ear, and he says, "Don't call *me* all the time," into hers, and then she is gone. Though she does turn back before she goes through the glass doors. Turns and blows him a kiss, and he waves back.

He pulls out into the traffic and blinks once, twice. Clears his throat. Then he turns on the radio and boosts the volume.

He thinks about whether or not he should make his next move with Amy Becker. Because what Sadie doesn't know is that he's already met someone. It was in a way he'd rather not share with his daughter. Or with anyone else.

ELIZABETH BERG is the author of many bestselling novels, including *Home Safe, The Year of Pleasures, The Day I Ate Whatever I Wanted,* and *Dream When You're Feeling Blue,* as well
as two collections of short stories and two works of nonfiction.
Open House was an Oprah's Book Club selection, *Durable
Goods* and *Joy School* were selected as ALA Best Books of the
Year, and *Talk Before Sleep* was short-listed for an Abby Award.
Berg has been honored by both the Boston Public Library and
the Chicago Public Library and is a recipient of the New England
Booksellers Award for her body of work. She is a popular
speaker at various venues around the country, and her work has
been translated into twenty-seven languages. Berg lives in
Chicago.

www.elizabeth-berg.net

Chat.
Comment.
Connect.

Visit our online book club community at
www.randomhousereaderscircle.com

Chat
Meet fellow book lovers and discuss what you're reading.

Comment
Post reviews of books, ask—and answer—thought-provoking
questions, or give and receive book club ideas.

Connect
Find an author on tour, visit our author blog, or invite one of
our 150 available authors to chat with your group on the phone.

Explore
Also visit our site for discussion questions, excerpts, author
interviews, videos, free books, news on the latest releases,
and more.

Books are better with buddies.
www.RandomHouseReadersCircle.com

THE RANDOM HOUSE PUBLISHING GROUP